WHEN LOVE CALLED

GLENFIELD SERIES—BOOK ONE
Second Edition

I0549679

ENDORSEMENTS

What a joy to discover this literary treasure! Travis W. Inman captivates with a powerful tale that is all at once thrilling, enchanting, and thought-provoking. You cannot help but be gripped by this enduring love story. Christian fiction readers who demand excellence will find that *When Love Called* delivers on every level.

—Alison Bryant

If you like a good love story, you will love this book. *When Love Called* is a beautifully written story of three very real characters, each suffering in their own way, who are brave enough to open their hearts again to find true love. I can't wait to read more from this talented author.

—Sara Vinduska, *author of The Drowning Man and Reflections.*

A fast paced love story. *When Love Called* gives glory to God, challenges you to look deeper into your own faith, and keeps you turning the pages. A terrific love story that I couldn't put down! *When Love Called* is a smash hit.

—*Shelly Tanner*

As a reader of Christian fiction for over 25 years, I can honestly say *When Love Called*, by Travis W. Inman, is one of the the best! It is an intensely emotional book, and I found myself falling in love with all the main characters—especially young Mariah, a precocious, precious child who just wants a mommy.

—Heather Ward

A good, inspiring love story. Inman is an excellent Christian fiction storywriter. This is a must read all the way to the end.

—Cindy Thames

Travis W. Inman developed enjoyable characters who are so real they could be someone you know, even a neighbor next door. *When Love Called* is a riveting love story that even a man would enjoy reading. I am looking forward to reading the rest of the series by this author!

—J.S. Bairrington

Travis Inman is not a typical romance author. He writes love stories that are both inspirational and exciting. *When Love Called* is a fast moving story that left me wanting more at the end. I truly cannot wait until the next book is released.

—G. McGrath

A charming romance that reads like a fairy tale, but with lots to ponder. A best seller!

—Amy Deardon, author of *A Lever Long Enough* and *The Story Template*

WHEN LOVE CALLED

GLENFIELD SERIES—BOOK ONE
Second Edition

TRAVIS W. INMAN

ELK LAKE PUBLISHING INC.
Plymouth, Massachusetts

Cover and Interior Design: Derinda Babcock

Editor(s): René Holt, Deb Haggerty

Author Represented by Amy

PUBLISHED BY: Elk Lake Publishing, Inc., 35 Dogwood Dr., Plymouth, MA 02360, 2018

Library Cataloging Data

Names: Inman, Travis W. (Travis W. Inman)

When Love Called / Travis W. Inman

238 p. 23cm × 15cm (9in × 6 in.)

Description: How does a widower overcome his past after the traumatic death of his young wife? How does a divorcée look into the future after heart-wrenching betrayal? How can a former Army surgeon embrace the trauma he experienced in Afghanistan? *When Love Called* forces Caton Harvey, Lily Demar, and Jack McCranie to explore these tragic events. Travis W. Inman takes these lives on a mysterious urn when they connect through a divine phone call.

Identifiers: ISBN-13: 978-1-948888-54-7 (trade) | 978-1-948888-55-4 (POD) | 978-1-948888-56-1 (e-book.)

Key Words: Romance, family, children, love story, death of spouse, music, beach read

LCCN: 2018954849 Fiction

DEDICATION

This book is humbly dedicated to my wife, Sarah, and my children, Caitlin and Seth, for their patience and understanding.

ACKNOWLEDGMENTS

I also want to thank Alison Bryant and Shelly Tanner. My special regards go to my agent, Amy Deardon, and to Deb Haggerty, René Holt, and all the staff at Elk Lake Publishing Inc. for seeing a diamond in the rough.

SPECIAL ACKNOWLEDGMENT

And a very special shout-out to Alex Wilson for his help and advice. He's my go-to-guy whenever I want to discuss trauma. Especially traumatic trauma!

TABLE OF CONTENTS

AUTHOR'S NOTES

A note before we launch … an explanation is required.

I first self-published this book several years ago under the title, *When Love Calls*. The story was much different and a tad sophomoric, so I seized the opportunity to rewrite and significantly improve the story line. So far, everyone agrees I made the right call. You might see *When Love Calls* listed on Amazon or other websites, but pay no attention. When I rewrote the story, I renamed it *When Love Called*. I promise, I won't rewrite this book again!

Caton, pronounced Kay-ton. An odd name, or so it seems. Many years ago, when I was a prison guard in Texas, I met a man whose last name was Caton. I liked the name and swore to remember it for a future storyline. I ran into him and told him, "Hey! I wrote a book and gave the character your name." He blinked at me and said, "You named the character Russell?"

A final, preemptive disclaimer. I use the word *ugh*. My intention is for it to be pronounced softly, like a sigh, not as if it has a hard *g* sound—a sigh of regret or dismay, not a caveman's guttural gasp when he sees his first mastodon and is fresh out of clubs.

And now, let us begin our journey … Lights, please … Queue the music … Action!

THE BEGINNING

Mary started the first chemotherapy trial right after the baby was born, but a moment later, her heart gave out, and she was gone.

Caton Harvey was numb at first. Everything happened too fast. It seemed he and Mary had just come home from their honeymoon, just built their first house, just celebrated their first anniversary—and now he stood by her hospital bed, watching her unmoving frame. The nurses and aides had straightened her room before allowing Caton to return, but the debris from her trauma code gave stark testimony to her final battle.

Caton's mind went back over the last eight years of their lives. He felt numb, disconnected from the reality that the love of his life was gone. And she was gone so quickly. They had tried for eight years to have a baby. The long line of specialists and treatments plagued his memory. He had trouble distinguishing which doctor served which role.

When Mary learned she suffered from polycystic ovarian syndrome, or PCOS, Caton knew she felt overwhelmed and depressed, knowing she might never conceive, might never know the joys of nurturing a baby within her womb. But that wasn't what happened. One day, God opened her womb, and she conceived. After years of struggling, she and Caton were going to be parents.

Mary was never more beautiful to Caton than those nine months before she gave birth. To the Harveys, their lives were in order. All was well.

"Excuse me, Mr. Harvey?"

A soft voice interrupted his nostalgic reminicences, forcing him to return to his wife's bedside. He didn't respond. He couldn't respond. He could only stare with eyes that couldn't see and a heart that couldn't feel.

The nurse spoke to him again, her voice compassionate. "Sir? We moved Mariah to the nursery. When you are ready to visit her, let me know. I'll show you the way."

He couldn't bear to look at the nurse. He nodded slowly, informally dismissing the young woman behind him. She turned and quietly left the room, softly shutting the door behind her. Caton looked down at his wife, still feeling nothing more than an empty, hollow, deadened void.

Mary was almost seven months pregnant when they discovered she had non-Hodgkin's lymphoma, the cancer that would ultimately take her life. It was unfair, and there was no escape.

They had the option of terminating the pregnancy to save Mary's life. Neither Caton nor Mary gave the option much consideration. To them, their long-awaited baby was a gift from God, and they would trust God, despite their impulse to blame Him. Mary chose to abstain from cancer treatments to give their baby the best chance at life. Caton knew she was forfeiting her life for her baby. Her sacrifice was heavy on his mind.

One specialist, working on a clinical trial, offered some hope that Mary might have a chance, despite the fact her cancer had advanced to stage IV. But Mary's life was forfeit when she reacted badly to the treatment. Even so, he knew she entered eternity with a song in her heart, for she was able to hold her baby and kiss her gently before her time came. In those precious moments, he could see Mary was at peace, and he loved her for making the right choice.

Hearing movement behind him, Caton turned to see his mother, Karen, reaching out to him. The moment her hands touched his shoulder, reality burst in, and he was hammered with the fact that his beloved Mary was gone.

CHAPTER ONE

CLOUDCROFT, NEW MEXICO

SOUTHERN ROCKY MOUNTAINS

LATER THAT FALL

The money from the settlement for Mary's death was cold comfort. Caton returned to his small home on the mountain where, surrounded by tall pines and the quaking leaves of the aspens, he could always think with clarity. He and Mary knew the risks involved with the clinical trial, so he resisted filing a wrongful death suit against the hospital. He changed his mind when his lawyers finally convinced him the medications used were known to have had similar reactions in other clinical trials, a fact ignored by Dr. Taylor and his staff. But for Caton, all that was all in the past. As he stood and surveyed his meadow, he was looking toward the future.

He and Mary chose to build their small, comfortable home in this meadow because they valued privacy. Sometimes, in the summer, Mary would spread blankets across the deck, and they slept under the stars. Once, they woke to the sight of a black bear poking her nose through the bars of the deck. That had been the final time they slept outside.

Caton slowly climbed the steps to the deck's upper level and gazed across their meadow. His thirty-five acres were boxed in by the national forest on the surrounding mountain slopes. He sometimes felt as though he owned the world. He found strength in the vision he and Mary shared. She had planned an enormous log home, set along the edge of the clearing near the base of the meadow, with stables and a barn on the opposite side of the narrow stream. Then she wanted to convert their current home into a guesthouse.

Finally, he would add a trout pond, along with a gazebo large enough for three picnic tables on the opposite side of the meadow. Mary wanted their home to look like a park when they were finished.

He often teased her about where she would get the money for her building projects. She always replied, "We'll see." She kept a detailed sketch of her plans folded in her Bible, now lying by her empty bedside, untouched ... unread.

The ache in Caton's chest burned against the memory. He inhaled slowly.

In the evening, a rain shower left spotted fog banks in the forest below. Caton sat in his office with a cup of tea, restlessly poring over the sketches Mary left behind. He sneaked into Mariah's room to make sure she was sleeping. She was lying in her crib, cooing at the ceiling fan. It was nearly time for her evening bottle, so he carried her into his office. She sucked on the rubber nipple, her little hands, curled into fists, resting against her chin. "Oh, you look like your mother, Baby Mariah. I wish she was here to see you." He carried her to the drafting table covered with building plans.

"See this?" Her dark eyes watched him. When he spoke, she quit sucking on the bottle, then resumed when he stopped speaking. "This is the memorial I'm gonna build for your mother. I'll build everything Momma wanted. You see?"

He pointed as if she could understand. "The big house will be right here, and the pond will be there. Then I will build you a playhouse near the stream and a real schoolhouse over by the barn. Right there. Your momma wanted to home-school you since it's impractical to drive an hour every day to school."

He sat in the rocking chair and stretched Mariah over his shoulder. Patting her back, he continued. "Now don't you worry about the money. I'm still bidding on jobs in Cloudcroft and Ruidoso, and we can afford to hire a live-in nanny and build this monstrous project. When we don't have any work, the crew can come out here and work on the house. Hopefully, I can do most of it by myself." Finally, as he stood to take her to bed, he was overwhelmed with grief, thinking Mary wasn't there to sing to her. Oh, how his heart ached for his wife. One moment she was lying in her hospital bed talking to him—and then she was gone.

He placed Mariah in her crib and switched on the CD player. Mary had read that playing classical music to a baby would develop the child's brain, so he faithfully played the music Mary picked out months before. He looked at the album cover. He'd never heard of the Boston Orchestra, but Mary immediately fell in love with the music and insisted their baby would love it as well.

Stepping onto the porch, Caton watched the moon stretching to peek through the tree tops. The night air was chilly, and the fog bank threatened to stay until morning. He involuntarily reached out to the hands that should have been there, but he felt only the splinters of the wooden railing. "Mary, I need you to be here." He shook his head sadly. "I'm going to add one last thing to your plans," he said solemnly, lifting his eyes to the back edge of the grass line. "In that farthest corner of the meadow, I'm gonna start a cemetery. And then, once you're back with me, I can start on your dream."

CHAPTER TWO

And Then It Happened

By the first snowfalls a year after Mary's death, Caton had moved into the big house he'd constructed according to Mary's plans. He now had a full time nanny, Mrs. Ruth Davis, an older widow from the Village, staying in the room next to Mariah. Caton provided Mrs. Davis room and board and a modest salary.

Even in the snow, he continued to work on Mary's dream. The stables and barn were mostly completed by the first thaws of spring. The heavy snows melted into his trout pond. He was pleased to see the fish meandering through the one-acre lake. By summer, he completed the schoolhouse and tennis court, and by the first snows of the next fall, he was working on the large gazebo in the meadow.

Weather permitting, Mrs. Davis strolled with Mariah, now old enough to walk, in the meadow, helping her pick flowers and holding her hand while she threw sticks at the fish. Then, at two o'clock, she brought lemonade to Caton, just as she'd done for her husband. She was fond of saying, "If it's good enough for Mr. Davis, it's good enough for Mr. Harvey."

Ruth Davis asked him what he was going to do once he finished building his little kingdom. Caton didn't know. He just knew he was dealing with Mary's death in a productive way. Building was better, he thought, than drinking himself to death or sleeping away his life in a depression. At least he'd have something to show for his efforts once he was finished.

Another winter came and went, and the spring thaw warmed the meadow again. Caton built a playhouse for three-year-old Mariah, now old enough to have a grand time in the miniature house. Only one thing remained to complete Mary's dream.

One day, four semi-trucks rolled onto the building site and unloaded a pile of paving stones and cobblestones. One by one, Caton placed the stones in a pattern he had designed. He and Mrs. Davis spent days planting flowers and trees. The final touch was the fountain in the garden's center that flowed around a tall cross built from the stones. The cobblestone paths led from the fountain to the big house, the stables, the guest house, and the cemetery. The fountain overflowed across a short waterfall into the small stream that fed the trout pond.

The day came when Caton sat down to supper and announced his project was complete. "We only need to name her," he said with a shy smile. "An estate like this deserves a name."

Mrs. Davis nodded as she spooned mashed potatoes on his plate. "Hmmm. I can't think of any names fit for a kingdom such as this," she said, laughingly. "Maybe Wonderland!"

They debated names until Mrs. Davis suggested Greenfield. Caton thought Greenfield accurately described the meadow but seemed to lack a certain luster. He suggested Glenfield.

Over breakfast one morning, Caton smiled at Mrs. Davis and asked, "Will you be okay out here when I go back to work?"

Mrs. Davis waved him off. "Pshaw. Don't you worry about me, Mr. Harvey. I've plenty of experience being by myself. We'll be just fine."

"All right," he nodded with satisfaction. "Then I'll get back to work tomorrow. The boys are working near the Ponderosa Pines Golf Course, so I won't have to go all the way to town. Whaddya think about that, Mariah?"

"I think good." Mariah was learning to talk in complete sentences. Caton marveled at how much his little Mariah had grown.

Every day, after Mariah and Mrs. Davis did school, they would go on walks through the forest. When they returned, Mariah played while Mrs. Davis did housework. Mariah had a habit of playing with the phone. She loved punching the buttons and pretending to talk to Mommy. Sometimes she would sing with the dial tone until the harsh alarm let her know to hang up.

Caton was in his office working on a bid to build a restaurant in Cloudcroft when he noticed line three on his phone was lit. He didn't think much about it, knowing Mrs. Davis occasionally phoned in a grocery order to the mercantile in town. However, when the line stayed active for more than a few minutes, he picked up his handset. Mariah was singing "Jesus loves me, this I know" into an active phone line. And, to his amazement, he heard a woman's voice talking back to her.

"Mariah, honey, who are you talking to?"

"Mommy!"

"Oh, my." He placed his hand over the receiver and called out, "Mrs. Davis, Mariah's on the phone again." Then he turned back to the receiver. "Hello?"

A cheerful, friendly voice answered back. "Hello. Who's this?"

"That's what I was about to ask you. Who have you called for?"

He could hear amusement in her words. "You called me—I didn't call you."

Caton was confused. "How's that possible? Mariah isn't old enough to use the phone."

The woman sounded pleased. "The phone rang, and a little voice asked for Mommy. I told her Mommy wasn't here, and she asked if she could sing for me."

"I'm so sorry! I can't imagine how she managed to dial a real number. She's only three."

"Oh, no worries. She's precious." She sounded delighted. "And she has a darling little voice. I've been sitting here enjoying her serenade. So, where are you?"

"In my office." He smiled. He was feeling mischievous.

"No!" The woman laughed. "I mean, where are you and your office located?"

Caton hesitated a moment before answering. "Um. We're near the Village."

"Which village?"

"The Village of Cloudcroft. New Mexico," he added for clarity.

"New Mexico? Wow! I'm in Chicago."

"Wait a minute! You're telling me that Mariah managed to dial a long-distance number? Do you know the odds against that?"

"It must be destiny." She sounded amused.

The conversation silenced, so, Caton grabbed at a straw to keep going. "Chicago?"

"Actually, I'm from Boston. I'm staying in Chicago for a month. Working, you know."

Caton smiled. "Well, happy working." He thought he should hang up, but instead, he added, "My name is Caton, by the way."

"It is a pleasure to meet you. I'm Lily DeMar." Her voice was comfortable and professional. He could imagine talking to a radio host.

"Listen, Mrs. DeMar …"

"I'm not married, DeMar is my maiden name," she replied casually.

"Oh, okay, Miss DeMar ..."

She interrupted him. "Hmm, I think I've misspoken. I was married a few years ago, but after we divorced, I took my maiden name again."

"Oh? Sounds like an ugly story."

Lily sighed emphatically. "You've no idea. He was the most self-centered, egotistical snob I've ever met."

Caton chuckled. "I can see why you married him."

Lily groaned. "Let's just say I was young and didn't know better. He seemed more charming when we were dating."

"That must have been a complicated time for you."

She sighed, "If only I'd known before the big day. I was studying in London, and he was the composer for the symphony ..."

"London? Symphony? Hold on, you used to live in London?"

"Yes," she replied informally. "I studied music theory there."

"London, England?"

"Of course. Is there another?"

"Actually, yes," he replied carefully. "There's a London, Texas, but I doubt you could study music theory there."

"London, Texas. I had no idea! Anyway, I was married to a jerk, but I didn't know until it was too late. It turned out I was not providing him the social standing he required, and he left me for another woman."

"I'm sorry," he said sympathetically. "That must have been difficult."

"I was crushed." She paused for a second, then asked, "Why am I telling you this?"

"I don't know," he said, "but I'm a good listener if you want to talk about it. Maybe you need an unbiased ear."

"Maybe. For some reason, I feel comfortable talking to you."

"I think it's my smile. Or maybe it's the way I comb my hair."

She laughed, and his face brightened. He hadn't joked much since Mary died and being distracted for a few minutes felt good.

Lily sighed. "So, who was the little girl who sang to me?"

"That's Mariah. She's my only child. Her mother died just after she was born, and she thought you were her mother on the phone."

"Yes, she called me Mommy. How sad. What happened, if you don't mind talking about it?"

He hesitated, then surprised himself by his answer. "No, it's okay." He ran his fingers through his hair. "Where to begin? We really struggled to have children—almost eight years, in fact. But after she got pregnant, we discovered she had cancer. She was stage four by the time Mariah was born."

"Oh, that's horrible. I'm so sorry. I shouldn't have pried."

"No," he responded quickly. "Actually, it feels kinda good to talk. I live in the mountains, and we don't get many visitors. I live with Mrs. Davis and Mariah."

"Mrs. Davis?" she softly inquired.

"Ah. The housekeeper." He felt he needed to clarify. "She's an older lady, a widow. Actually, she's only in her fifties, but she seems much older. She's one of those people who was born older, if you know what I mean." His fumbling fingers found a pen to play with, and he clicked it open. "She's very wise and mature." He laughed. "That sounds better than old, right?" Without waiting for a response, he continued. "She does our cooking and cleaning, as well as caring for Mariah. Wonderful lady. She lives here since it's so far from town."

"It's hard to find people like that. You're lucky."

"She's the greatest. It's like having a built-in grandmother."

Another pause as the conversation stopped. Finally, Caton asked, "So, Lily, what do you do?"

Lily seemed to smile. At least he imagined her smiling. "I'm a concert violinist. I play with the Boston Orchestra."

"You must play very well. Even I've heard of the Boston Orchestra!"

They laughed together, and suddenly, Caton was full of enthusiasm. "I just thought of something! I'll be right back." Caton placed the receiver on the desk and walked away. He was back in a flash. "Are you still there?"

"I'm here."

Caton knew for sure she was smiling. He could hear it in her voice. "I thought I remembered the Boston Orchestra. I have your CD here."

"You're kidding!" Lily laughed. "We knew someone bought one, but we had no idea who. Wait until I tell the producer."

"Seriously!" He laughed with her. "It's labeled *Baby's First Symphony*."

She gasped. "Oh, I remember that. I have a violin solo in it."

"Maybe I should send this CD to you for an autograph?"

She laughed. "What's your favorite selection on the CD?"

"We really enjoy Pachelbel's "Canon in D." It's our favorite."

"Mine too!" She was delighted. "That was the first piece I learned to play when I was a little girl."

"Have you played long?"

"Almost all of my life. I started on the piano when I was five. My mother danced ballet, and I would watch her for hours. I was so saturated with classical music that it became my life. By the time I was eight, I started playing stringed instruments."

"Mary and I used to go to the ballet."

"Mary? Was she your wife?"

Caton didn't want to start crying, but it was hard to ignore the lump in his throat. He took a breath. "Yeah, she loved the ballet," he said slowly. "It was okay for me, but she really loved it. Every time a ballet troupe arrived in the area, she'd want to go, but I seldom took her."

"Shame on you," Lily teased.

"I do regret it now," he replied sincerely. "There's so much I would do differently if I had the chance. But, it was also a good opportunity for her and her friends to spend an evening doing girl stuff. However, I faithfully attended the *Nutcracker Suite* every year. I didn't miss the *Nutcracker* until recently."

"Why did you stop going?"

He could feel his ears turning red with the confession. "It's hard to go to the ballet by yourself, especially if you're a man."

Lily snorted. "Ah, yes. I can appreciate that. Why don't you take your daughter?"

"I took her when she was still an infant. She slept through the performance, and I took her home. But now, there's no way she could sit that long. Do you have children?" The moment the question was out, he realized he might have been insensitive.

"No, I don't have children."

"I'm sorry. Was that a bad question?"

"No. Well, not really." She sighed. "It's just that … it's a hard thing for me. Ah—that's why my husband left me. He had a social standing in London, and he needed a young pretty wife to sire him a legacy. I was unable to have children, so he found a mistress who could. The minute she confirmed her pregnancy, I was issued divorce papers and sent home."

"That's horrible. I'm sorry. I imagine it's hard to talk about."

He could hear her sniffle. "No, like you said, it actually feels good to say it aloud. I don't talk about it much, and I travel too much with my work to be in therapy, so it stays with me. Thank you for asking. You have no idea how hard it is on a woman who can't bear children."

"Mary was infertile for many years. We finally gave up on having our own child."

"She had the same problem?"

"Well, she had polycystic ovaries."

Lily immediately became interested. "How long ago was that?"

"Around eight years. We were about to give up. I saw how hard trying was on her, and I know that it's hard on you also."

"How long were you married?"

"Almost nine years."

"Wow, nine years? What an accomplishment. Most marriages don't last that long anymore."

"Oh, she was so wonderful."

"Tell me about her," Lily said softly.

Caton exhaled slowly, steeling his heart. "I met her on the tennis courts in college. I just had to meet her, so I walked up to her and said—you're going to love this—I said, 'Hey, baby, got a match?'"

Lily groaned. "You're kidding."

"Well, it seemed funny at the time. Anyway, she agreed to play me. But I had never played tennis in my life. She slaughtered me out there, but I was hooked."

Lily laughed. "What did she look like?"

He inhaled sharply. "She was beautiful. She had the softest brown hair you've ever seen. Her green eyes sparkled when she laughed, and she had an amazing athletic figure ..." He stopped suddenly, realizing he was talking to a stranger.

The pause stretched. "Go on," Lily urged.

He relaxed. "Oh, I loved her. We got along so well together. We shared such a connection. We were compatible in every way possible."

"That could prove to be boring," she observed.

"I suppose it could be for some. There were enough subtle differences that kept us balanced. She hated broccoli, and I hate pecans. She hated linguini, and I hate cold pasta ..." His voice trailed off.

Lily said, "It sounds like you two really had it together."

"I'll never find another woman to love the way I loved Mary."

Lily agreed. "Probably not." Then she suggested, "But, love can be different."

He sighed deeply. "No, I could never love another woman. Not like that. I just don't have it in me anymore."

"But what about Mariah?" she protested. "Doesn't she need a mother?"

"She has Mrs. Davis, who's a terrific nanny."

"No, a girl needs a mother," she pushed.

"We'll make do." Caton was through with that subject. "So, do you have a boyfriend?"

He could almost hear her frown. "Not now. It's hard. I have to travel around a lot with the orchestra, and I'm not in one place long enough to meet anyone." She paused. "When I'm bored, I try to date, but I don't have much luck with finding keepers. In fact, my last real boyfriend was a pianist, but he ..." Her voice trailed off.

"He what?" Caton asked gently. "You can't start that kind of sentence and not finish it!"

"He left me for someone else."

"Oh. Did you know her?"

"Him." Her voice was flat.

"Oh, wow." Caton cringed, having no idea what to say.

"Yep, it was a bad situation, and no, I didn't know him, but it didn't change anything." She groaned. "I have the worst luck with men," she admitted.

"I'm sorry that happened to you."

"We weren't dating all that long, just a couple of months."

"Still, it had to hurt."

"A little. It seems I'll never find the fortune in love that you once had. I would give everything I have to experience what you had even for just one month."

"God can give it to you."

"God?" She seemed surprised.

"Well, sure."

"My family isn't religious, but I do believe in God," she added.

"I understand," he said. "My faith in God has gotten me through the last few years."

"You seem so normal, not like some other religious people I know. Oh! I wish I hadn't said that."

Caton chuckled gently. "You must not have had many positive encounters with Christians."

"Not really. My husband was a member of the Church of England, but he was the biggest hypocrite who walked the earth."

"I'm sorry."

Her voice was soft. "Why would you be sorry about that?"

"Well, God is so good to us, and there's no way that I could have endured Mary's death without him."

"You don't blame God for taking her?" She gasped. "Oh! There I go again. I'm sorry. I didn't mean to imply that God killed her."

He was more amused by her retreat than offended by her suggestion. "Not at all. Maybe I struggled at first, but not for long. When she was diagnosed with cancer, it felt very unfair, but God soothed my pain." He paused, changing direction. "I believe there's a day marked for each of us to die. Whether you believe in God or not, someday you'll die. It was Mary's time. I was thankful for the opportunity to be with her in her final days. God didn't take her from me; He gave her to me."

He sensed her smile as she changed the subject. "What do you look like?"

"I have a face that's perfect for radio."

"Somehow I doubt that." She laughed. "You sound like a great man."

"Thank you, Lily." He paused. "Son of a gun! Look at the time! We've been talking for almost an hour?"

"I feel like we're old friends." She hesitated. "Caton? You were good for me today. Thank Mariah for dialing my phone."

"I am still amazed at the odds of that happening."

"I know. But truly, thanks. I feel better having talked to you. I'm sorry you lost Mary."

"Thank you, Lily."

For a moment, neither of them spoke, and neither attempted to hang up. Caton went first. "I guess this is good-bye."

"Yes, I suppose it is."

"We won't ever talk to each other again, I suppose."

Lily sighed. "Maybe not, but I'll remember this conversation forever."

"Me too." He frowned at himself, feeling silly. "Goodbye, Lily. I enjoyed meeting you."

"Me too. Goodbye now."

CHAPTER THREE

Hearing a minor uproar, Caton went to the kitchen. Mariah was sitting on the counter, her face and arms covered with stripes from a blue magic marker. Mrs. Davis, obviously distressed, was frantically scrubbing her with a washcloth, fussing over the lines on Mariah's face.

Caton couldn't help laughing. "Mrs. Davis, how is everything this evening?"

"Dear me," she muttered sheepishly. "I only turned my back for a moment and look what happened."

"Don't worry," he reassured her. "These things happen."

Mrs. Davis placed the cloth on the countertop and frowned. "No, you don't understand. I could hear you on the phone, and I heard you laughing." She winced. "I was curious, so I stood by your office for at least five minutes," she admitted, her face flushing with embarrassment.

He suppressed a grin. "Were you hiding around the corner or standing in the doorway?"

"I was in the doorway. Oh," she gasped, clearly horrified. "You saw me eavesdropping?" She went to work with her cloth again, trying to hide her embarrassment.

He waved his hand dismissively. "I don't care about that. If my conversations are private, I'll close the door." He shook his head in amazement. "Check this out—that phone call?" He grinned. "Did you know Mariah dialed a number in Chicago?"

"Why, no, sir, I didn't. But I won't let it happen again."

"Mrs. Davis, you aren't in trouble! In fact, whatever you are doing is working great." He grabbed a cloth to help her erase stripes from Mariah's arm. "You're raising a child prodigy. She randomly punched numbers and called a working number. We should play the lottery today."

She lowered the cloth. "Are you telling me Mariah called whoever you were talking to on the phone?"

Caton nodded, then turned to Mariah. "Honey, how did you call the woman on the phone?"

"I push numbers. Like this." She made a show of pushing buttons on an imaginary keypad and counted while she did. "One, two, tree, fowah, two, six, seven, one." She was proud of herself. Caton knew Mariah couldn't recognize which number went with the symbol. "I talk to Mommy," Mariah said, obviously pleased.

Caton smiled at her. "No, baby, Mommy is in heaven with Jesus. Remember?"

Her eyes hardened. "No, I talk to Mommy."

He started to correct her again, then he saw Mrs. Davis shrug. "I suppose it won't hurt her to think she talked to her mother," she said. "It's not like it'll happen again."

He sighed with resignation. "Did you sing for her?"

"No, I *talk* to Mommy."

Caton needed to relive the moment so he could process it. "You wouldn't believe it. I looked at the phone and line three was lit. I thought you must have been phoning in a grocery list, but the light stayed on for a long time. So I pushed the line, and I could hear Mariah singing. I chatted with the woman a few minutes and then hung up."

Mrs. Davis fought back a smile. "You talked for nearly an hour. Who was she?"

"Her name is Lily, and she's a violinist from Boston. She performed on the classical music CD we play for Mariah every night. Isn't that amazing?" He rubbed his fingers in his hair. "I can't figure it out. There were dozens of baby music CDs, and we ended up with the same one Lily plays on. What are the odds?"

Mrs. Davis's eyes sparkled. "I don't know, but you certainly seem excited by it."

"I am not." He shrugged, still unable to contain his enthusiasm. "It's just interesting to see the coincidence, that's all."

Mrs. Davis smiled. "And all this time I thought you believed in divine providence, not coincidences."

That stopped him for a moment. "Hmmm, so I do, but why would God have me talk to her?" he mused aloud. "After all, it's not like I'll see her again ... or talk to her, for that matter."

Mrs. Davis turned to wet her cloth. "You can lead a horse to water, but you can't make him drink."

His eyes narrowed suspiciously. "And what's that supposed to mean?"

"It's just something Poppa used to say."

"I know the phrase. What are you drivin' at?"

She smiled affectionately. "You hung up on a woman who made you laugh?"

He looked up at the ceiling. He already regretted not pursuing further contact with Lily. "So? It's not like I'm going to marry her. It was all an accident, anyway—right?—that she was on the phone."

"Accident or divine providence?" Mrs. Davis smiled.

"Well, whatever it is, it doesn't mean I'm gonna get involved with this woman."

"God has a way of working out these things. You could find her through the symphony listing if you wanted to," she suggested.

His face flushed. "I don't wanna hunt her down. It's Mariah who called, not me."

Mariah, pulling at the string on her sweater, said, "I talk to Mommy."

"I know, baby doll. You told us already," Caton replied.

One evening, Reverend Montgomery made a special trip to Glenfield to collect a pledge from Caton to help a missionary family in South America. He greeted Caton with a smile and a hearty handshake. "How in the world are you?" he asked.

Caton shrugged. "I've been staying busy."

"We wanted to invite y'all to join us for lunch after the church service last Sunday, but you disappeared immediately after the benediction."

Caton shook his head. "Are you telling me I missed out? I'm truly sorry to hear that, Reverend."

"Mesquite-grilled baby back ribs," he taunted. "Maybe next time you won't leave just because I'm taking up an offering," he replied with a friendly jab. He turned his eyes to the house. "Oh, my!" he exclaimed. "This place gets bigger every time I come out."

Caton looked down. "Sometimes I think this house owns me. It's a lot to keep up with by myself."

Reverend Montgomery placed a hand on his shoulder. "We never have to be alone." He patted Caton on the back. "You say the word, and we'll get a work crew up here on Saturday to help you out."

Caton met his gaze. "I'll keep that in mind." He glanced at the sun. "It's a bit hot out here. Why don't you join me in the kitchen for some lemonade?"

"Well, that depends," he replied. "Did Ruth bake any cookies?"

Caton laughed. "When Mrs. Davis heard you were coming, she put on her apron!"

They sat around the table in the breakfast nook while the good reverend greatly reduced a platter of chocolate chip cookies. " Ruth," he spouted between bites. "These cookies are crispy and chewy at the same time."

Mrs. Davis' eyes beamed. "It's an old baking trick. You use brown sugar and double the amount called for in the recipe."

"Magnificent," he crowed. "If I weren't a Christian, I'd worship at your feet!"

"My soul, Reverend! You do go on! You know you don't need a reason to come out and eat cookies."

He shook his head. "That's not a good idea, Ruth. I'd be as fat as the prophet Eli in no time at all."

Caton placed an envelope in front of him. "Are you sure that's enough to buy a new plane?"

Reverend Montgomery popped a cookie crumb in his mouth. "Between this and the money we raised, not a brand-new plane, but a used one. You are certainly being a blessing to the Ashworth family."

Caton pursed his lips together and tried not to look bashful. "I'm glad to help. The Lord's blessed me. I'm just paying it forward, so to speak."

"Well, I'm praying God will bless you in return."

"Thank you," he replied graciously, "but that's not why I give. After I received the settlement from Mary's death, I invested a portion and did pretty well." He shrugged. "I got lucky and caught some tech stocks as they were going up. God was good to me."

"Quite an accomplishment in this economy," the pastor agreed.

"Well, the investments have paid for this house, and I've got all I need." He glanced at Mariah, who was coloring a picture of a phone with a red crayon.

"The Ashworths appreciate your help. The government officials in Venezuela seized their plane in retaliation for all the 'spying' they were doing." He laughed. "Can you believe that? Spies! Ha!" He sipped his lemonade. "Your gift will make a difference, Caton."

Caton shook his head. "Oh, don't make me out to be a saint."

"Do go on, Reverend," Ruth interrupted. "Mr. Harvey will never call himself a saint, but that's what he is." Caton opened his mouth to protest, but Ruth held up a hand to silence him. "He simply has a good heart and loves to be generous."

"And I seem to remember a missionary family in Haiti who wanted to start an orphanage," the reverend added. "Caton practically funded the operation by himself."

"Oh, that's not true," Caton replied. "Besides, a little money in Haiti goes a long way."

"Yes, it *is* true," Montgomery shot back. "And there was that family in China." He picked up another cookie.

Uncomfortable with the praise, Caton wanted to change the subject. "I have my faults too, Mrs. Davis," he asserted. "Before you knew me, I spent plenty of money on myself, and bought plenty of trouble at the same time."

Montgomery laughed. "Is this about those guns you bought?"

Caton laughed. "You know it. Mary was so mad at me."

"I haven't heard this story," Ruth hinted.

Caton traced a circle on the table with his glass. "A few years before Mary got sick, I went on a gun buying spree."

"A spree?" Mrs. Davis didn't believe him.

"Oh, like most mountain folk, I bought a gun here and there. But one day, the good Reverend here invited me to an estate auction in Artesia."

Montgomery laughed. "He thought he'd died and gone to heaven!"

"A firearms collector put together a large array of antique firearms, including a gatling gun and a blunderbuss …"

"A what?" Mrs. Davis asked.

"You know what a blunderbuss is, Ruth. It's a pilgrim gun," Montgomery offered.

"Do you mean the gun with the fluted end that looks like a trumpet?"

"Yes, I suppose so," he replied with a chuckle.

Caton continued. "Anyway, I picked up some old dueling pistols and an assortment of nineteenth-century military arms."

"When he saw those guns, his eyes bugged out like in a Bugs Bunny cartoon," Montgomery howled. "He had to buy them!"

Caton smirked. "You should have seen Mary's face when I showed up with more than thirty different guns. She kept pressing me to see how much I'd spent."

"Did you tell her?"

"I did." His eyes sparkled with the memory. "And that's when I thought she would use those guns against me!"

Montgomery burst into laughter. "It was a good thing none of them were loaded!"

Ruth shook her head. "And what came of all those guns?"

Caton shrugged. "Actually, we ate 'em."

"You *ate* them?"

"In a manner of speaking. Well, heck, I didn't need them. We went through a few lean years, and I needed a spot of cash to build a spec home. I sold the guns and used the money to finish the house. When I sold the house, we used that money to live. So, yes, we ate them."

CHAPTER FOUR

ONE TUB OF ICE CREAM COMING UP

Lily sat on the balcony of her apartment pensively sipping her Earl Grey tea and trying to forget her miserable luck with finding a quality date. She'd managed to find a man who still lived with his mom, whom he called his roommate, and claimed to have property on the English Riviera. In ten minutes, she'd seen through his façade. The evening was disappointing on so many levels, and regret hung in the air. She was lonely and growing tired of drinking tea by herself. But tomorrow, she would pack her clothes and fly to San Francisco again. She was tired of traveling, but this was the life she had.

Lily finished her tea and walked back inside. She noticed Jayne had called. She pressed a button on her cell. "Hey! I'm sorry I missed your call. Everything okay?"

"I'm okay. I just called to see how your date went. I was hoping you got lucky!"

Lily groaned. "Don't bother."

"Bad, eh?" Jayne, who played cello in the orchestra, was her friend— her "wild Canadian friend," as Jayne liked to say.

"Yep. I walked out on him at the restaurant and went to a movie."

"Why, what happened?"

"Oh, I'll tell you about it tomorrow. I'm not up for the conversation tonight. I only want to go to bed and suck my thumb."

"That's too bad. Sounds like an ice cream night."

"Chocolate. With chocolate chips and chocolate syrup."

"Want me to bring some over?"

"No," she exhaled. "It's too late. Can I ask you something?" Without waiting on her answer, she asked, "Am I gullible?"

"What? You? Are you kidding me?"

Lily sighed. "Oh, I'm just tired of finding men who only want to impress me. And I'm irritated that I seem to be attracted to such buffoons."

"So, one of your standard dates, eh?"

"You know it."

"Well, tell me tomorrow, okay?"

"I promise."

"What movie did you go see?" Jayne asked.

"*Direct Access.*" She awaited Jayne's predictable response.

"Oh! That's the one with Brent Jacobs! He's your old beau, eh?"

"Don't be silly. We only dated twice, and he couldn't keep his hands off me either time. Dating an octopus would have been better."

Jayne exaggerated her reaction. "You're crazy. Any normal woman would be grateful to have his hands all over her. I know I would have."

"That might have been my biggest concern. How many women had he been pawing? Who knows? Well, I certainly don't want to know."

Jayne groaned. "You've got to get over being such a prude. You need to loosen up some."

Lily sighed. "I'd rather have a man who respects me," she replied softly.

"You'll never get a ring with that attitude."

"Don't you turn into my mother," Lily scolded playfully.

"You just need to find an old-fashioned man."

"Sure, but where do I get one of those?"

"Have you tried the nursing home?"

"Ha, ha."

"What about that lumberjack-slash-mountain-man who called you and talked for an hour?"

"Oh? Caton? The phone was dialed by accident." She smiled at the memory. "And I hardly ever think about him."

"Don't you get tired of lying to yourself?"

"Well, it's better than thinking about how lonely I am."

"You don't believe in accidents; you believe in destiny. Remember?"

"Fine, I believe in destiny, but my conversation with Caton wasn't destiny. It was something else."

"Like what?"

"Something similar to ice cream on a hot day."

"Wow, he really got to you, eh."

Lily stared wistfully across the lake. "Well, he is a special man. If only I could meet him, or a man like him."

"Why not him?"

"For one thing, he's still in love with his dead wife. You can't have a man who's in love with a memory. The competition's too strong. And perfect."

"Yeah, I can imagine." Jayne agreed.

"Jayne! You aren't the one he talked to."

"Maybe, but you aren't going to pursue him, and we both know it."

"I'd love to speak to him again," she whispered, and inhaled deeply. "He was so easy to talk to … like we knew each other already."

"I still wonder what he looks like," Jayne mused.

"It doesn't matter." Lily looked up at the stars. "A man who can love with that kind of passion doesn't need good looks."

"Maybe for you. I like a strong and rugged man."

"Like I don't? What if he were both rugged and passionate?"

"Then marry him the minute you find him, eh."

"Right. It's too bad I'll never hear from him again."

Jayne yawned. "What time are you going to the airport tomorrow?"

Lily yawned. "Oh, around one o'clock or so. I'll come by and pick you up, okay?"

"Okay, I'll see you then."

CHAPTER FIVE

How She Lost a Man She Never Had

Lily hardly noticed the flight to San Francisco. In a few hours, she was sitting on the veranda of Rutherford, her San Francisco home, looking out over the bay. Beautiful and historic, Rutherford offered a commanding view of the Golden Gate Bridge and the waters beyond.

She had a few days before the next performance, but she had a rehearsal later in the afternoon. She had a craving for Ivar's Seafood in Santa Clara, so she called Jayne and invited her along. After dinner, they went to rehearsal. Although Jayne always stayed in Santa Clara when they were in the area, Lily didn't see much of her because of Jayne's local boyfriend who dominated her free time.

The phone rang just as Lily was about to leave. She cringed when she read the caller ID. *Sneed!* Her face contorted at the thought of talking to him. She allowed the phone to ring twice more before summoning the energy to talk to her boss.

"Lily? Sneed, here."

She hated how his voice was almost a hoarse whisper; she got chills. "What can I do for you, Jerry?" She knew he preferred to be called Mr. Sneed, but the entire orchestra refused to grant him that small accommodation.

Amidst several profanities, he snapped, "We have to move tomorrow's rehearsal to the high school theater. Some freakin' idiot double booked the facility. Apparently, the Governor rates higher on the list than we do." He sounded genuinely confused by this revelation. Lily rolled her eyes.

"Okay. This is the theater on 19th Avenue?"

"Of course."

Are we done?

"And I saw on the list you were supposed to wear the studded V-neck black dress for the performance in two days. Have you seen how the stage lights reflect? I don't want my musicians looking like some confounded disco ball."

"Okay." *Now are we done?*

"Instead, I want everyone to wear the halter neck waistband dress." He was breathing heavier now.

I'm sure you do, you dirty old man. He seemed to love that dress because of the low cut and display of more cleavage. And backless. He was always looking at the women with too much enthusiasm. The thought of his ogling made her skin crawl. "Fine, Jerry." *Come on, take a hint and bother someone else.*

"Oh, and I'm making a change to the program, so bring your music to Guitar Concerto Nos. 1-3."

"Sure thing." She loved that movement, one of her favorites from this tour.

"And don't be late," he snarled.

"Goodbye, Jerry," she said politely.

"Out," He hung up.

She rolled her eyes again. Lily recalled how Jerry once fired a cellist for missing a performance due to an emergency appendectomy. They had to buy out the rest of her contract, but once he decided she was fired, the decision was final. The entire ensemble turned against him, but they wouldn't fight him on small issues any longer. Most lived in fear they would catch him on a bad day and get fired.

Lily had better things to do than dwell on painful memories. She had plans with Jayne, which always made for an interesting evening.

Jayne continued to invest all of her time into her boyfriend, so Lily continued in her loneliness. She spent some time gardening, but mostly she spent her days daydreaming. One afternoon, while she was considering life improvements, her cell phone rang.

"Hello? Mamma!"

Instantly, Lily's heart soared as she recognized the tiny voice. "Mariah, is that you?"

"Hi, Mamma. Are you in heaven?"

She stood. "No, sweetie, I'm in San Francisco. Mariah, how did you call me?"

"I push numbers. One, two, tree, fowah, five, six, seven, fowah, ten!"

Lily's head was spinning as she imagined the impossibility of Mariah playing with the phone and finding her twice. No, there must be a redial button on the phone. Somehow, her phone number had been hidden in Caton's phone-bank memory.

"That's great, sweetheart! You can count so very well! Is your daddy home?"

"Uh-huh. Do you want me to sing to you?"

Lily's heart gushed to realize Mariah had found her again. "Oh, what a wonderful idea!"

Mariah started out with "Twinkle, Twinkle, Little Star," then "Row, Row, Row Your Boat." Next, she sang "Jesus Loves Me."

"Mariah, you sing so pretty! Honey, could you go and find your father? I want to talk to Daddy."

"Okay." Lily could still hear her soft breaths over the phone.

"Do it now. Put the phone down and go get Daddy."

"Okay." She heard the phone being dropped, then a small voice faintly calling out, "Daaaaddy!" After a moment of silence, she could hear heavy footsteps on a hardwood floor.

"Hello?" A familiar voice.

"Good evening, Caton—this is Lily. How are you?"

Silence prevailed for a moment; her heart jumped into her throat. *What if he doesn't remember me?*

"Lily? From Boston?"

"You do remember." She was relieved.

"How did you get this number?" He sounded more concerned than interested.

"Mariah called me."

"Again? How's that possible?"

Lily laughed gently. "I know, an impossibility but true. My cell number must be somewhere in your phone's memory bank. I was sitting in my garden when my phone rang, and I heard that sweet little voice."

"Incredible. I didn't realize we still had your number. I'm sorry she bothered you again."

"Oh, no bother!" she replied, a little too quickly. She paused. "I like nice surprises."

"So, how's Chicago?"

"I'm at my home in San Francisco."

"California? How's that possible? How did she call you there?" He sounded dubious.

"Well, the number's for my cell. So, all she had to do was hit redial."

She heard him chuckle, but his voice was flat. "Yes, that would explain everything."

"Gee, Caton, you sound disappointed."

"Oh, no!" he responded too quickly. "I just didn't expect to hear from you again."

"I know. Wonderful, yes?"

Caton finally laughed. "I suppose so. So how have you been?"

"Well, since I've spoken with you, I've relocated to California for a few weeks. How about yourself?"

Caton paused. "I've been busy. We have a lot of work, and my one crew has been increased to two crews."

"That's fantastic!" She grinned, clearly overjoyed at talking to him again. "What do you do?"

"Hmm? I suppose we never covered that in our last conversation. I'm a general contractor. I build homes and office buildings."

"Do you make a good living?"

"Sure. I manage to keep my employees with food on their tables."

"How's Mariah?"

She could almost hear him smile. "She's grown even since you've seen her last."

"Caton, can I ask you a silly question?"

"Go ahead, take your best shot."

"What do I look like?"

He chuckled. "How am I supposed to know? I've never seen you before."

"Exactly," she said, "But you just said she's grown since I've seen her last."

"I did?"

"Yes, you did." She twirled a strand of hair in her fingers.

"Why would I do that?"

"I don't know. Maybe we just had a good connection the last time we talked."

Lily's heart warmed—maybe he'd been thinking of her also.

Caton reflected. "I wonder how we keep finding each other?"

"I think a better question is why?"

"Why?"

"Yes, why."

"No, I'm asking you why you think that's a better question."

Lily hesitated. Where to begin? "Well, Caton, do you believe in destiny?"

He thought for a moment before answering, and when he did, he spoke carefully. "Yes, I think I must. What about you, Lily?"

Lily sighed softly when he said her name. "Maybe it's not time for us to know yet. But I can tell you that I've missed talking to you."

Caton cleared his throat, clearly uncertain what she was getting at. "I enjoyed our conversation too. I liked talking with someone who had no vested interest in being polite."

"Oh, I managed to destroy a day trader's future—yes, pun intended," Lily started. "He was a humongous jerk."

"What happened? Do you want to talk about it?"

Lily grinned, excited for him to invite her, and began to tell the story of her date with Rees, and how he tried to impress her by lying about everything and insisting he had lived on the British Riviera and visited the Fletschhorn Hotel in Switzerland. Caton laughed at each stage of his lies and how she trapped him into revealing the truth.

"So, you've experienced the champagne breakfast at this Fletch Hotel?"Caton asked.

"The Fletschhorn Hotel." She giggled.

He joined her laughter. "That sounds better. Fletch sounds like a place Chevy Chase would own."

Lily hesitated. "We went there all the time. Rodney took me because I loved that part of Switzerland." She was wistful. "It's all very *Sound of Music-y.*"

"Nice," he said, appreciatively, "but it sounds expensive."

"Well, the hotel is pricy, but money was no big deal to Rodney. Of course, living in London, we could take a train through the Chunnel and be there in a few hours. We didn't have to fly over the ocean to get there."

"True. I've never been to Europe, but I would love to visit. I'll take Mariah someday."

"I would love to go back, myself. What you need is a guided tour." Then her face turned red as she realized how she must have sounded. She immediately stammered, "What I mean is—not that it should be me …"

Caton was laughing and managed to comment, "It's cool. I know what you mean. When I go, I won't invite you."

Lily grimaced at the apparent step backwards. "What? You mean I can't go with you? How rude!" She laughed to hide her discomfort.

"Well, I'm not in the habit of traveling to other countries with strange women."

"Oh, so now I'm a strange woman?"

Caton laughed again. "Yes, Lily, I'd have to say you're a little strange. But, maybe that's what I like about you."

Lily's smiled returned. "Caton, how are you doing?"

She heard him take a deep breath. "Gee. How do I know? My heart still cries out at night, and sometimes I reach across the bed only to feel an empty, cold pillow. I try to move on, but I seem to have no ability to do anything but hurt." Suddenly, he was in a mood to talk and he engaged without looking back. "Sometimes I get these haunting dreams, as if we're together again, and then—I wake up." He hesitated. "Everyone tells me I'm doing all right, but I don't know."

She flushed at hearing him speak so. "What have you been doing to help you deal?"

"Well, I built the home Mary always wanted across the meadow from my old home. She wanted something larger, but we never had the money." He started telling her about old vacations and laughing about Lily's two dates with the actor Brent Jacobs.

Then they started talking about religion and God, their favorite foods and books, and, finally, love and marriage. When their discussion turned to politics, Lily laughed at Caton's shock that she was a staunch conservative. "How is that possible? All this time, I assumed you were a liberal."

She contrived annoyance. "Just because I grew up in Massachusetts doesn't mean I'm a liberal. There are a dozen or so conservatives living there, and we have support groups to help us deal … when we're not hiding under our beds, that is." She enjoyed hearing him laugh. "Actually, my father was one of those tax-paying property owners. He fought the liberals who wanted to increase his taxes every time they funded another project."

Before she realized, almost two hours had passed. Lily said, "Caton, what if we exchanged emails?"

Silence.

"Caton, are you still there?" She bit her lip, realizing she'd overstepped his comfort level.

"Yeah, I'm still here." A few seconds of awkward reticence followed. "But ... I don't know."

She closed her eyes, willing the correct words to come forth. "Caton, I've had lousy luck with men. You're the most open and gentle man I've ever talked to in my life. And I mean, ever." She laughed to hide her discomfort. "I'm not asking you to marry me or anything, but I want to know you better. Please, please, forgive me if I'm pushing too hard, but I want to keep in contact if we can."

His silence scared Lily.

"Caton, say something."

Several seconds passed. "I don't know, Lily. I'm just—really confused right now. I love Mary as if she were still with me." She bit her lip in anticipation of what he would say next. "I sort of feel I'm betraying her for talking to you." Then his voice grew stronger. "I'm not sure I can do this."

Well, he was honest with me, which was what I wanted. Lily brushed away her tears. "I understand."

He sounded both alarmed and concerned. "Oh, Lily, please don't take it like that."

"I'll be okay." She sniffled, wishing she had a tissue. "Thanks for being honest."

"Look, the reason I'm so confused is because, for the first time since I met Mary, I'm attracted to another woman, and it feels strange. Heck, I don't even know what you look like, but I've got a feeling I'm seeing you in my dreams." He stopped for a moment, and then continued when she offered no response. "Just don't tell me that you're a blonde with green eyes and very slender."

"Oh!" She sat upright in her chair.

Caton was suddenly very alert. "What do you mean, 'oh'?"

"Caton, you've never asked me what I look like—and yet you just described me." She thought for a moment. "Did you look me up on the internet?"

He almost chuckled. "No, I promise. Maybe a lucky guess."

"Ya' know? I don't think so. Have you been dreaming about me?"

He was in full retreat now. "Look, I don't know. I can't imagine I'd dream about you. I've no idea what you look like."

"Yes, you do," she insisted, "and you know it!"

There was a pause in the conversation, then Caton continued. "Look, Lily, I haven't enjoyed talking to anyone as much as I have you, but I'm not ready to betray—no, that's not the right word." He was walking through a minefield. "Be romantically involved with anyone after Mary. Not yet." He swallowed. "I don't think we should talk anymore."

Suddenly her hands were shaking. "Caton, don't let me go." *Please not without a fight.*

"I just don't know what to do. I need time to think."

"Well," she was scrambling. "Write down my number so we can talk to each other again."

"I don't know … You can't imagine how hard this is for me."

"Why? Explain to me, so I can understand, so I can have peace," she explained. She heard him sigh in acceptance of her request.

"I was so in love with Mary. I barely noticed other women. We were so good together I never once thought about straying from her. Now, I feel like that's what I'm doing."

Careful, Lily. "What if I promise not to call you, but to let you call me if you change your mind?"

Silence.

Lily decided she'd insist. This was her do or die moment. "Caton, I'm going to lay my cards on the table. I've never met a man I cared for more than I care for you. I barely know who you are, but I feel our hearts and our lives are connected in some way, as if destiny, or God, is trying to connect us. I think you and I could be very happy together. I don't want to replace Mary, but I do want to be a part of your life. Now, if you've been dreaming about me, then something's going on. Shouldn't we find out what this is?" Unable to believe what she just said, she sat, stunned and shaking, until Caton spoke.

"Lily," he said, " I think I could probably love you some day, but that day is not now. And it's not tomorrow. It might be five years from now, but it's not today."

I'll wait, she wanted to scream, but the words wouldn't come out of her mouth. "Goodbye," Caton said, and hung up.

She'd lost him. She sat trembling in her chair until she found herself crying uncontrollably, as if she'd lost her best friend.

Finally, she grew weary of wiping her nose on her sleeve and moved to the kitchen. She removed a container of chocolate ice cream from the freezer, grabbed a spoon, and collapsed on the couch. She wasn't hungry, it was late, and she had to work tomorrow. In addition, she might have trouble fitting into her dress in the morning, but she cried and ate until the ice cream was gone.

Eventually, Lily retired to her bed. With a deep sigh, she picked up a photo sitting on her nightstand, a picture of her holding a steaming mug of cocoa on a snowy landscape in front of the Fletschhorn Hotel.

She had lost a man she never actually had.

Caton stared at his phone, completely denying his sense of loss. The house was stifling, so he moved to the balcony and watched the wind bending the aspen trees. The full moon allowed him to see all the way across the valley. The aspens had a suggestion of yellow in them. The first autumn snows would arrive within a month. The air had a nip, but he didn't acknowledge the bite. He was beguiled by his emotions but couldn't decide whether he was experiencing grief or loss. He couldn't tell the difference. He simply stared across the meadow, his gaze set like a mask.

His recurring dream remained in his memory. He and Mariah were picking flowers in the garden, when Lily walked up and shared a flower with Mariah. He looked into her eyes and saw a clean, crisp green, a shade he'd never before seen. Her hair was arranged neatly on top of her head. She wore a formal black dress. She was so beautiful he couldn't stop staring into her hypnotic eyes.

As he stared across the meadow, Lily dominated his thoughts. He couldn't stop thinking of those dream eyes. He walked down the outside stairs to the bottom deck where the wood gave way to stone. Guided by the soft, glowing moonlight, he moved through the garden to Mary's grave. As he often did, he sat down on the stone bench, built for just such an occasion. "Father," Caton prayed, "what's happening? I don't think I've ever been so confused. Things were simple with Mary, and things were simple without her. But now, nothing with Lily is simple. Please show me your path. If you want me to start something new ..." He felt his voice catch. "then I ask You to heal me from the old."

CHAPTER SIX

The Highest Golf Course in the United States

The orchestra would be leaving San Francisco soon to tour several key cities. The current schedule would give Lily almost two full weeks in Boston before Christmas. She couldn't wait to get home to be with her mom.

While the rest of the world was shopping for Black Friday sales, she was rehearsing in a downtown theater in Seattle. While others were hanging Christmas ornaments, she was performing in Las Vegas.

In a few more days, they would be in Phoenix, then she would be home. She desperately missed her family, even her edgy sister, Ivy, who was continually in and out of trouble with the law. She was ready to be home in Boston. However, upon arriving in Phoenix, the orchestra members learned that Jerry Sneed had extended their tour for an additional week. They would be in Albuquerque as a last-minute substitute for the Dallas Pops Orchestra. An outbreak of the flu among the Dallas musicians had spread rapidly through the woodwind section, then severely impacted the percussionists. With little regard for his musicians, Sneed had callously agreed to fill in, garnering favors from several people in the business.

Gloomy faces peered out the windows as the plane lifted off the ground. Lily loved the stark, naked mountains jutting upward, standing as sentinels to those who live the hard life in an arid climate.

Lily sat by Jayne, who was glaring through the window. She returned her gaze to the clouds, but no joy would come to her as she contemplated the coming week.

"I can't believe we have to do this," Jayne whined.

Lily rolled her eyes. "Tell me about it."

"You tell me about it, eh. Where is home anyway, right?"

"Wherever my contract tells me to live," Lily moaned.

"I feel like the finale will never come," Jayne groaned. "But, I'm sorry we left Phoenix so soon."

Lily frowned at her. "Does this have to do with a man named Dwight?"

Jayne smiled.

"Jayne, you're incorrigible. He's a scary man." Lily couldn't hide her disapproval.

Jayne was in the mood to press the issue. "Go ahead—get the scolding out of your system, Miss Goody-Two-Shoes."

"It's simple. You want to be in a solid relationship, but you sabotage them all before you can get them going."

Jayne picked up the in-flight magazine. "What's that supposed to mean?"

"Look, Jayne, there's nothing as precious as a woman with virtue, even if you don't believe me. Once that virtue is lost, it's difficult to recover."

"Look who's talking!" Jayne accused her. "You're no saint yourself."

"When have you seen me go home with a man?"

"You're kidding, right?"

"No." Lily was unflinching.

"Wait a minute," she twisted in her seat to face her. "Are you telling me that you've never slept with a man since your divorce?"

Lily swallowed. "Yes."

"Liar." She returned to her magazine.

"Jayne, that's why Brent Jacobs stopped going out with me."

She lowered the magazine. "You mean it's true? You really didn't sleep with him?"

Her eyes were soft. "That's not who I am. And it's okay for me to be this way," She grinned. "I'm a romantic at heart. Why would I sleep with him?"

"Because …" she said in disbelief, "Lily, the man is a god!"

"Ugh. Whatever." She looked out the window and then back at Jayne. "And you know what? Your demi-god would have had fun that night and then moved on. I'd just be another meaningless conquest for him."

"Oh, cool!" She flipped the magazine toward Lily. "I could use a remote-control grill that flips my burgers for me, eh." Jayne flipped the page. "I can't believe you didn't sleep with him … unless you have some kind of psychological disorder." Her lips pressed together. "Seriously. Why not?"

Lily sighed. "If you have to ask the question, you won't understand the answer."

"Try me."

Lily thought for a second. "Imagine you're given one gift that you can give to the most special man in your life, your future husband, but you decide to give it to the first man you meet. What will you give to the man you want to marry? The memory of having compromised and given his gift to a man you didn't love?"

Jayne frowned. "Hello, Jayne, my name is Lily, and I'm a wet blanket."

Lily stuck out her tongue. "You're only upset because I'm right, and you know it."

"Whatever," Jayne retorted childishly.

"Jayne, I've made mistakes in my life. Rodney was one of them. But, I chose to remain celibate because I do want to remarry, and I want my husband to be the right man. I might not be able to give him my first special gift, but I can make my gift meaningful to him. You know ... special."

"But, how can you go so long? I mean, that's like ... years! I couldn't do it." She was exasperated. "Why would I want to?" Her voice rose. "That's insane."

"You just do. Just say no. Besides, I know he'll be worthy."

"Yeah, right," Jayne moaned. "I've never met a man who's worth that."

"I have," Lily stated with conviction.

"Who?"

She remained silent.

Jayne's eyes widened. "Your mystery man in New Mexico. Right?"

Lily turned and looked out the window.

"I thought you were over him. At least you stopped putting on weight, eh."

"Jayne!" Lily patted her stomach. "I took it off again. And I don't think I'll ever get over him," she replied with a sad smile.

"Careful, these perfect men will hurt you."

"You're right about that."

"Why don't you go see him?"

"Oh sure! I'll go see him. Just like that?" Lily snapped her fingers. "Are you insane?"

"Look, if you don't at least try, you'll regret it for the rest of your miserable, spinsterly life." She smiled warmly. "I know you, eh? You'll never let this go until you can drive the last nail into the coffin."

"How?" she asked with exasperation. "Where is he?"

"You said he was in New Mexico, right?"

"It's a big state, Jayne."

"What town did you say he was from?"

"I can't remember. Some village. Some place up in the mountains."

"Well, there you go. How many towns can there be in the mountains, eh?"

"Hello? The whole state is one big mountain."

"Well," Jayne wasn't giving up so easily. "Is there anything you remember?"

She tapped her lip. "He told me he was building a home on the highest golf course in the United States, or something like that."

"The highest golf course? What does that mean? Wait, are there millenial deadheads in New Mexico?"

Lily ignored her. "I think it means the golf course with the highest altitude. At least, I think that's what he said."

"Well, there ya' go. What more do you need?"

Lily was exasperated. "A lot more!"

"Coward." Jayne turned around in her seat and peeked at the couple sitting behind her.

Lily, sensing Jayne was about to go off road, glared at her. "No! Whatever you're about to do, stop!"

"Trust me!" Jayne said flippantly, and then made eye contact with the man behind them. "Excuse me, sir, I'm Jayne from Canada, and this is Lily from Boston. Are you from New Mexico?"

Lily buried her face in her hands. "Oy," she mumbled.

The man turned to his wife and shrugged, indicating he didn't initiate contact with the two hottest women on the plane. He stammered. "Y-Yes, I'm from Roswell," then added, "that is, *we* are from Roswell." His wife nodded in approval of his revision.

"Good. Can you tell me where the highest golf course in the United States is?"

He nodded. "Well, I don't know about the US, but the highest one in New Mexico is in Cloudcroft."

Lily's face was ashen as she immediately recognized the name of the town. *What if it is possible? What if I have learned the location of the one man on earth I want to see?*

Jayne looked from the man to Lily, then back again. "Is it a village?"

He blinked. "Well, they call it the Village of Cloudcroft." He glanced at his wife. "That's its name."

"Honey, when we land, I'm gonna give you super big kiss to show my gratitude. You just be ready."

The man looked horrified. "If it's all the same to you, I'll pass." He shifted awkwardly in his seat, clearly wishing Jayne would leave him alone. Jayne smiled sweetly at his wife and turned around in her seat.

Lily's mind was just short of an overload, processing both her horror at Jayne's embarrassing her on the plane and the intriguing information they'd learned. Caton, from Cloudcroft. A contractor. Jayne was right—enough information to discover where he lived.

In the months following their last phone call, Caton's torment was growing. He continually returned to the idea he had betrayed his wife by talking to Lily. No, by *enjoying* his talk with Lily. He knew the idea was nonsense, but those were his feelings, and he couldn't escape them.

He refused to wonder about what life would be like with her. In truth, the idea left him nauseated and excited at the same time. He tried to convince himself he was no fool for letting Lily go. He had done the right thing. However, he refused to pray about his decision because he was afraid God would want him to pursue a new relationship. The only way he could distract himself from longing to hold another woman—that is, Lily—was to channel his energy into making Glenfield a better place.

He continuously started more building projects, seemingly incapable of accepting the estate as it was. He made sidewalks from paving stones, an arching bridge over the stream, a gazebo near his bedroom balcony, and installed a hot tub. He then built a fountain in the garden and a sitting area nearby.

One afternoon, as he was connecting the plumbing to the fountain, Mrs. Davis said to him, "You'll go bankrupt if you don't get Lily off your mind."

Caton was angry with himself for spending so much time working on his monstrous home, even though work was therapeutic. *Am I being ridiculous? Probably. Definitely.* He could justify his actions by saying he was honoring Mary's wishes, but he was only fooling himself. Mary would never endorse such an extravagant home. The house was incredible, but he wasn't ready to be happy, at least not yet. He found comfort in his grief and misery.

He had been driven to create an entire village of empty buildings and call the estate a memorial. Finally, he realized he simply needed to pray.

He walked through the garden and into the cemetery, quite extravagant by now, but still a peaceful place. Seated on his bench, he slowly, methodically took inventory of his motives, then poured them out before God.

"Father, I'm lost in my pain. I can't get past my feelings. Mrs. Davis tells me that I'm only grieving. She says once my heart is whole, I'll stop building this little kingdom. But how can I be sure? Why am I not healing? And what if I'm simply obsessed? In my mind, I only want to serve you, and I want to do so honestly. But, I'm not sure what's in my heart. Please heal me."

Caton shook his head, irritated at himself. He still hadn't gotten to the root of his concerns. After a moment, he continued: "Father, I've become lazy. I send my crew out to work. I used to go with them, but now I just send them out. I go over figures, order material, and seek out new jobs, but I should be on the worksite with them. Ugh!"

No, that wasn't right, either. He was lying about being lazy. No lazy man could build Glenfield and run a profitable business. So, what was truly in his heart?

He hesitated a moment. Could it be? Could God be trying to tell him something, but he refused to listen? And then, deep in his spirit, he heard the familiar voice.

There's more.

But there couldn't be more. Not for him. He'd had his chance, and Mary was gone. He'd loved once, and he didn't want any more.

Or do you? Be honest with yourself.

No, he couldn't deal with honesty. He had tried to squash the notion until nothing existed. "Father, I don't even know where she is or how to find her. It's not possible. She's gone."

Is she?

"Of course."

Why don't you press redial on the phone?

Well, why didn't he? A valid question. He steadfastly refused to use that phone, so he hadn't erased the redial to Lily's phone.

You're being like Peter when he had a vision on the rooftop. I'm setting something good before you, but you are too selfish to see it.

Selfish?

Yes, selfish. You enjoy the pain. You enjoy the suffering. It's your way to hold on to the past. Mary wouldn't want you to hold on to empty pain, and neither do I.

Selfish? He'd never considered that. Slowly the pain began to lift from his shoulders and heart until he got up to leave. Maybe he wasn't ready to release the control.

The control? What was he thinking? Control of what?

You're still angry.

"No, Father," he said aloud, "I'm not angry."

Silence.

"But I'm not angry. I understand what you're doing."

Do you?

"Of course. At least I think I do."

Your ways are not my ways. Your thoughts are not my thoughts.

"Well, of course, I know that."

Then how can you understand what I do? Are you able to guide me with your understanding?

"No, of course not."

Then you can't understand what I'm doing.

"Then I should just accept?"

Give me your pain. Give me your anger. Give me your denial.

"But … what will I have left?"

Silence.

"I can't let go."

Trust me.

"I can't." Caton left the cemetery and entered the garden. He intended to place some stonework around the trout pond and plant more trees near the stream. He had work to do. And winter was coming.

CHAPTER SEVEN

The Granite Shower

In Albuquerque, Jerry Sneed could feel the tension building among the orchestra members. After the musicians assembled, they confronted him about the extra week. He conceded they had a right to be concerned, then he further ruffled their feathers by calling for an early morning rehearsal. Ultimately, he had a change of heart and surprised them, saying, "We don't have a performance for three days. Why don't you take some time for yourselves. Be back here on the morning of the twenty-second for rehearsal."

For Lily, the days off were liberating, though she didn't have time to go home. One group invited her to join them for a day trip to Santa Fe, but she decided she wasn't up for group activities. Jayne was planning to spend the evening touring night clubs, but Lily didn't want to go dancing. She knew Jayne would ditch her for the first cowboy to make a pass at her, which wouldn't take long.

In the hotel lobby, she thumbed through some travel brochures. *Caton lives in New Mexico. No, don't think about him ...*

On a whim, she stopped at the hotel's front desk. "If I rent a car, what's there to see around here?"

The young man reached under the counter and produced a pamphlet. "What are you interested in?"

"I don't know." She glanced around the room and saw a map of New Mexico pinned to the wall. "Make a recommendation."

"Okay, if you like history, Indian ruins are nearby. The town of Lincoln is the site of the Billy the Kid shootout and the home of the Lincoln County War. If you like to sightsee, the Carlsbad Caverns are close by ..."

She interrupted him. "I've never seen the Caverns."

"Oh, they're a must see," he said with conviction. "Then, when you get done, you can either go down to El Paso and into Mexico, or you can cross over the mountain and visit the Indian casinos in Ruidoso, or you can drive over to White Sands National Park."

"Sounds pretty good. Where would I stay the night?"

He shrugged. "Depends on what you like. There are tons of little log cabins in Ruidoso. Or, if you want a little more opulence, you could go to the Lodge. Well, that's in Cloudcroft, not Ruidoso, but they're close together."

She gasped. "Where did you say?"

"Cloudcroft. Why?"

"Is that nearby?"

He smiled. "It all depends on how you view distance. It's roughly a three- to four-hour drive. You could be there in the early afternoon."

Her mind was spinning; excitement tugged at her belly. "I'll need directions on how to get there."

During the three-and-a-half hours on the road, Lily chided herself for being silly, yet she felt compelled to at least talk to Caton. Who was she kidding? She had to see him. She had to know what he looked like. She chastised herself that a proper lady should never initiate contact with a potential suitor, but she had limited options if she chose to listen to her heart. She knew she couldn't make him love her. He was still hurting and didn't know what he wanted.

The desert gradually gave way to foothills, and the foothills gave way to the mountains. The mountains were replete with pine trees, and large patches of snow covered the ground in the shaded areas. Lily rolled down her window. The scent of pine and cold, damp air was wild and free. She drove even faster. A state trooper flashed his lights at her and motioned her to slow down. Luckily, she was passing through a narrow corridor on the mountain, and he had no safe place to turn around and write her a ticket.

She entered a quaint village nestled on the top of the mountain. Stopping at the Allsups gas station, she stepped out of the car. The town was alive with Christmas lights and music. A horse-drawn sleigh jingled, moving around the corner and out of view.

The Village of Cloudcroft was folded in and around the pine trees. A long boardwalk full of shops and cafes catered to tourists. The village was fashioned after a frontier town, with tall, false-fronted buildings, and long, wooden sidewalks. Following the aroma of fresh-baked bread across the street, Lily found a teashop that was open. She had left Albuquerque quickly, forgetting to eat. She headed for the bakery and bought a loaf of warm French bread. She then walked to the teashop.

"May I help you?" an older lady inquired.

"Do you have any Earl Grey brewed?"

"Of course. Would you like that to go?"

"Yes, please."

As the elderly lady busied herself with the tea, she inquired, "So, where are you from?"

"I'm from Boston."

"That's a long way to come for tea … unless you've dumped the chests in the ocean again." she quipped with a grin.

"Yes, it is, and no, we didn't." Lily was polite, but she had too much on her mind to chat about the Boston Tea Party.

"Are you visiting friends?" the woman asked casually.

"I'm not sure," Lily replied distantly.

"It sounds like you're confused."

Lily sighed. "Well, I'm looking for someone."

"What's the name? I probably know them."

"Caton Harvey."

The woman stopped working and looked up, almost glaring at her. "What's your business with Caton?"

Lily, taken aback by the woman's intense stare, said, "Well, I met him once and wanted to say hello."

The woman held her hard stare for several more seconds, then returned to her work. "Where did you meet him?" she asked.

"On the phone."

"The phone?" she repeated, somewhat dubious.

Lily hesitated. "Yes, his daughter accidentally called my phone."

The woman gasped. "Oh, my!"

"Are you okay?"

"Are you Lily?"

Lily stopped, suddenly on edge. "How do you know my name?"

"Everyone knows your name," she replied matter-of-factly.

"That's not possible. I've never been here before."

The woman shrugged. "It's a small town. Caton told us how Mariah called your phone. Twice."

Lily was embarrassed. "Well, it was strange."

"I'll say. But God works in mysterious ways."

"Yes, I suppose He does."

After pouring the tea, the woman placed a lid on the cup, then held it out. Lily tried to accept the container, but the woman refused to let go. "What are your intentions?" she asked.

Lily could hardly believe what she heard. "I beg your pardon?"

"What do you intend to do? We all love Caton, and we loved Mary too."

Lily cautiously accepted the cup, "I'm not certain. I just know I had to meet him. You know … in person."

"Well, far be it for me to interfere with your personal business, but you need to be careful. Caton's experienced a great loss, and he doesn't need to be trifled with."

"I appreciate your concern. You must be a good friend."

"My name is April Poe."

Lily held out her hand and nodded. "It's a pleasure. My name is Lily DeMar."

April shook her hand. "We go to church together, you know. You need to be mindful of his relationship with God."

Lily didn't know what she meant and said, "Thank you. I'll keep it in mind." She stirred sugar and milk into her tea, then asked, "Could I trouble you for directions to his home?"

"Glenfield?" She frowned.

"What is Glenfield?"

"That's the name of his place. Some kind of big home, so I've heard. He doesn't like people bothering him out there."

"I don't plan to stay long."

April reluctantly scribbled directions on a scrap of paper. "Now, you better get going. The days are short, and the nights are cold. It'll take you an hour to get there, so buy gas now, seeing that you're already at the Allsups across the way."

The snow season forced Caton to take on a new project, decorating Glenfield for Christmas. He placed lampposts along the drive, beginning where his driveway emerged from the woods and entered the meadow. He strung lights along the edge of the road, illuminating both sides of the drive, hung lights on every building, and placed lawn ornaments randomly across the snowy lawn. In the big house, he erected a sixteen-foot spruce, decorated entirely with gold ornaments. Mrs. Davis grew weary of climbing the ladder to add the balls. She swore Caton would have to find a better method next year.

Next, he wired speakers to every building, broadcasting instrumental Christmas music throughout the meadow. He traced the pathways in the garden with lights, and placed a Christmas tree near the fountain. His decorating project took several days. He winced when he realized all of this would have to come down and again at the thought of his electric bill.

When the sunlight dimmed and the Christmas lights could be seen properly, he gathered with Mrs. Davis and Mariah in the center of the meadow. When Caton flipped the switch, Mariah gasped in delight. Mrs. Davis could only say, "Oh, my!"

"Have Yourself a Merry Little Christmas" played over the speakers. "I think it came out okay," Caton commented.

"I should say so, dear," Mrs. Davis said, slightly bewildered.

Mariah pointed at the light atop the cross. "Look, Daddy! A star!"

"Isn't it pretty?"

"Uh-huh, now the traveling people can find the baby."

"Don't you mean the wise men?"

Mariah nodded.

They stood, marveling at the majesty of the scene until the cold forced them to return to the big house.

Lily was lost. She grew more than frightened as darkness descended on her, engulfing the forest in dense shadows. Somehow, she had missed the forest road that would take her to Glenfield Meadow. "Oh! Where am I?"

She remembered passing a turnoff a little way back, so she decided to return to that place and try again. When she reached the turnoff, she looked for the marker that said FR 1229, but failed to see a sign.

She started to panic. Would she freeze to death?

Lily had never been a religious person. She didn't know how to pray. Yet, she stopped her car and said, "God, I don't know if you can hear me, but I need some help." Was that enough? She didn't know, so she added, "and I'm scared. Could you, uh, point the way for me? You know? Like send a sign, or something?"

Suddenly, a light appeared through the trees, and she heard Christmas music. Amazed, she turned to look and saw the light was a star. She stepped out of her car and walked toward the lights coming from beyond the trees. The snow covered the edge of the road. Not watching her steps, she slammed into a snow-covered road marker, knocking the snow off the sign—FR 1229.

Astounded, she climbed back into her car and drove on to Glenfield.

The Harveys were still walking toward the big house when a car emerged from the forest. "Who on earth is visiting us this late?" Mrs. Davis wondered aloud. "Why, it's already after dark."

"I don't know." Caton frowned as he examined the car. "And who would be driving a large sedan like that out here in the woods?"

"Maybe it's a flatlander," Mrs. Davis suggested.

"It would have to be. Especially this time of year. A sedan like that could cost you your life. Shoot, if they got caught in a snow bank, they could freeze to death before help could get to them."

They watched the car approach, driving slower and slower. They could tell the driver was a woman and seemed at a loss for what to do.

"Maybe she's lost," Mrs. Davis commented.

"Maybe."

Lily was grateful to see the lights and hear the music, but her gratitude was swept aside by the awe she experienced as she turned onto the driveway of the estate. The lights lining the road and outlining the buildings created a wonder. Even the grand estates in London were no match for what she saw. She was so enthralled by the incredible view she failed to notice she was being observed from the far edge of the circle drive. As she pulled up to the front of the house and parked, she was startled when a hand reached out to open her car door. She jumped, then looked into the eyes of a man. Her heart began to swim.

"How may I help you, ma'am?" he asked, neither friendly nor hostile, but direct and to the point.

She stepped out of her car and stood straight before answering. "I'm looking for Caton Harvey."

He glanced at the woman standing near him. "You've found him. What can I do for you?"

She had to take everything in before continuing. He was rugged and unshaven, his dark brown hair was disheveled, and he was wearing a red denim shirt under a leather coat. His smile brightened his face. Holding out her hand to him, she said, "It's a pleasure to meet you. My name is Lily DeMar."

Caton could not have been more shocked. He was absolutely speechless and failed to take her outstretched hand.

Mrs. Davis exclaimed, "Oh my, Lily! It's a pleasure to meet you." She accepted her hand and remarked, "You'll have to forgive Caton. It seems the cat has his tongue."

Caton nodded a moment, and then said, "Lily? What …? How …?"

She smiled at him while he spoke, then glanced down at the little girl next to Caton. "You must be Mariah."

Mariah, recognizing her voice, exclaimed, "Momma!"

Lily bent down to her level. "No, Mariah, my name is Lily. And you're as cute as a bug in a rug!" Mariah reached out and hugged her.

Caton swallowed hard. "Lily, it's a pleasure to meet you. Won't you come inside? I'm certain Mrs. Davis has some hot chocolate on the stove."

Mrs. Davis took her hand. "Come inside, dear. I'll get you fixed up." Patting her hand, she began to pull her toward the house. Lily glanced back at Caton.

Caton couldn't help but notice what a beautiful woman she was. She wore her blonde hair pulled back from her face, and the cold made her cheeks glow. She wore a form-fitting red-and-green sweater and an ankle-length black skirt. He had never seen a prettier woman in his life.

They sat in the kitchen nook around a small table; Mariah nestled into her father's arms. Lily, glancing awkwardly around the room, commented, "What a beautiful home, Caton."

"It's comfortable," he replied clumsily.

"And such a lovely tree. I've never seen a prettier tree in my life."

"You can thank Mrs. Davis for the tree. That was her project."

"It's quite remarkable."

Mrs. Davis nodded at her. "Thank you, dear."

Caton watched as she gazed around the room.

Mrs. Davis said, "Mr. Harvey has apparently lost his senses, so I'll ask—what brings you to Glenfield?"

Lily flushed. "I was traveling through New Mexico and wanted to meet you. All of you."

"How nice."

"Did you have trouble finding us?" Caton finally spoke.

"Well, I had some trouble at the last turn, but the star guided me here." Her cheeks turned even redder.

Then he shook his head. "Please excuse my rude behavior, Lily. It's just a shock to have you sitting in my home. I wasn't expecting this."

"I know," she blushed deeply. "I wasn't expecting to come either, but I found myself close to the area, and I just had to try and find you."

Caton was staring at her.

Lily sighed. "You're exactly what I imagined," she said.

"I've seen you before." He looked bewildered.

"I know," she replied softly. "In your dreams."

"How's that possible?" Caton seemed to be in a dream while they spoke.

"I don't know."

"Me either."

Lily responded, "How is it Mariah called me twice?"

"I don't know." Caton shifted in his chair and leaned toward her. "I want to know why I've dreamed of you."

"I can't answer that," she said softly. "I wish I could."

Mrs. Davis said, "Well, I'll see about some refreshments."

The nook was wide and comfortable—and inviting. From the adjacent window, the estate sprawled out before them, Christmas lights illuminating the ground as far as they could see.

She caught and held Caton's gaze. "This place is like a winter wonderland," she marveled.

Mariah snuggled deeper into her father's arms. Then suddenly, Caton's face brightened, and he exclaimed, "Lily! I just can't believe you're here. In my home!"

She smiled broadly. "I can't believe it either. It was a crazy idea."

Caton didn't know what to do next. "Um. Well, how about a tour?"

"I'd love that."

She followed him deeper into the kitchen. Caton tried to see his house from her eyes. There were two stoves with countertop ranges that matched the two side-by-side refrigerators. In the center of the room stood an island with pots and pans suspended from the ceiling. The room was larger than it appeared from the nook.

Caton began, "As you can see, this is the kitchen."

"I'm jealous. What a wonderful set up," Lily gushed. "Do you cook?"

Caton laughed. "Who me? Not a chance. I can grill some, but I'm no cook. That was Mary's department." His face clouded, and he looked down at the floor. Lily pretended not to notice. "Mrs. Davis is in charge of the kitchen. Do you know your way around a kitchen, Lily?"

She shrugged. "I'm not home long enough to do much cooking."

"Sure, I get that." Caton continued through the room and into a hallway. "This hallway either takes you to the downstairs or to the bedrooms and the grand room." Turning to speak to Mariah, Caton realized that somewhere along the way, she and Mrs. Davis had disappeared.

"What's downstairs?"

"Well, all kinds of things. The game room is there, and the workout room is next to the lap pool."

"You have an indoor pool?" She was amazed.

"It seemed like a good idea at the time, but it takes too long to fill. My well isn't productive enough for the houses, the pool, and the barn."

"I see."

"We'll end our tour downstairs since that opens up to the patio and the garden." He turned down the hall and passed several bedrooms, each with its own bath. When they entered the grand room, Lily stopped and stared, her face filled with awe.

"Oh my goodness, Caton! This is fantastic!"

They toured the rest of the house quickly, but Lily paused when she saw the living room and the library built into the walls. With the fireplace, the room was warm and inviting.

A Christmas tree stood against the back wall. Several boxes of ornaments lay around it. "Mrs. Davis is still working on that tree. It'll be as pretty as the one in the parlor," he explained.

Lily nodded. Caton walked up the stairs first, then pushed open a door leading to the master suite, which filled the entire upstairs. Her jaw dropped as she stepped into the bathroom and saw the gargantuan shower made from granite faces.

Caton opened a doorway in the far corner and stepped onto the deck. Lily followed as Caton moved to the edge of the deck, flipped a switch hidden behind the post, then walked into the forest. She soon spied a hot tub under a gazebo. It was covered, but she could imagine how luxurious sitting in the tub on a night like this must be.

Caton didn't stay there long, nor did he have much to say. Lily followed him back into the bedroom, where she noticed several art pieces on the walls but had no time to stop and appreciate them. They wound down the staircase to the living room, emerging from the hallway into the downstairs.

Caton paused. "I wonder if it's too cold to go out on the patio?" He glanced at Lily. She nodded her approval, so Caton opened a door she assumed led outside, but she was stunned to be standing in a small greenhouse running the width of the house. "This room is for me," he confided. "I love plants and trees, and I wanted to have my own place to hide."

Lily nodded, "What I lack in cooking, I make up for with a green thumb." She walked through the greenhouse, the only room she felt wasn't dedicated to Mary's memory. The humid warmth of the room was a nice change of pace from the cold winter air outside. She saw a potted plant with long, soft pink, fluted flowers. "Is that an Angel's Trumpet?"

He seemed impressed. "Yes, it is. You know your plants."

She pointed across the room. "And that's a justicia brandegeana, right?"

Caton nodded eagerly. "It is! Also known as a shrimp plant."

"Because the flowers resemble shrimp." She guessed his next question. "I used to work at a nursery when I was in high school."

She was embarrassing herself, but Caton saved her by plucking one of the arching, coppery flowers and with a smile, handed it to her. "Thank you," she mumbled.

Caton led her to the patio. Once again, she was delighted to see the Christmas lights outside. A stage rose gently from the patio. She said, "Oh, Caton, it's large enough to host a ball with a live orchestra."

"I have to admit I never considered such an idea. I'm not really into parties."

"Well, now's your chance." The patio seemed never-ending. "How big is it?"

He pointed over her shoulder. "Do you see the star?"

"Oh, that's the star that guided me to your home."

"Well, the star is in the center of the garden."

Her eyes bulged. "It's too big to see tonight. How disappointing. It's getting late."

"I know. I was just getting used to the idea that you were at Glenfield. You must be tired from your travels and probably hungry by now. How about some supper?"

She laughed. "Is supper anything like dinner?"

"To a Yankee, I suppose it is."

"Am I a Yankee?"

"Many times over," he said with a gracious smile. He held out his arm, which she gratefully accepted and walked with him back into the house. She smelled something delicious. "Mmm. What is that?"

"That's Mrs. Davis's beef stew. I really hope you're not a vegetarian."

"Not me. I'm a foodie! I like my steaks a little pink."

He nodded and winked. "I knew I liked you." He patted her hand as they entered the kitchen. They exited the kitchen and turned the opposite direction into the dining room. The room was perfect, down to the small wet bar in the corner.

The large table was set for four, and she was seated next to Caton. He asked if she cared for hot tea or coffee.

"Some Earl Grey, if you have it."

"Our favorite. Just a moment, and I'll brew a pot." He walked into the hallway and disappeared around the corner. She was relaxed now, with no regrets about coming.

Suddenly, Caton's head popped around the corner. "Sugar?" he asked.

"Yes, please. And cream, or milk, if it's available." He nodded and disappeared as quickly as he came.

She smiled and leaned into her chair. Caton was everything she imagined. He was witty and kind, but he also possessed the strength to be strong and stubborn. He was a little taller than she imagined, and he was unshaven, both of which were pleasant surprises. The look was right for him. She arose and moved closer to the painting hanging over a buffet.

Caton returned with her tea. "Do you know art?" he asked.

"I studied art in college for my electives, but I don't recognize this painting or the artist. It reminds me of Thomas Kincaid."

"That's what drew me to him. We were traveling through Arizona. When we stopped for lunch, I noticed an art gallery next door. We decided to explore the gallery and discovered a man named Joseph Gulick. He specializes in sea and ocean paintings, and we loved his style. I bought three of his pieces, and I've been a fan ever since." He pointed to the opposite wall. "All three of the works in this room are his."

"He's marvelous."

"He lives in Ajo, Arizona, and doesn't paint as much as he used to. But he's a kind man with a great soul."

Lily sighed with regret. "I just came from Phoenix. I could have visited him."

"Oh, well. Next time. Come on, your tea will get cold. The stew will be ready in fifteen minutes."

Lily could hardly take her eyes off the seascape. "What's the title?"

"I believe it's titled *Pacific Coast*. If you like art that much, I'll take you through the house again, and you can see the rest of my collection."

Lily pulled herself away from the painting and sat next to Caton. "I would love to see everything else. That is, if you can spare the time."

"What else do I have to do but entertain my guest?"

"I'm sure it must be late. It took me an hour to drive here. Actually, a little more than that, so I should be going soon."

Mrs. Davis entered the room and said, "Nonsense. You left your car unlocked, so I moved your bag from the back seat into the guest room just down the hall."

"But I can't stay here tonight," she protested. "I don't want to impose."

Mrs. Davis shook her head in protest. "Oh, no, I must insist. The mountain is no place for a stranger, especially at night."

Lily stole a glance at Caton. He nodded and said, "I have to agree. The roads are icy and dangerous. Please stay. I would never forgive myself if you got hurt."

"Well, if it's not too much trouble."

"Then it's settled." Caton slapped the table. "Woman of the house, where's my supper?"

Lily jumped. Mrs. Davis hollered back, "Keep your shirt on; I'm working on it."

Dinner was wonderful. Lily never enjoyed a stew as much as she did that night. After Mariah had entertained them with counting and alphabet recitations, Caton whisked her to bed. The adults retired to the grand room and settled in front of the fireplace. Caton stirred the fire, and Lily explored the room, filled with art from around the world. *Who is this man?*

Inspecting the paintings, she was pleased to find a piece she immediately recognized. "It's a Tomasz Rut," she exclaimed. "*In Externo.*"

"Do you like Rut?"

"He may be my favorite contemporary artist. He will be remembered as a significant American painter."

"I really like his work, but my favorite artist may be Bellet, for his color schemes. He pointed to a lithograph near them. "See, this one is called *Mediterranee*. We liked the purple look."

She laughed. "A purple look! I can tell that you're a connoisseur."

He chuckled. "Actually, the art lover of the house was Mary. She minored in art in college and set all this up." He motioned with his hands across the room. "She made art fun, and I learned a little myself."

Lily pointed to another piece. "Look! A Rembrandt! What's the title of this one? Wait; is it *Christ at the Well?*"

"Close. Actually, the piece is *Christ and the Woman of Samaria—Among Ruins.*" He returned to the fire and added a log. "You should see the piece by Hua Chen that I hung in Mariah's room. I don't know the title, but it's a ballerina."

Lily nodded, "Oh, I like Chen also. How did I miss seeing all of this when I walked through the first time?"

"Oh, about that," he stammered. "I actually ran through the house when you were visiting with Mrs. Davis about the stew and hung these up really fast."

She laughed. "You did not!"

"It's true! You thought I visited the restroom, but I was running like a madman through the house."

Lily enjoyed laughing. "I think the room is so incredible that the details are missed on the first run through."

He almost seemed embarrassed. "You say incredible, and I say overstated."

"Aren't you the one who built the house?"

"Guilty. I just didn't realize the place was going to be so over the top."

After Mrs. Davis retired for the night, Caton and Lily sat up for another hour, getting to know each other. Lily was captivated by Caton's charm and demeanor.

Around midnight, Caton showed Lily to her room. He turned on the light, and she paused near her valise. "Would it trouble you to get my violin out of the car? The instrument's a little sensitive to the cold."

"No problem. I'll be right back." He hurried out of the room and through the parlor. The air was colder now, and he wished he had donned his jacket. Once he had the violin, he walked back to her room. The bedroom door was still open, and he started to step inside when he saw Lily letting her hair down. He couldn't take his eyes off her beauty. She was a remarkable woman to see with her hair up, but when her hair fell across her back and shoulder, she was stunning. The way she brushed her hair was so provocative he was immediately ashamed of himself. He leaned the violin against the door and said, "Well, if you need anything, I'll be upstairs."

Unable to move, he remained for a moment as she ran her fingers through her hair again. He couldn't stand more. He disappeared down the hall and stayed in his room the rest of the night.

CHAPTER EIGHT

BEFORE THE STORM

Caton paced in his room for half an hour before getting ready for bed. "I'm such a fool! What am I thinking?" He knew he couldn't mourn his wife forever, but for the life of him, he couldn't let go.

Let go.

"I can't. I just can't let go," he whispered back.

Trust me.

"I want to, but I …" He never finished his sentence. To whom was he lying? Himself? God? Lily? Mary?

"Why can't I let go?"

Because you're angry at me.

"No! You're my Creator, you're my life, my Sovereign. I worship You freely."

Then let go.

"Show me how."

Nothing happened. Frowning, he muttered, "What were you expecting, Caton? For God to come and rock you in a chair? Get a grip." He looked up and saw a painting by Tomasz Rut, *Campaspe*, hanging near his bed. The painting portrayed a woman dressed in a light robe modestly covering her body. She was sitting in curled position on the floor, fixing her dark brown hair. When Caton first saw the painting, he had to buy it because it reminded him of Mary. He often stared at it for hours. Mary would sit on the bed and fix her hair, just as Campaspe was doing.

Take it down.

"I don't think I can."

Take it down.

"I like it too much."

The painting's not Mary.

"I know!" he said too quickly, then in a softer tone, "At least I think I know. Mary's with you."

Then let her go.

"Why?" His question wasn't one of rebellion but of inquiry.

I have something else for you.

"Yeah, but what I have is …"

Dead. You need to move on with me.

"I want to."

Silence.

Caton lay in his bed, focusing on the painting. He was in love with that woman.

Wait? He was what?

He sat up and considered those words for a moment. He was in love with whom? With the painting? Or with Mary?

The painting was safe, for Campaspe could never do anything to him, nor could she die. His memory of Mary could remain complete and perfect.

The high places.

Caton wasn't sure what God meant by that. The only high places he could think of were in the Old Testament of the Bible. The Scriptures recorded when the majority of the kings of Israel and Judah tried to restore righteousness to the people, most of them failed to remove the high places, which he always thought of as idols. So, what did that have to do with him?

He went down to the library and searched until he found a Bible commentary on First Kings. The commentator proposed the high places were like an unhealthy emotional bond which should be broken in order to embrace true freedom. One example was when a married person kept old letters from a former love.

He closed the book and returned it to the shelf. Was the painting a form of the high places in his life, or was his refusal to release Mary a form of the high places? Or both?

He sat in front of his smoldering fire and reflected on what God was speaking to him. Why did he have to release Mary?

He leaned back in his chair and thought about Lily. She was smart and witty, and he enjoyed the time spent with her. Her smile brightened the room. He wanted to—"

Why do you run?

"What do you mean? I'm not running."

Silence.

Caton sat still for a moment, then leaned forward. "Okay, maybe I'm in denial. She is attractive. All right, I said it. She's a knockout."

Silence.

"Well, why did you send her to me? I was doing okay without her."

Is everything about you?

He exhaled with regret. "No, I suppose not. So, what's it about?"

First, you must let go.

Caton stumbled to his feet and returned to bed. He stole one last glance at the woman in the painting. Could he really let her go?

No. Not even if there was something better.

As usual, Caton awoke before sunrise, growling at himself for staying up so late. He stumbled to the shower, lathered his face, and shaved. Stepping out of the shower, he was ready to meet the day.

The day ... or Lily?

He nearly skipped down the stairs but was disappointed to find the room empty. Entering the patio, he was surprised to see flames roaring in the firebox. He heard the melancholy sound of a lone violin serenading the forest. Lily sat with her back to the door, facing the fire. In the darkness before sunrise, the fire illuminated her silhouette. Lily's body moved with each change of the bow as she masterfully maneuvered her fingers over the strings. He stood silently, mystified that such a wonderful sound could come from such a small instrument. When she concluded the final note, she sat with her eyes closed.

Caton approached her respectfully. "That was fantastic!"

If Lily was startled at his sudden appearance, she didn't show it. "Thank you. It might be one of my favorite tunes."

"I didn't recognize it."

"Ashokan Farewell." She smiled sheepishly when he didn't recognize the title. "It's from a CD called *Fiddle Fever.*"

"It was inspiring," he agreed.

She lifted her chin, thoughtfully considering his words. "Funny, I think of it as haunting."

"I didn't realize classical violinists would allow their violins to be called *fiddles.*" He watched her smile. "So, what's the difference between a violin and a fiddle?"

"A fiddle is fun to listen to," she replied with a grin, and then comically exhaled. "Sorry, a little orchestra humor. A violin *is* a fiddle, but a fiddle is not necessarily a violin. Technically, any bowed string instrument can be called a fiddle." She held the instrument for him to see. "There can be a difference in the bridge though. Most violinists only play one string, while fiddlers play multiple strings at the same time. So, the bridge for a dedicated bluegrass musician would be flatter."

She glanced at him, as if caught off guard. "Sorry," she said shyly. "My dad used to say, 'I asked you what time it was, and you built me a watch'. That was probably a lot more info than you expected."

"Not at all. You answered a question I've wondered about, but never had anyone to ask. So, you can play either bluegrass or classical. Is that typical?"

Her lips twisted in thought. "You'd be surprised at the varieties musicians enjoy. But ..." She rolled her eyes. "there are plenty of classical violinists who would never condescend to play bluegrass on their instruments. I'm not typical. My father loved bluegrass music and insisted we listen. Bluegrass holds a special place in my heart."

"Your dad sounds like a great man." He squatted by the fire, holding his hands to the flames.

She gazed wistfully into the flames. "He was a man of great determination, but his family always came first. He was well respected in his circle, and he did well with his career." Her face dropped. "He died a few years ago."

"Oh. I'm sorry."

"I miss him tremendously." She sighed. "He would have loved this place." She shifted in her chair, clearly changing the subject. "I hope it was okay to build a fire."

"That's what all this wood is for." He savored the morning as if he had never tasted morning air. "I love living here. This will always be home to me."

"I don't blame you. I'd feel the same in your place."

"It'll be light soon. Would you like to walk down to the garden ... I mean ... at sunrise? I'll show you the rest of the place."

"Sounds great." Her eyes found his, and she held his gaze for a moment, inviting him to seek her.

Caton felt his stomach swim. Her hair was pulled back again, and he could see the soft skin behind her ear. He felt a devilish desire to brush his lips against her neck. Slowly, he realized they were still locked in a visual embrace, and he felt his own skin flush from the intensity of the moment. He was grateful it was too dark for her to see his reaction.

"Well," he said, trying to clear his mind, "I, uh, need a cup of coffee. Would you like some too, Lily?"

"I'd love some, thank you."

When he returned, she was playing again. He recognized her selection. "That's Pachelbel's "Canon in D." She nodded and continued to play. "It sounds so different without the other instruments."

"That's why they call the piece a symphony and not a concert," she said playfully.

"Ah." He glanced at his watch. "Mariah should be getting up any minute now."

"A little early, isn't it?"

"That little girl never sleeps late."

Lily nodded. "That's the hardest thing about my work. Most theaters and performances flourish around the nightlife of a big city. I wake up early by nature, but I'm forced to be a night owl. Of course, that works great for my friend, Jayne, who loves the darkness. She's always trying to drag me along, but I'd rather be home with a good book and a roaring fire." She sipped her coffee. "Well, what passes for home, anyway. I can't really say I'm ever at *home*. I'm always on the road … or so it seems."

"It must be hard, being away so often." Caton sympathized.

Lily sighed. "It is, although I've done it for years. Of course, when I left for London—that was the hardest time."

"You weren't happy in London?"

"No, just the opposite. I was a college girl in a foreign country full of castles and chivalry. What's not to love? I would hardly study because I was so busy sightseeing. That's what led to meeting my husband. He owned an estate in Yorkshire, and I was researching a local legend of a man called Bold Robin of Bouthwaite, who single-handedly captured criminals breaking into his home, Bouthwaite Grange. Bold Robin was something of a legend in the area, and I wanted to explore Yorkshire." She stopped, suddenly self-conscious. "Listen to me, going on about places you probably don't care about."

He shook his head. "I'm enjoying your story. Please continue."

"My friend, Clarisse, and I noticed an estate viewing was available, so we took advantage of the opportunity. The owner of the home is seldom present when the house is opened for tourists, but Rodney happened to be home. I immediately recognized him. He was the conductor of the Royal

Symphony Orchestra, which I'd applied to a month earlier. He asked us to stay for dinner that evening. Clarisse was uncertain, and I should have listened to her. But I didn't, and we stayed. The following week …"

Caton interrupted. "What was Clarisse worried about?"

Lily shook her head. "Clarisse thought Rodney was self-absorbed and arrogant. Of course, she was right. But he was also handsome and rich—and a conductor," she added innocently. "A conductor of the very orchestra I'd applied for! Well, I fell in love. And, I never imagined he would arrange for my employment the next week with the orchestra. Furthermore, I should have foreseen my position being removed after the divorce. But that's a story for another day." She pointed excitedly. "Look! What's that? Is it a deer?"

Caton leaned forward and peered into the first grey hints of morning. "Probably. It's either a deer or an elk. Those deer give me fits by eating my garden."

"Have you tried hair?"

"I beg your pardon?"

Lily grinned. "What I mean is, back home in Boston, the locals collect their hair when it's cut … you know … at the barber shop. They spread the clippings along the rows of the garden. It's supposed to deter deer from coming in and eating the plants."

Caton shrugged. "I wonder if it works."

The patio door burst open, and Mariah appeared with Mrs. Davis, who was carrying a tea set. "I thought you might enjoy some tea, now that you've both overindulged on coffee."

"Oh, thank you! That would be nice."

Mrs. Davis winked at her and removed the lid from a dish in the center of the tea tray. Lily gasped when she saw four crumpets set on plates, with the traditional butter and jellies. "Is that? … No way! Are they really crumpets?"

"Oh, absolutely," Caton responded. "Mrs. Davis has an affinity for crumpets. That's why I let her to stay on. She makes them perfectly."

Mrs. Davis waved him off. "Don't you listen to him, dear. Enjoy. I have more in the kitchen when you finish those." Then she disappeared into the house.

"I do miss living in London because the tea and crumpets were so wonderful," Lily reflected. "I haven't had crumpets since I left England, except for the one week I spent in Seattle. I found a little tea shop at Pike's Market that makes them fresh."

Mariah stumbled over to Caton, clearly not fully awake. She crawled into Caton's lap and snuggled close to him. He smiled down at her. "Are you cold, baby?" She nodded, so he covered her with his coat. "The fire will keep you warm." Mariah pointed at the flames.

Lily reached for a plate. "May I get you a crumpet?"

"Thank you, no. I'll let Mariah wake up a little first. But, please help yourself. They're much better when steamy hot." Caton glanced at the thermometer on the wall. "It seems like we always get hit with a big snow storm around Christmas. This might be the day."

Lily studied a small bowl of jelly. "Is this gooseberry?"

"I believe so."

"I love gooseberries on my crumpets." Her eyes were dancing.

"I prefer smoked salmon and eggs."

Lily spread the jam over her crumpet. "Mariah's so pretty. Does she favor her mother?"

Caton stole a glance at the little girl curled up in his arms. "She does. She has her mother's eyes and her hair. She'll be a heartbreaker someday." Mariah tried to snuggle closer to her father. "Are you still cold, baby?"

"Maybe we should relocate?" he suggested. Lily nodded agreeably and grinned when Mariah also waggled her head up and down. "Let's go inside to the breakfast nook."

By the time they were settled inside, the morning was light enough for them to see across the meadow.

"I don't like the look of those clouds."

"Snow would be pretty." Lily glanced at the clouds. "I love a fresh snow."

Mrs. Davis came in the room. "But up here, we don't get a little snow. We usually get a couple of feet."

Lily's eyes grew large. "Feet?"

"The mountain is no place for the weak of heart."

Caton was busy preparing a crumpet for Mariah and missed Lily's expression, but he could hear fear in her voice. "Is it safe up here in the snow?"

"We'll be fine. The roads are usually closed for a couple of days."

Lily blinked. "A couple of days?"

"Unless it's a big storm," he added casually.

"But I can't get snowed in for a couple of days," Lily responded quickly, her concern growing. "I have a performance in Albuquerque tomorrow night."

Caton studied the sky again. "I think it'll snow. But it probably won't start until late this morning. Maybe around noon."

She tapped her finger on the table. "Since we're through with our breakfast, why don't we quickly tour the grounds, and then I'll be on my way?" When Caton agreed and reached for his coat, Lily approached Mrs. Davis. "The crumpets were a pleasant surprise. I really enjoyed them and the gooseberry jelly."

"I'm glad, dear."

They walked across the patio, then followed the cobbled pathway and entered the garden. Lily stopped suddenly.

"What's wrong?"

She looked around with wonder. "Nothing's wrong," she assured him. "I just didn't expect it to be so ... very grand!"

"Very grand?" Caton smiled. "What an adequate description. Mrs. Davis has spent a lot of time here. Most of it is her work."

Lily teased, "She said you would say that. And she said not to believe it. She also insisted you are the chief designer."

"Well, I don't know," he replied bashfully.

"This must have taken a long time to build. There's a colossal amount of planning, designing, and building that went into this place."

"I'm glad you like it."

"Like it? I love it! Why, it's even better than the house!" she exclaimed. She glanced around. "A fishpond?"

"I stock it with trout. Want to take a closer look?"

They passed through the garden and down the pathway to the small stream.

"What a quaint bridge."

Caton scowled. "I'm not too happy with it. This is such a little stream that it hardly deserves a big bridge."

"I like it. It reminds me of Germany."

"You've been everywhere, haven't you?"

Lily was embarrassed, "I'm sorry. There's nothing nearly as boring as a show off."

He laughed. "Are you trying to show off?"

She was slightly alarmed. "No, of course not. I so dislike being around a know-it-all, and I don't want to become one, especially not with you."

"Don't worry about it. I like you just as you are."

Her face flushed. Then she saw him blush as he realized the implication of his words. They hurried over the bridge and took a few tentative steps along the pond, their feet crunching in the remaining snow. "I don't see any fish."

Caton leaned forward and pointed to an opening in the thin layer of ice. "See that long greenish-brown stick?"

Lily squinted. "I think so."

"That's not a stick; it's a trout."

"Oh, they're not at all what I expected. I thought they were rainbow colored."

"Well, I stocked it with bull trout and cut-throat trout. They are better sport fish than the rainbow."

"I see." She glanced around and saw the barn. "Are those the stables you mentioned?"

He nodded and shrugged, "We have no horses. I enjoy riding, but they're a lot of work. I didn't want to start messing with them until I was finished working on the place."

She curiously glanced around. "When will that be?"

"Well, I plan to buy three horses this spring."

"That won't be long." Lily pointed across the garden to a grassy slope. "What is that?"

"Where?"

"That place up there, with the picket fence around it."

"That's the cemetery." He tried to keep his voice conversational. "It's where I buried Mary."

"Oh." She clearly didn't know what to say.

Caton noticed that Lily looked cold. "Shall we make our way back to the garden?"

"I wish I had enough time to sit in your hot tub. This would be a spectacular morning for it," she lamented, looking back over her shoulder.

Caton nodded, but offered no comment. When they arrived at the fountain, they paused a moment. Lily asked why there was no water in it.

"It's too cold," he replied. "The fountain would ice over and the lines would burst."

She nodded and slowly circled the fountain, with Caton close on her heels. She glanced at her watch. "I'll have to be going soon." They sat on one of the benches facing the fountain.

"The clouds are growing heavier. It'll start snowing within the hour."

"Then I should leave now," she replied, regretfully.

Neither of them moved. The moment was growing awkward. Finally Lily spoke. "It's getting colder."

"Yes, it is."

She watched Caton brush a snowflake off her black coat. "See, this has the marks of being a bad storm," he said.

"I can't risk getting stranded here for three days, as much as I would love the idea. Mr. Sneed will fire me if I miss my next performance."

"Sounds like a nice guy."

"He's the last of the great ones," she said sarcastically. "I can't wait until my contract expires. Then I can stay in one place for a while."

"If you have a contract, how can he fire you?"

"He has that much discretion. Of course, the company would buy out my contract, but I only have about ten months left. I'm sure he'll tolerate me for a few more months."

"You don't sound very happy with it."

She sighed. "No, I'm not. I think that's what was so disappointing about my divorce in London. I really wanted to be a wife and mother, not a career woman. Don't get me wrong, I enjoy my work and I love playing, but I don't want to do it the rest of my life. I want my life to matter."

His eyebrows rose. "You don't matter now?"

She had never considered the idea. "Well, that's not what I mean ... I don't think."

"Of course, you matter. If not to the world, you matter to God."

"God?" Lily was surprised at the sudden introduction of religion. "What does He have to do with anything?"

"Everything. Whether you know it or not, God has a purpose for you."

"Well, at least somebody does," she said playfully.

His eyes laughed. "I'm serious. God really intends for you to have a meaningful life."

She looked at him. "Caton, do you have a meaningful life?"

He nodded. "I do. But that's not why I serve God."

"Why, then?"

"I serve him because he's God. I recognize how significant he is. One day, you and I and the entire world will have to stand before him and give an account of our lives. I want to be on the right side of the fence when it all comes about."

Lily huddled under her coat. "You sound like you really believe that."

"I do! Don't you believe in a Creator?"

"Well, I don't disbelieve in God; I just don't make him an issue in my life. We never really went to church when I was a growing up, and I mentioned how horrible my husband was."

"Yeah, he sounds like a pill." He paused a moment in thought. "Lily, whether you want him to or not, God will judge your life. What will he discover?"

She lifted her chin. "An honest woman. I'm a morally sound woman. I don't sleep around. I don't steal. I don't lie—and I'm not going to do those things."

"So, you're a good person?"

"Yes, I think so."

"Have you ever told a lie?"

She glanced at Caton and chuckled. "What is this, the inquisition?"

He shook his head. "No, I just really want you to know God is a significant part of my life, and he wants to be in yours. My faith is very important to me."

"Sounds like it." She shifted on the bench. "As I said, I'm not opposed to God. I just don't know anything about him."

"So," he pressed her further, "have you told a lie?" He held up a hand to silence her. "Don't tell me, I already know the answer. I simply want you to understand that it only takes one virus to kill a healthy body. If a grain of salt falls into a bowl of sugar, it's no longer pure sugar."

Lily sat silently for a moment. Caton pressed her again. "Imagine how white a sheep is when it's against a green, grassy hill, and then imagine that a great snow falls all around the sheep. Now you can see the dirt in its wool once you have something to compare it against."

That's sufficient.

Caton lifted his hands. "Forgive me for preaching. I just …" He paused and carefully considered his next words. "I care for you too much not to share my deepest beliefs with you."

Lily gasped. "Is that what you're doing?"

He nodded again. "Yes. Not only so you'll know who I am, but so you can find out who you are."

She placed a hand on his shoulder. "Thank you, Caton." She glanced around the meadow, as if trying to memorize it. "I'll miss you when I leave."

"It was such a surprise to see you. I knew who you were the moment I saw you, but I couldn't bring myself to believe it was possible."

"I know." She suddenly realized the snow flurries were increasing. She brushed a flake off Caton's coat. "I should be leaving."

As if waking from a dream, he looked around. "I don't know." He turned and watched the clouds. "This is an aggressive storm, much more than I figured. It could be dangerous. It looks like it's snowing heavier between here and town."

"You sound as if you care." She tilted her head toward him, her eyes open and inviting.

"Well, I would care even if I didn't know you." He immediately regretted sounding so disengaged, but he was unprepared for this moment. He tried to salvage his words, "No, that didn't come out right … I mean …"

She nodded and placed a hand on his shoulder. "I think I know what you mean," she replied, disappointed.

The moment was clumsy. Slowly, Lily rose to her feet, and Caton followed. She wanted him to take her into his arms and beg her to stay, but he was unmoving. "Well," she said, "I should be leaving."

He nodded, then reached out to hug her good-bye. She melted into his arms and held him tightly. Not expecting her to latch on to him, he almost released her. He lowered his face as she looked up, their lips almost brushing. Lily held her position for a moment, waiting, but Caton glanced over her shoulder. She saw him looking at the cemetery on the slope. He released her. Her heart shriveled, rejected.

She saw in his eyes that he was going no further, so she turned on her heels, disappointed and embarrassed at having exposed herself so. Caton reached for her shoulder. "Hold on, okay?"

Lily stopped and turned to face him. "It's not going to happen, is it?"

Caton hesitated, then swallowed. "I just can't."

"Why? What are you afraid of?"

"I'm afraid I'll love you." He stared at his feet.

She frowned. "And would that be so wrong?"

"It might." He looked up. "I don't know."

"Then, I should leave. Sorry I intruded into your life," she said with more emotion than she intended. She needed all of her concentration not to fall apart as she stood there. She marched down the path, her footsteps lively and sharp. Caton stumbled along behind her.

When they reached the house, he said, "You should wait until the storm passes before you try to drive. The snow's already picking up."

"I'll be fine."

"You should stay."

Turning to face him, she asked "Why? Why should I stay?"

He hesitated. "Because the storm …"

She coolly interrupted him. "I should stay because of the storm? That's why you want me to stay?"

"Well, I …" he stopped. She could see he was conflicted and trying to say something, but the words never came.

"Goodbye." Lily entered the house and went straight to her room, retrieving the valise and violin case. She met Mrs. Davis in the hall but said nothing, unwilling to see the disappointment in her eyes. She was too close to the edge of losing control. She kept telling herself she couldn't cry until she was down the road.

"Are you okay, dear?"

Her eyes swelled with tears. "It's time for me to say goodbye."

Mrs. Davis smiled sadly. "Give him some time. This is happening very fast."

Somehow, she managed to stick her finger back in the dam, momentarily steadying herself. "It's been three years since Mary died. I can't wait another three. I'm going to leave now while I still have a chance."

"Please change your mind, if for no other reason because of the storm. These roads are dangerous."

"It'll be too awkward. He's already said no."

Her shoulders fell. "I see." She called for Mariah, who hugged Lily warmly and said, "Bye-bye." Lily returned her hug and handed her a CD from her bag. "Here, I made this one special for you, okay?"

Mrs. Davis prompted Mariah. "Well, what do you say?"

"Thank you."

"You're welcome." Lily placed a hand on Mariah's head, gently straightening a loose strand of hair. "I'll miss you both very much."

Lily returned to the parlor where Caton was waiting. He offered to carry her valise, but she refused. She only wanted to leave as soon as possible. He walked her to the car and opened the door. She hesitated, then said, "I'm sorry to have intruded."

Caton shook his head. "It was good to meet you. I'm sorry you're leaving."

Lily closed the car door and turned the ignition. The car lurched forward. Once on FR 1229, she pulled over and released bitter tears. She would not return to Glenfield. She could never compete with a perfect memory.

CHAPTER NINE

THE WOMAN FROM BOSTON PREFERS TEA

As Lily emerged from the forest and turned onto the highway, she noticed the road was already slippery. She drove slowly, and her car was handling okay. Then the snow began to fall faster, and she had trouble seeing the highway through the gargantuan snowflakes bouncing off her windshield. Within minutes, an inch of snow had accumulated on the road.

Lily started to worry. Should she return to Glenfield? She pulled over and thought her options through. No, returning would be too humiliating. She tried to pull back onto the highway, but her tires spun on the snow. Finally, the car inched forward, but to her dismay, she skidded sideways onto the pavement. She was thankful for no other traffic.

Having grown up in Boston, Lily wasn't immediately concerned about driving in bad weather. "Come on, Lily, you got this," she told herself. She turned her wheel and gassed the engine enough to reposition her car on the road. She was still moving slowly, but gaining ground, when a large pickup suddenly entered the curve. The pickup's horn blared as it bore down on her. Lily stared into the headlights of the oncoming vehicle. Suddenly, the truck veered to the left, narrowly missing her. Horrified, she once again pulled to the side of the road and waited until her heart stopped hammering in her chest. The pickup slowed down, and the driver reversed, returning to check on her.

A short, balding man emerged from the red truck and cautiously stepped toward her. "Hey, lady? You all right?" he called out.

She rolled down her window and shouted back to him. "Sorry, I lost control there for a minute, but I think I'm okay."

He waved, returned to his pickup, and slowly pulled away. Lily's nerves had settled, so she pulled the gearshift into drive, and began to move forward, trying to stay in the tracks of the truck in front of her. "Holy cow, they weren't lying when they said the mountain is dangerous!"

The snowfall was increasing, approaching whiteout conditions. Lily knew that in another few minutes, she wouldn't be able to see at all. Then what would she do? Barely able to make out the tracks in front of her, she knew in a short while they would be completely covered. She tried increasing her speed, but when she went around a curve, she realized she was driving too fast, so she pressed her brakes. The car slid sideways and began to spin. She tried to turn her wheels into the skid, but she was too late. The car slid completely off the road. Next came a gut-wrenching drop as the car slid down a steep slope and slammed into a tree. Lily was thrown forward into the steering wheel. A loud crack followed, and the car dropped again, coming to rest against a tree, at least forty feet below the highway.

When Lily came to, her head was resting against the passenger seat. Blood trickled from her nose and dripped sideways across her cheek. She tried to lift her head, but a tree limb pressed against her. She managed to push the limb to the side and sit up straight, but when she realized blood was dripping from her nose, she panicked, struggling to move. She screamed as pain shot across her leg. When she probed the source of her pain, she felt something hard and cold protruding from her leg. Pulling her hand back, she saw more blood. Slowly, the pain and blood loss took its toll, and she passed out. Snow slowly covered the top of her car.

For a while, Mrs. Davis left Caton alone as he moped around the house, but she finally grew irritated with him. She wondered what happened between Lily and him that forced Lily to flee Glenfield so hastily. She could tell he regretted letting Lily go, but she had no idea how to help him. When she'd first met Caton, well before Mary died, he laughed all the time. Years had elapsed since he'd laughed, and she feared he would become even worse now.

Caton tried to dismiss the unpleasantness of the morning's departure. He was haunted by the scent of Lily's perfume and the memory of her smile and laughter. She had brought a few moments of light-hearted laughter to their home, and he'd pushed her away.

Was Mariah destined to grow up without a mother? He turned away from the question, for it posed a more threatening question—would he live the rest of his life alone?

He fled outdoors after snapping at Mrs. Davis when she brought him tea. He knew she was offended. He wanted to sit by the fountain, but that was the site of their ill-fated last meeting, and he couldn't bear to relive their conversation. To think, he had held the most beautiful woman he had ever seen, and he had let her go. Remarkable. Absolutely remarkable.

Why did he let her go? Because he still loved Mary? Because she was prettier than Mary? Perhaps. Maybe he felt guilty.

Let her go.

"I want to, but she won't leave me."

You won't let her go.

"Show me how."

Just do it.

"What do you want from me?"

Your anger.

"My anger? But I'm not angry."

Silence.

"Really, I'm not angry she didn't live."

You're angry she died.

"No, I accepted she was going to die, and I was grateful for the chance to say goodbye to her."

Nice sounding words.

"But it's not true?" Caton asked sincerely, his voice growing smaller.

Silence.

"Why isn't it true? Didn't I trust you through the process and through the sickness and death?"

Let her go.

For the first time since Mary's death, Caton didn't argue with God. For the first time, he sat silently and actually thought about anger. Was he angry? Deep in his soul, was he angry with God for Mary's death? He wanted to say no, but when had God ever been wrong? If God told him he was angry, he was angry. But why didn't he know it? Why was he lying to himself?

Because of pride.

Caton remained silent. Because of pride? What did pride have to do with his anger?

Slowly the picture began to take shape in his mind, and the lens on his soul began to focus. Caton was always seen as a leader in the church and in the community, even as a young man. Because people chose to see him in that manner, Caton accepted that vision. Once he accepted everyone else's view, there was little room for God to shape him further. When Mary died, he was forced, no—he allowed himself to stay collected and in charge. Well, at least he appeared to be calm and collected. But inside, he …

Caton began to tremble. Inside, he was afraid of being alone. Caton portrayed the image of a super Christian so well that no one doubted the lie. While he was frantic on the inside, he was leading the masses into God's grace—at least that's what he wanted everyone to think.

That was the chief problem with standing on a pedestal—it's harder to get down than to get up there. Once Caton admitted he was portraying the image of a super Christian, invulnerable to fear and doubt, he unintentionally accepted this falsehood.

"Father, forgive me for lying." He began to weep. By the time he said, "Please forgive me for the pride that caused me not to trust you," he was sobbing.

Go on, say it.

Caton continued. "And I'm scared and lonely, and I don't know what to do. I'm not angry with you for taking Mary home; I'm angry you didn't leave her with me." He stopped. "That doesn't make sense." His voice faltered. "Because …" He wiped the tears from his.eyes. "Because it's all about me." The dam burst as a flood of emotions spewed forth.

Caton allowed God to cradle him while he sobbed. After a few minutes, he prayed, "Thank you, Father, for your patience and mercy. Thank you for the blood of Jesus that washes away my sins." Peace flooded his soul—he felt clean and honest and, for the first time, vulnerable and naked. He didn't try to hide. Finally, he could trust God with Mary's death, and he determined, from that day forward, he would never return to the cemetery to mourn his dead wife. For the first time in a long time, joy returned to his heart as peace invade his soul.

"What about Lily?"

What do you want?

"I'm so lonely."

You don't have to live alone. I'll open your heart if you want.

Caton shrugged. "I think I do want that." He breathed deeply in the fresh air filling his soul. He was free, and he was enjoying it. He admitted he wanted to move on with his life, and he was attracted to Lily. "She's so beautiful, Father. Could someone like her really love me?"

She's not perfect, either.

He smiled. "No, I expect she's not perfect."

You'll have to apologize to her.

"Yes, I suspect so."

You need to go get her now.

"Right now?"

Time is short.

As if in a dream, Caton was standing in the middle of the big curve near Spring Cave Road on the highway to Cloudcroft. He could see skid marks on the pavement and the guardrail crumpled under the weight of a car. He could see where the car went down the slope and lodged in a tree. Lily was alone and scared and cold. Then Caton woke up.

He had fallen asleep while he was crying before God. Was the vision just a dream?

Hurry.

No, he hadn't been dreaming. He leapt to his feet and ran into the house, almost knocking down Mrs. Davis. He hugged her and said he was sorry for the way he'd been acting earlier. He promised to explain more when he returned.

"Where are you going, dear?"

"I'm going to get Lily back."

"Yes," she nodded, "I expect you should."

He ran into the grand room and picked up the phone to call the teashop. "Hello? Mrs. Poe, this is Caton Harvey. I'm well, thank you … Yes, I know a woman was looking for me … Yes, she made it all right … Yes, she is rather fetching, but … Yes, I appreciate your helping her with directions, but … April, wait a minute! I called to ask if you've seen her. Lily? Well, no, but I expected her to stop and buy gas and maybe a coffee or something before hitting the road. Yes, I know she prefers tea, which is why I called you. She shouldn't have left in the storm, but she did, and I want to make sure she made it to town in one piece … About two hours ago … Okay, good, ask Chip—he lives on this side of the mountain. If he just drove into town, then maybe he saw her on the road … Yes, I'll hold."

He could hear the front door on the teashop open and April calling Chip to come to the phone. Then he heard a confused man answer. "Hello? Who's this?"

"Chip, this is Caton."

"Oh, hello, Caton. How are you? Did that woman ever make it to your house?"

Caton could hear April telling Chip she made it to the house, but not back to town. "Chip? Can you hear me? Chip?" Suddenly, Chip's attention returned to Caton. "Chip, did you just drive into town?"

"Yep, I wanted to get some groceries before we got snowed in, but I might be too late to get back home. It's bad out there."

"Okay, did you see a woman driving a grey Toyota sedan on the road?"

"What did she look like?"

"Does it matter? How many women could there be out there in a grey car in this weather?"

"Well, if she's a blonde, I saw her just the other side of Spring Creek Road, near the cave turn off."

"Was she okay?"

"Hmm, she seemed all right, but I almost ran her over. She hit a slick spot and wasn't moving very fast. I came along behind her and hit the same spot and barely missed her. Scared me all colors of purple. But when I got out, she said she was okay, so I got back into the truck and came to town. Gee, she should have been here by now. Do you think she's all right?"

Caton's mind was racing. "No, I think something went wrong. Get your stuff done and start back. I think she was in an accident down by Spring Cave. I'm on my way right now."

He slammed the phone on the cradle. Instantly lifting the receiver again, he punched in 911. "A car just went off the curve on Spring Cave Road. There's a single occupant, and she's injured. How do I know? I saw it. Hurry. The snow's bad, and it's getting worse."

Caton hung up and started Blue Boy, his pickup. Within seconds, he was grinding his way to the Cloudcroft highway. He slid onto the shoulder in several places but managed to maneuver Blue Boy down the road.

Regaining consciousness, Lily slowly came out of the fog she had been suspended in. Remembering she had been injured, she gasped when she saw the tree limb jutting from her leg. She had to do something.

She felt around until she found her bag, then tied the strap of her valise just above where the limb impaled her leg. Though light-headed, she knew she was in trouble and needed to focus on staying awake.

As the initial shock of the accident began to wear off, the throbbing pain intensified. She tried to move, but the pain in her leg ripped through her like hot coals. No one knew where she was, and Caton thought she had returned to Albuquerque, so she wouldn't be missed for five or six hours. The old pickup that nearly hit her was the only vehicle she had seen on the entire journey. The odds of her being found were slim.

Lily tried to start the car and run the heater, but the ignition wouldn't turn. Frustrated, she considered building a fire in the car, but she couldn't move around to find any fuel. Moreover, if the smoke got too bad, she wouldn't be able to open the windows to vent the cab.

Her leg was throbbing. She was cold and scared. "Don't cry, Lily," she said aloud, mostly for the comfort of hearing a voice, even her own. "You need to conserve your energy, and you don't want to dehydrate." No matter what she said, however, she couldn't stop crying. After a few minutes, she felt slightly better. Then, in the distance, she heard a vehicle coming. By the roar of the engine, she knew it was a truck.

Caton drove as fast as he could manage, but he wasn't covering ground quickly enough. As he neared Spring Creek, his pickup hit the same patch of ice Chip described. The vehicle jammed into the retaining wall of the curve, preventing him from plunging over the edge. He tried to move the truck, but he was stuck. The more he tried to move, the more his tires dug in.

He slapped his steering wheel. "Confound it!" The truck was firmly pressed against the retaining wall. Normally he would have unlatched the winch on the front bumper and tied it to a tree to pull himself free, but he would have to cross the highway with the steel cable. If another vehicle hit the steel cable, everyone involved could be killed. He stood in the middle of the road and listened. No one was coming. He unlocked the winch and began to uncoil the steel cable, stopping often to listen for other vehicles. Silence. He stretched the cable over the pavement and tied onto the nearest tree. He ran back to Blue Boy and pressed the switch, activating the winch. When the truck started to vibrate, he gassed the engine enough to get some traction. Slowly, with a loud scraping sound, Blue Boy edged away from the retaining wall, ripping the passenger mirror off the door. Just as Caton was pulled far enough into the roadway, to his horror, he saw headlights from a snowplow churning toward him.

Lily listened as the vehicle roared closer to the spot where her car had left the road. She could only hope the snow hadn't covered the evidence of her wheels sliding off the pavement. As the vehicle neared, she heard it shifting to a lower gear. Her heart soared, but just as quickly, she was thrust into despair as she faced stark reality. The truck was a snowplow and had just covered the guardrail she had crashed through with a foot of snow. All hope faded as she sank lower into the seat.

Caton bit his lip as the winch painstakingly inched his vehicle forward onto the pavement. In another few seconds, he would be free, but the snowplow was closing in on his location. He pressed on the accelerator. The truck lurched forward and turned sideways on the road. He leapt from the cab and ran across the highway to unhook the cable before the snowplow slammed into his truck.

The driver in the snowplow barely missed hitting Blue Boy. Caton felt the steel cable rip from his hands as the truck's cord rewinder snatched it from his grip. Relieved, he worked his way back to the highway.

"Are you all right?" the operator hollered.

Caton waved. "I'm okay! Did you see a gray sedan on the road anywhere?"

The driver shook his head. "No, I haven't seen anyone for miles. They'd be crazy to be out in this weather."

"Did you see anything indicating a car went off the road?"

The operator scratched his head. "There was some disturbed snow down by Spring Cave, but it looked old. The snow had covered it up pretty well."

"How old would you say?"

"Oh, a couple of hours ago … maybe less … judging by the snowfall. But that's a bad place … almost a straight drop off at the curve."

Caton jumped into Blue Boy, spinning his tires into the snow-packed highway.

After the snowplow dropped more snow, almost burying her car, Lily reached full desperation. She wanted her leg to stop hurting, and she certainly didn't want to die. But what could she do? She remembered Caton mentioning every person has an appointment with death, and all would be judged by God. She'd refused to answer his question about telling a lie, but she knew the truth. Who hadn't lied at some point in their life? She knew many people who were worse than she. Jayne moved from one illicit affair to the next. *I'm nothing like Jayne, so I can't be all that bad. Right?* She bit her lip

Pressing against her leg, she felt the blood oozing out of her wound. She leaned forward and saw the floorboard was covered with muddy, bloody snow. What a mess! That snow had been white only a few minutes before, but now, with only a little dirt mixed in, was filthy.

Maybe Caton was right when he said it only took one blemish to ruin the complexion. If one lie was sufficient to condemn her, then where did she stand? She didn't want to find out.

She rarely prayed, but she instinctively knew if she wanted to live, now was the time to start. Unsure how to proceed, she managed to say, "God, I know I don't know you, though I'm not opposed to you. Caton really seems to find meaning in his relationship with you, and I wonder if there's any way you could help me get out of this mess? I'm not ready to die."

Her words sounded hollow. She felt foolish for even speaking to someone she had ignored her whole life. Why should God care about her? Who was she to deserve his interest? Caton had made the relationship seem so logical and easy, but was it? She wept until fatigue and dizziness forced her to stop. Gradually, the dark crept in around her, overtaking her consciousness. She slowly drifted into an almost comfortable, warm darkness.

Caton slowed as he approached the curve he had seen in his dream. The plowed snow completely covered the roadside and the guardrail—there was no way to know if anything had gone wrong here. He now faced an impasse—should he press on in hopes of finding her farther down the highway, or should he stop and search the immediate area. Time was precious. If he made the wrong choice, Lily could die.

Stop here.

Caton parked on the shoulder, got out, and walked along the roadside, looking for evidence of an accident. On the drop-off side of the highway, the snowplow had pushed a colossal pile onto the guardrail. He climbed up the snow pile and peered over the edge. He gingerly stepped over the edge and peered down. He could see the shape of a car under a pile of snow.

Caton's blood ran cold. "Lily!" he hollered. "Lily, can you hear me? Where are you?" He heard nothing but Blue Boy's gentle idling. Jumping into his pickup, he turned his wheel sharply and stepped on the gas. The tail end of his truck about-faced, pointing in the opposite direction. He unlocked the winch, threaded the hook under his belt, and flipped the button to extend the steel cable.

The cable slowly lowered him forty feet to the car. When he reached the car, he realized it was partially suspended in a tree, keeping the vehicle fairly level and preventing the car from somersaulting to the bottom of the canyon. The steel cable on his winch was fifty feet long. He had used most of that length to descend to the car.

When his foot touched the trunk, he felt the car's weight shifting backwards with a low groan. Brushing snow off the back window, he tried to look in, but the window was frosted over.

With every movement, he changed the balance of the car. He delicately stepped off the trunk into the tree, then felt around until he found the towing hook mounted to the car's frame. He unfastened the strap from his belt and gently snapped the hook on the car. He barely had enough cable left to use, but the car wouldn't slide too far if it moved.

Caton climbed back onto the trunk and inched his way to the locked front passenger door. He scraped enough snow off the window to see a silent form lying awkwardly against the steering wheel.

"Lily?" He shouted to her. "Lily? Are you injured? You'll be okay."

When she didn't respond, his heart sank. He glanced at his watch. A quick calculation told him the emergency crews wouldn't be on the scene for at least fifteen minutes.

He knew he had to bust out the passenger window to unlock the car. Since he had nothing to break the glass, he returned to the trunk and searched for anything capable of making a fist-sized hole.

The storm had covered everything with eight inches of snow. How was he supposed to find something useful?

Look up.

He glanced into the tree supporting the car, and saw a rock wedged in the branches, probably deposited there from road construction done years ago. As he maneuvered the rock to loosen it, Caton discovered a sharp point on the edge. He hoped the rock had enough weight to take on the window. As he worked his way back to the passenger door, the car shifted, pulling the steel cable tighter.

Holding the point of the rock facing the window, Caton slammed the glass. It bounced off. He tried again with the same result. "Father, help me get into this car." Smashing the rock into the window for the third time, he heard a splitting sound, but it was the tree, not the window. The car shifted forward, sliding to the right; the steel cable was now taut with added weight.

CRACK.

The car lurched to the right and slammed into the tree. A branch punched through the passenger window. Caton pawed at the shattered window with the rock and managed to remove enough glass to unlock the door. At that point, he realized he couldn't open the door as the car's weight now rested on that side of the tree. He continued ripping out the glass until he could peer into the car.

"Lily? Can you hear me? Hold on, sweetheart, we'll get you out. Stay strong."

Sweetheart? Did he really say that?

The only way to enter through the window was to slide off the car's roof and through the window in one fluid movement. If he missed, he would fall off the car and end up another ten or fifteen feet down the slope. Carefully, he leaned over the roof on his belly and wiggled through the broken window. The car shifted with the sudden weight change, and the branch began to pull away from the window.

Caton's coat snagged on the branch. He pulled off his glove with his teeth, then found his knife in his pocket. He opened the blade with one hand, then tore frantically where the coat had snagged on the branch. His movement caused the car to shift farther to the left, pulling him back through the window.

CHAPTER TEN

MUSHROOMS?

Caton heard a rip, then felt a searing pain in his side. With a twist, he broke free from the branch, and tumbled back through the passenger window. With a snap, the branch fell free of the car. "Lily, can you hear me?" She was unresponsive. He twisted again, drawing his feet into the car and positioning himself next to her. Her head dangled awkwardly against the steering wheel. Blood had dried on her face, and he could see where she had placed a makeshift pressure bandage on the puncture wound in her leg. She had bled profusely from the wound. Her breathing was labored.

The back-and-forth shifting of the car's weight had wrenched the branch from Lily's leg, leaving an open wound. Blood was flowing from her leg at an alarming rate. Caton reached across her body and found the switch that moved her seat farther back, trying to get access to her leg. He gently eased Lily back into her seat, then leaned forward to adjust the strap around her leg.

As he reached for a scarf in the back seat, the car shifted again—forward this time. Caton braced himself against the dash in anticipation of impending doom. Lily was still wearing her seatbelt, so she wouldn't be thrown out of the car, but he might.

The steel cable attached to the car pulled harshly against Blue Boy. Under normal, drier, conditions, the pickup would have held the weight without sliding forward, but the pickup had no traction on the icy pavement. The weight of the car was slowly pulling the truck closer to the edge.

With stark realization, Caton felt the car inching closer to the point of plummeting down the slope again. He knew if the car kept pulling Blue Boy closer to the edge, the pickup might come crashing down on them. He frantically cut a smaller length from the scarf and wrapped it around Lily's wound, all the time looking forward at the shifting horizon. He managed to create an adequate pressure bandage that would stop the oozing blood, then strapped himself into his seat and prepared to launch down the slope. He was starting to get dizzy himself.

Blue Boy was now in contact with the snow pile created by the plow, poised to enter the hole in the guardrail created by Lily's car. Another foot and the pickup would be dangling off the road.

Caton cried out to God. "Father, if you have a plan, now would be a great time, 'cause this is gonna leave a mark!"

Chip, a volunteer firefighter for over fifteen years, was munching on a cream-filled cupcake when he heard the emergency tone on his radio, informing him an accident had been reported near the big curve on Spring Cave Road. He immediately stepped on the gas, but he was having a hard go. The snow was heavier in the village, so he was not making good time. He was at least twenty minutes ahead of the emergency crews. He breathed a sigh of relief when he spotted where the plow had cleared the road. He would make better time now.

Caton struggled to breathe—his mind started to drift. He managed to pray, "Father, please take good care of Mariah." The car started sliding forward faster, reminding him of the last second before the big drop on a roller coaster. He and Lily were minutes away from the car's weight snapping the branches, sending them tumbling down the mountain, followed by Blue Boy.

Rounding the curve at Spring Creek, Chip blinked when he saw Blue Boy slowly sliding off the pavement. He stopped his pickup immediately behind Caton's truck and leapt from the cab. The winch on his bumper was stuck, but when he kicked it soundly, released. He quickly unlocked it and tossed the hook around the trunk's bumper. Allowing fifteen feet of slack, he threw his vehicle into reverse. The cable tightened with a snap, halting Blue Boy's slide. He gasped as he realized Blue Boy was resting on three wheels, the fourth dangling over the edge. Another few seconds and the truck would have gone over.

Caton felt the car's momentum stop. Sticking his head out the window, he yelled, "Is anyone up there?" He felt nauseated from the effort—pain cascaded over him.

"It's me, Chip," he heard from above.

"Thank God," Caton whispered. He drew as much breath as he could and yelled, "Man, am I glad you're here! What's our situation?"

"It's pretty bad," Chip shouted back. "I had to tie onto your truck to keep it from going off the mountain. What do you need down there?"

"Lily is unconscious." Caton paused to gather more strength and brace against the pain. "A tree branch in her leg," he yelled, gasping, "and it bled a lot. I've got a bandage on it … but I couldn't stop much of the flow."

"Are you okay?"

"Yeah, for the most part … scratched up my side … out of breath … I'm managing."

"I'll see what I can do from up here." Chip disappeared from the edge.

Caton prayed silently. "Thank you, Father, for your mercy. Please help Lily with her injuries." Reaching back to touch his painful side, he blanched when he saw his fingers were covered with blood. "What in the world?" He probed until he found the wound. Gasping loudly, he realized he was in trouble. He leaned back, trying to fight the blackness that threatened to overtake him. Snowflakes continued to fall through the open window as he slowly drifted into unconsciousness.

Caton stirred. Voices were repeating his name. He was walking—no, he was floating. No, that wasn't right either. Then he heard, "I think he's coming around."

Opening his eyes, Caton saw a large mushroom. He felt something wet brush against his face. *Is the mushroom licking me?*

"Caton? Are you in there?"

The mushroom slowly came into focus. He realized the puff was a helmet, and he was looking into the face of a paramedic.

"There he is. Try to stay with me, Caton."

Caton wondered what was happening. Had he been dreaming about Lily?

Lily? Suddenly he remembered being in the car … and the pain in his side.

"Don't fight us, Caton. You're hurt pretty bad, but we'll get you through. You're gonna be okay."

The pain in his side burned, and he couldn't breathe. He began to panic, squirming and trying to move his head, but the man with the helmet held him still. No, that wasn't right. He was tied to the bed, and he was very uncomfortable. Darkness beckoned him, offering relief and peace. He embraced the warmth.

Lily was being rolled down the hall in the hospital's trauma center when she started to revive. She couldn't believe she was safe. She wondered who had found her. Slowly, she began to realize she was strapped to a gurney. She felt no pain at all.

"Ah, there you are," said a pleasant voice. Lily twisted enough to see a young, pencil-thin nurse step into her vision. "We were a little concerned about you. You lost a lot of blood. In fact, we gave you a transfusion about an hour ago. But, everything looks much better."

Lily glanced at her leg.

The nurse put her hand on Lily's arm. "The doctor cleaned the wound and stitched it up. Your biggest problem was the blood loss." She pulled out a syringe.

"What's that for?" Lily asked.

The nurse smiled. "Just something to help you sleep. I'll put this into your IV."

Lily watched as the nurse injected the medicine. She felt so weak.

The nurse moved back. "My name is Terri. I'm your nurse tonight."

"Tonight?"

"Yes, you've been here several hours. We're going to admit you for a couple of days."

Lily shook her head. "No, I can't stay here. I have to be in Albuquerque tomorrow." Her voice was thick, and her words were deliberate as she fought the medication.

Terri smiled compassionately. "Don't worry, Lily. I'm sure your date will understand why you can't go to the theater with him."

Lily knew she was not communicating, but her mind was drifting. The harder she fought, the deeper she sank. The next time she opened her eyes, she was in a private room. Her door was closed. She pressed the nurse call button, and a gruff voice asked, "Can I help you?"

"Could you send the nurse to me, please?"

"I'll give her your message." Within five minutes, Terri popped her head in the door.

"Welcome back. How're you feeling?"

Lily thought carefully. "Okay, I guess. What's going on?"

Terri nodded with understanding. "You were injured in an accident and lost a tremendous amount of blood. We got you stitched up, and we cleaned your wounds."

"So, I was rescued after all."

"A very dramatic rescue from what I hear. The first responder to the scene was injured and flown to Lubbock by MEDEVAC."

"I hope he's okay."

"He'll be fine. They do good work in Lubbock. He needed some pretty serious surgery we aren't equipped for here."

"Good," she mumbled and looked around. "Look. I have to be going. I'm expected in Albuquerque tonight."

Terri shook her head in a kind, but sincere denial. "You were seriously injured. Is there someone I can call for you?"

Lily groaned. "What time is it?"

"It's just past noon

"Ugh." She rolled her head back in dismay. "Noon?"

"Yes, just past twelve. Are you hungry?"

"Not really." She closed her eyes, bracing for the inevitable. "I do need you to make a phone call for me, if you don't mind."

"Of course not. Who should I call?"

Lily gathered her fuzzy thoughts. "Can you write this?" she asked. "Mr. Sneed. I was injured and unable to attend performance. In hospital now."

"Do you know the phone number?"

Lily thought for a second, then rattled it off.

The nurse nodded. "OK."

Lily moved. "And then, if you can, call my mother at this number. Tell her what happened, that I'll be fine, and I'll come home as soon as I can." She exhaled regretfully. "I have a feeling I'm about to have lots of free time on my hands."

"Okay, Lily. You be still. I'll be right back."

Lily looked at Terri carefully. "Weren't you my nurse last night?"

She nodded. "I was! This is a small hospital, and I'm the RN for the floor, the ICU, the ER, and long-term care. You'll have me for the rest of this week." She folded the paper in her hand. "I'm going to make these calls now."

An hour later, Lily was poking at some Jell-O when Terri stuck her head in the door. "I talked to Mr. Sneed. He seemed unpleasant."

She rolled her eyes. "You have no idea."

"He said to tell you, and I quote, 'You're fired.' Who is this guy?"

Lily nodded with acceptance. "Yep, that's what I expected." Her face flushed scarlet as she thought about it. *I'm certain my attorney would be glad to offer him a course correction. I'd love to hand a juicy law suit right back to him. I'll call about that later.*

"He didn't even ask if you were okay."

"He doesn't care. Now, the orchestra has to pay the rest of my contract." She smiled. "It'll work out fine."

Terri shrugged. "Oh, and I talked to your mother. She'll be here in the morning."

"Oh, she doesn't need to do that. I'll be okay."

"She said she has to actually see you with her own eyes."

Lily smiled. "Yes, I half expected that."

"She sounded wonderful."

Lily nodded. "She *is* wonderful." She hesitated a moment. "Have I had any visitors?"

Terri shook her head. "No. I understood you were from out of town. Were you expecting someone?"

Lily lowered her head. "No, I have no reason to expect any visitors. I was just hoping a former friend of mine would stop by."

"Who's your friend?"

"Caton Harvey. Have you heard of him?"

"Heard of him?" she exclaimed. "He's practically a celebrity around here. He's a widower, you know."

"Yes, I know."

"Well, every eligible woman in the area has set her sights on marrying him, but he won't have anything to do with anyone. He rarely leaves the mansion he built. People hound him when he's in town—the girls are the worst."

"Why do they bother him?"

Terri straightened the tray sitting next to the bed. "Well, he's a dream. The women all want to marry him—and his money, of course."

"Oh?" Lily played dumb.

"He got some kind of big insurance settlement from a lawsuit. He's worth like thirty million, or something. Not only that, but people are always trying to get to his place to see the mansion he built. I have heard it's like three stories tall and has thirty rooms in it."

Lily smiled at how the rumors had twisted the truth. "What about you, Terri? Do you have your heart set on Caton Harvey?"

Terri stared out the window. "Who wouldn't? He's quite a catch. But he's kind of religious," she added with a frown.

"Does he date?"

"Him? Never. He lost his wife a few years ago." Terri thought a moment. "I did hear some fancy chick showed up in town and moved in with him. But I also heard he kicked her out."

Lily frowned. "That sounds horrible."

"Doesn't it though? I hope it's not true because that woman was beautiful and rich. If he turns her down, none of us stand a chance."

For a moment, Lily thought she would cry. "I guess I won't bother to try and contact him, then. Sounds like he's happy just as he is." She suppressed a yawn. "You seem to know a lot about Caton."

Terri snorted. "In a small town, everyone knows everything. There are no secrets." She adjusted a wrinkle on the bed sheets. "You look tired, Lily. You'd better get some sleep." Terri turned to go, then changed her mind. "Has Dr. McCranie made his evening rounds yet?"

"I don't know. What does he look like? I did see a younger doctor walking around. Sort of playboyish."

"That'd be Dr. Fox. He and Dr. McCranie are polar opposites."

"Well, I haven't seen McCranie yet."

Terri sighed again. "He must be running late again. He's very busy. Now close your eyes and get some rest. I'll see you in twelve hours."

Lily did as she was told. Before she could drift off, she felt the whisper of a tear on her cheek. "Good-bye, Caton." She turned over to go to sleep, but then came a knock on the door. Looking up, she was startled to see a very handsome man with a scowling face.

"I'm Dr. McCranie. How are you feeling today?"

CHAPTER ELEVEN

CHIP'S CUP CAKE SAVES A LIFE

Caton had no idea what was happening, except someone was talking to him from far away. The voice sounded like his mother—or maybe Mary. No. But who? Someone was instructing him to breathe.

"Come on, Caton." A woman's voice.

He breathed, which hurt. He stopped.

"You can do it. Take a deep breath and let it out."

Again he took a deep breath, and pain seared his lungs. Breathing was very unpleasant. Why were they doing this to him? He was warm and comfortable and only wanted to be left alone.

His mother spoke to him. "Come on, Caton. Breathe deeply."

He breathed, and it hurt. He stopped.

"You can do it. Take a deep breath and let it out."

Again he took a deep breath. Pain seared his lungs. Why were they doing this to him? He only wanted to be left alone. His mother spoke again. "Come on, Caton."

This time was easier but still hurt.

His mother said, "He's doing better, Mandy."

Mandy? Who was Mandy? Where was he? Why did he have to breathe? Why wouldn't they just leave him alone? He only wanted to go back to sleep.

"Caton?" A hand caressed his hair, stirring him from his drowsiness. "You have to keep breathing. Don't stop."

Mary! I must be at home.

The woman said, "Take a deep breath, Caton. That's it, good job!"

His mother sounded relieved. "I think he's getting the hang of it."

The woman replied, "The body wants to remember how to function. Being on a ventilator is hard. Getting off is harder."

"He looks pretty good, considering what he's been through."

She agreed. "Yes, he does. I think he'll recover quickly. I imagine he'll be up and walking by tomorrow."

Who cares? He drifted back to sleep.

Caton awoke to see a tall woman with a long, brown ponytail leaning over him, examining his chest. He looked up at her, and she smiled.

"Hi, my name is Mandy. I'm your nurse for the day."

"Hi" was all he could say for the moment. He wasn't certain the word actually came out.

"Do you need anything? A sip of water, maybe?"

He didn't even know where he was, much less if he needed anything, but when she said water, he was suddenly thirsty. He nodded yes, and Mandy produced a small cup with a long straw. "Here you go … easy now. You can only have a few sips. I don't want you to get sick."

That water was the best he had ever tasted in his life. He wanted more, but Mandy wouldn't budge. "You'll thank me later." Then she looked him in the eyes. "Do you know where you are?"

"No," he croaked.

"You're in Lubbock Methodist Hospital. Do you know why?"

It was like trying to remember a dream. "No." His voice was scratchy, and he couldn't move. Were his arms and legs tied to the bed? He tried to lift his head, but there were tubes on his neck and an oxygen mask covered his face. He couldn't see anything.

"You had a bad accident in the mountains. I understand you're from Cloudcroft?"

He nodded yes. Some of his memory was coming back.

"I envy you," she said wistfully. "My husband and I go camping up there every summer. I'd love to live up there."

"What happened to me?" He could speak, but doing so hurt.

"Well, when the paramedics found you, you had a chunk of wood sticking out of your lung."

He blinked at her several times. "What?"

"It's true." She picked up a damp cloth and started to wipe his face. The cool felt good, and he wanted to drift off again. But he needed more answers.

"Where's Mary?"

"Who?"

"Mary, my wife. She was here yesterday."

"No, I'm sorry. The only people here yesterday were your parents."

He was crestfallen. He'd been dreaming after all, and now he was stuck in a hospital. "What happened?"

"They don't know. The best they could figure was you rolled up on an accident and fell when you tried to reach the victim."

"Lily!" He tried to sit up, but he was restrained.

"Careful, you're tied down." She began to unbuckle his arms and legs. "You have to stay in bed. If I untie you, do you promise to stay in bed?"

He nodded. "How is Lily?"

"Who's Lily?"

"The woman in the car. Did she make it?"

"I'm sorry," she sounded sincere. "I don't know. I'll ask the medics if they know. She's not here in the surgical recovery ICU."

"I'm in ICU?"

"Yes, the piece of wood collapsed your lung. You almost died. When the medevac people arrived, the hole in your chest had been covered up by a plastic covering for a cupcake."

He looked confused, and she continued. "The plastic helped create a vacuum in your lung. It probably saved your life. You owe that EMT your firstborn child."

"Chip."

"What's that?"

Caton thought back. "Chip. He arrived just after I punctured myself with that wood. You don't know about Lily?"

"No, but I can ask."

"Did I hear my mother's voice earlier?"

"Uh-huh. You had family here this morning. In fact, visiting hours begin in a few minutes." She turned and picked up some papers. "I only have three patients today, so you'll have my full attention. Right now, I'm going to chart. I'll be back after visiting hours." She turned away and then faced him. "Actually, it's only one hour, but you know what I mean."

He went back to sleep but woke up when he heard his mother speaking. "Caton! How are you feeling?"

"Just swell. I don't really feel anything except pain, but only when I breathe. Hey, Dad," he said, looking past his mom. "Pardon me not getting up."

His dad laughed. "No worries. Keep your seat."

"You were in surgery for a couple of hours." Karen, his mother, sounded irritated with him.

"What happened to me?"

"You were playing hero and fell off the mountain." His mother scolded in a nice way.

"No, I didn't fall."

"Actually, you did. The weight on the winch was too much and tore loose from her bumper. The car fell ten feet. You don't remember?"

"No, not at all."

"It almost brought your truck down with it."

Caton's father, Harry, spoke. "They say you saved her life. We're proud of you, son."

Caton moved his head. "Thanks, but it doesn't sound like I did much except get myself hurt."

"No, everyone is still wondering how you even knew she went off the road."

Caton shrugged. "I guess God wanted her to be saved."

"From now on, you need to leave rescuing to the professionals." Karen said.

He smiled at her. "No problem. I've learned my lesson. What happened to Lily?"

"The woman in the car? No one even knew who she was. Then someone found her purse on the floorboard. She's from Boston."

"I know. How is she?"

Karen's mouth twisted, and she shook her head. "I think she's already been released."

"How long will I be here?"

"The doctor said it depends on you."

"Good," he nodded. "So, Lily wasn't injured too badly?"

"Apparently not. I don't think anything serious happened to her."

"Already gone home?" He was discouraged. "How's Mariah?"

"She's doing well. Mrs. Davis is snowed in at the house, and the phone lines are down, but the two of them are holed up and sitting out the remains of the storm."

"How bad was it?"

"Twenty-eight inches."

"I knew it was a good storm."

"You look tired," his father said. He turned to Karen. "Let's leave him alone so he can rest."

Karen shook her head. "I'm not leaving. I only have an hour to see about my son, and I won't leave after twenty minutes."

Caton closed his eyes and wished he knew how to reach Lily. He doubted even Mariah could find her this time.

Dr. McCranie stood over Lily's bed, scribbling on his clipboard. "You almost got yourself killed." He had a deep, strong voice, matching his strong, square jaw. His gray eyes seemed angry with her. "You shouldn't have been on the road in a blizzard."

Was she being scolded? "Yes, a bad choice."

"Well, next time you probably won't be so lucky," he admonished. "People get killed doing stupid stuff all the time."

Wow, this man is angry about something. "I was lucky."

"Don't depend on luck. You've used all of yours, and you don't have any left."

Lily watched him closely. "Are you okay?"

He exhaled loudly and ignored her question. "I need to examine your leg. Would you lift your bed sheets please?"

"Of course." She revealed her leg.

He leaned over her for a second, then reached for a rubber glove from the dispenser on the wall. "This wound is getting infected," he growled. He pressed on the incision and frowned. "I'll need to keep an eye on this to make sure it doesn't get worse."

Lily watched him carefully. "Are you the doctor who stitched me up?"

"Yes," he mumbled. He was writing on his clipboard again. "I'm going to start you on some antibiotics. Are you in pain?"

"Not really. My leg aches some, and I'm sore all over."

"So you are in pain or you aren't?"

Gosh! Lighten up! "I'm not in actual pain. Just sore."

He nodded. "Which happens when you drive off a cliff." His scowl was never ending. "I'll check your labs in the morning. In the meantime, rest."

"Yes, sir," she snapped, which she immediately regretted.

He watched her carefully. She could feel his steel gray eyes burning a hole deep into her own. Why was he so angry with her? Finally, he turned and exited the room.

Terri knocked softly. "I'm gone for the night. Do you need anything before I clock out?"

Lily shrugged, "How about a new doctor?"

Terry entered the room. "Jack's a good man and a great doctor. Don't take him personally. He's just really gruff sometimes."

"You think?"

There was little chance of Lily leaving the hospital for the next few days. Her infection concerned Dr. McCranie. Lily's mother, Susan, sat next to her bed and held her hand.

"You don't have to be here, Mother. I'll be all right."

"Shush. You're in a strange town and in the hospital. If you needed something, who would get it for you?"

Lily didn't argue. "Actually, it's nice to have you here. I was lonely on the tour, and I missed home more than I cared to admit. I guess we'll do Christmas in Cloudcroft."

Susan glanced out the window. "It's so pretty. I can imagine worse places to be for Christmas. Did you know they have a horse-drawn sleigh running up and down the streets? And an ice-skating rink in the middle of town? This is a charming little village."

"I know! I like it a lot."

Susan nodded. "This could be a great vacation place." She was silent a moment but obviously curious. "Lily, why were you here?"

Lily sighed, ready to get this part of the conversation over. "Do you remember the little girl who called me in Chicago? And later, she called me in San Francisco? Well, that family lives here, and I wanted to meet them."

"A single man and his daughter, if I remember correctly."

"Yes," she admitted, waiting for the shoe to drop.

"Lily, you're a grown woman. I wonder, have you overstepped that relationship?"

Lily perceived no threat in her mother's inquiry, for they had always shared an honest relationship. She bit her lip. "Well, I shouldn't have initiated contact with the man at all, but it was the only way I could know for sure." She glanced at Susan. "I suppose my behavior might have been unorthodox."

"Maybe." Susan's voice softened. "And you stayed the night at his home?"

Lily rolled her eyes. She knew where this was going. "Yes, I did. And we both slept with one foot on the floor and the door open." When Susan didn't flinch, she sighed. "We were chaperoned, and the weather was inclement. I really had little choice in the matter."

"Did you accomplish what you needed to do?"

Her voice was small. "Yes. I found out he's in love with his dead wife and won't let go of the past."

"I see. Well, that wasn't such a good idea was it?" A smile crossed her lips. "At least you got to meet a handsome doctor."

Lily grinned. "I'll say! He's a fine-looking man, isn't he?" she said sarcastically.

"For a young lady who needs a good husband? I'd say he was about perfect."

She scowled. "Dr. Jerk? Wait until you actually meet him. If he's so perfect, why isn't he already married? I would imagine these local women would be all over him, if not for his looks, then for his money … but it won't be for his charm."

"Who knows?" Susan mused. "Maybe it's destiny."

"Perhaps." Her lips curled. "But I think I'm done with destiny."

"Maybe so. But destiny may not be done with you." Susan stood and walked to the window to avoid the glare Lily shot her. "This small-town hospital is so foreign to what we have in Boston."

"I know!" Lily agreed emphatically. "I've had the same nurse for several days. Apparently she's in charge of … well, everything. She even manages the nursing home next door."

"It's not a very busy hospital. There are only twenty beds."

"Twenty? That's very small." Lily tugged at her hair. "I must look like a monster."

Susan smiled. "You could use a shower. But for now …" She reached for her purse and pulled out a brush. "I'll put your hair into a ponytail." She sat on the bed and went to work.

"I've only seen two doctors, a nurse, and some nurse's aides. I guess they don't need a large staff."

Susan brushed her hair with long strokes. "There's a woman in the next room who has some kind of chronic pain. And a teenage girl who had an appendectomy is in the room across the hall. Down the hall, there's a really old woman who appears to be dying, judging by the amount of family standing around her room."

Lily laughed. "And how do you know all of this?"

"Well," she said, bunching Lily's hair, "when you were napping, I went to the cafeteria to get something to eat. Two of the nurse's aides were chatting about their patients, and I was sitting close enough to hear what they were saying."

"Mother! You were eavesdropping?"

Susan shook her head. "I was not. It's a very small cafeteria. We all sat close together because there was nowhere else to sit. They talked about their workload and what they had to do for the day. Everything around here is so … personal, not much privacy. Everyone knows everyone." She got off the bed and returned to the chair next to the window. "Do you want to know what else I learned while I ate lunch?"

Lily grinned. "My mom, the gossip."

Susan feigned innocence. "Well, there's nothing else to do around here. So, I discovered this is not a place you want to be for super serious medical issues."

"Meaning what? Should I be worried?"

"Not at all," she said dismissively. "But, Dr. McCranie was fired from his last job, and this was the only place that would hire him. And the other doctor—Fox, the young one—is not very impressive either. He's a new doctor and very unprofessional. And he supposedly eats the Jell-O off the patient's trays if they don't eat it."

Lily rolled her eyes. "Well, aren't you full of information?"

"Like I said, there isn't much to do but watch everyone else."

A shadow darkened the door and they looked up to see Dr. McCranie, reading a chart. His tall frame almost filled the doorway. "Good afternoon, Miss DeMar." His baritone voice was comfortable to hear, but his tone was short. "I stopped by to let you know your lab results indicate the infection in your incision is improving." He placed the chart on the end of the bed and added, "Do you mind if I take a look?"

"Not at all." When he sighed impatiently, she said, "Oh!" and lifted the bedding from her leg.

Frowning, he slipped a glove over his hand and pressed the incision carefully. "This should heal nicely. There shouldn't be much of a scar either."

He removed his glove. "I'm fairly cautious. You're going to stay overnight, just to make sure the infection doesn't get worse. If everything looks good in the morning, you can go home." He looked at her, and again his sharp gray eyes seemed to pierce her soul and left her breathless.

"Thank you," she replied sweetly.

He dropped the glove in a trash bin next to the sink, then turned his gaze to Susan, who smiled awkwardly. He frowned as he held out his hand. "My name is Jack McCranie. How do you do?"

"Susan DeMar. Pleased to meet you."

"Are you Miss DeMar's sister?"

Susan flushed. "No, I am her mother."

He looked at the chart again. "Well, my apologies for the mistaken identity." He turned to Lily. "I've ordered a final round of antibiotics to be administered through your IV. I'll make my rounds just before noon tomorrow. Until then, have a good night."

"Good night," Lily replied cheerfully. She stole a glance at her mother, whose face was still red. "How do you like my doctor?"

Susan waved her hand in front of her face. "Wow, I've never seen eyes like those before."

"I know!" Lily smiled. "He's a dreamboat."

"You said he was handsome, but you never mentioned he was so ..."

"Yes?"

"Abrupt? Is that the right word?"

Lily nodded. "Yep, I think so. He's not burdened with a lot of charm. But, his eyes are like lasers, and his voice is so commanding."

"He acts like he should be the president," Susan replied cautiously.

"You're sure he killed a patient?"

Susan shrugged. "He must have burned them with his laser eyes."

"Or maybe someone tripped and fell into that granite jaw and died." She looked at her mother. "I'm glad you're not my sister, but he seemed disappointed."

Susan shook her head. "Not my type. I like men who smile. Besides ..."

"Besides, what?'

"Well, look at him. He's incredible. Why isn't he already taken?"

"Maybe he hasn't found the right woman."

"That doesn't seem likely. And in my experience, if you meet a man like him who isn't already married, then they're broken."

Susan frowned slightly. "You found a rich widower."

"Yep," she agreed, "and he's broken."

"But is he fixable?"

"Only if he wants to be." She looked into the hallway and wondered where Jack McCranie went. "Men like them are dangerous. They're single for a reason."

Susan nodded. "You're probably right." She returned to the window. "And you'll be discharged tomorrow?" She didn't wait for a response. "Why don't we spend Christmas and New Year's here?" She turned to Lily. "Would you mind terribly if we extended our stay here past the New Year?"

Lily shrugged indifferently. "But what would we do? Where would we stay?"

"My room at the Lodge is comfortable, but I also found this pamphlet about a bed-and-breakfast just down the street … The Crofting." She fished the brochure from her purse and handed it to Lily.

"This looks nice. And very quaint." Lily thought for a moment, then nodded. "I'm tired. My ordeal has exhausted me." She examined the back of the brochure. "But what would we do for an entire week?"

"I don't know. We could go skiing."

"Mom?" Lily lifted the covers and pointed to her stitches.

"Ah, yes. Well, we could build a fire and roast marshmallows?"

Lily smiled. "Sounds great. I could sit around a fire and simply read, for that matter." She thought for a moment. "Would you mind terribly if Jayne joined us?"

Susan's smile faded. "Isn't she going back to Canada for the holidays?"

"You know she doesn't have any family to speak of. That's why she joins us almost every year. And the tour will be over tomorrow. Would you mind?"

Susan shook her head. "Of course not. I enjoy spending time with Jayne, as long as I don't have to go out with her at night."

Lily laughed. "Why, whatever do you mean?"

Susan mockingly rolled her eyes. "You know full well what I mean. She has the morals of an alley cat."

"She just enjoys meeting new people, that's all." Lily's defense of her friend was pointless, as neither of them believed a word.

As far as Caton was concerned, Mandy was torturing him. She insisted he get out of bed and walk around, but he refused to do so. He had painful tubes and wiring coming out of him, and a large incision in his side where the wood had jammed between his ribs. The incision in his chest was drained through a tube. Mandy promised if he would get up and walk for a few minutes, she would ask the doctor to take out some of the tubes. He demanded she remove his catheter or the deal was off.

Mandy grinned. "Deal!" She extended her hand to confirm the bargain.

When Mandy removed the largest chest tube, Caton felt as if his lungs were being pulled out of the hole. When she pulled the smaller tube, he thought that his bowels were being pulled out also. Once the drain tubes were removed, he felt like a new man. The doctor told him if he could walk a full circle around his wing, he could go home. He immediately set his mind on staying out of bed.

The next morning, after Caton suffered through his nondescript breakfast, Mandy walked him around the hospital floor. Holding tight to the doctor's promise, Caton held a slow, steady pace until he passed the nurses' station, where he stopped in his tracks. His blood suddenly ran cold.

He was looking at room 941, the same room where Mary had died three years earlier. He swallowed hard, regarding the room for a moment before slowly walking to the open door. An old man watched *Gunsmoke* on the television, oblivious to Caton's presence. Caton stood in the doorway, gaping into the room, then stepped back into the hallway.

He could still hear Dr. Taylor shouting, "Clear!" over and over again. Caton had retraced his steps to the waiting room where he received the news Mary was dead.

Discouraged, he returned to his own room and collapsed onto his bed. He offered Mandy no explanation for his surrender.

He was not prepared to be on the same floor where Mary died. He sat on his bed and stared out his window into the empty sky beyond.

Susan visited The Crofting to arrange better accommodations, leaving Lily to watch *MacGyver* reruns on the ancient TV in her room. Growing tired of the program, she decided to stretch her legs for a moment. She pressed the call button and summoned Terri to see if she was available to walk the halls.

Terri popped her head in the door and cheerfully asked, "Who's up for a walk?"

Lily took a second to slip into her house shoes and placed a free hand on her arm. "I'm ready." She grabbed her IV pole, and they stepped into the hallway. The corridor was not as long as she remembered. With the family pressed together at the end of the hall, the whole building felt congested.

"Let's walk to the cafeteria and back," Terri suggested.

"That's a big family group," Lily observed.

"They were called in this morning. And now it looks like they'll be here a little longer."

"Why's that?"

Terri opened her mouth to reply, but then snapped it shut. "I'm not supposed to talk about it. You know, patient confidentiality?"

"Sure, I understand." They reached the cafeteria and turned to walk back the way they came. She paused a moment and rubbed her incision.

"How's the leg?"

Lily considered her question. "It feels tight and sore, but I guess it's okay."

"It'll get better."

They could hear shouting from inside the cafeteria. Lily glanced through the open door and saw Jason Fox squaring off with Jack McCranie.

"What's best for my patient is my business, not yours, Jack."

McCranie pointed at him. "The way you treat your patients is my business."

Fox glared at him. "The problem isn't yours. She needs to die."

"What's wrong with waiting until her family gathers before turning off life support?"

"Don't give me that," Fox shouted at him. "She's got family coming out of her ears. They're all crowded at the end of the hall right now. How many people have to be here to watch her die?"

"How about her children, Fox? Why can't you wait until her children arrive?"

"Come on!" he pleaded. "How many more children can she possibly have?"

Jack growled at him. "She has eight children. Eight. And the last one will be here on Christmas Day. Why can't you give them some time?"

"Because it'll do no good. She's just as dead today as she will be tomorrow. It's not my fault they live in freakin' China."

"Grow up, Fox," McCranie snapped. "It's not as if we need the bed. We have five patients tonight." He held up his hand. "Five! And three of them are mine. So what's the real problem?"

"It's pointless to delay the inevitable. Her body can't go forever."

"Is this so you can fly to Breckenridge and go skiing?"

Fox flinched. "Of course not."

Jack softened his tone. "Because if it is, I'll take care of her. You can take off, and I'll make sure her family is with her when she passes."

"You want me to go? Fine! I'm outta here. But when the hospital administrator asks why we're spending money on her life support, you can answer him."

Jack shook his head. "This isn't about money. It's about people. And people have to come first. So, go on your trip and leave us in peace." He turned to leave. "I've fought the bean counters for as long as I've been a surgeon, and they always think the bottom line is money. Is that the kind of doctor you want to be?"

Fox lifted his hands in mock surrender. "Oh, the mighty surgeon has spoken." He lowered his hands and glowered at him. "I'll bet the bean counters at Parkland Hospital loved you. How much did they have to settle for to keep from being sued in open court?"

For a moment, Lily thought McCranie was going to punch Fox in the face, but he shook his head in dismay and replied, "Nice." As he turned to leave, he spoke over his shoulder. "Enjoy Colorado, and if you can find work, don't come back." He walked into the hall, almost running over Lily who was caught red-handed gawking at the disturbance. He didn't acknowledge her as he stormed past and disappeared around the corner.

"Wow," Terri muttered. "They've been going at each other for the last few days. Fox is such an unprofessional doctor, and Jack cares too much about his patients."

Lily was surprised. "Jack does? He seems so gruff. And disagreeable."

Terri nodded. "He has a horrible bedside manner. But he really does care. He has the emotional aptitude of a turnip, but he's two hundred times the doctor Fox will ever be."

Lily looked down the hall where he disappeared. "First impressions must be deceiving." She started walking again. "What was that comment about being sued?"

"Oh, Jack McCranie comes with baggage. But who doesn't? He had some trouble when he was a trauma surgeon in Dallas. We don't know what really happened, but someone died and the hospital was sued." Terri frowned. "We shouldn't be talking about this. We need to focus on your recovery."

Lily walked in silence. Who was this mysterious doctor who seemed to dislike patients, but fights with his colleagues to protect them?

Lunch was served before Dr. McCranie made his rounds, an hour later than he first projected. He entered the room with a light tap on the open door. Ignoring Susan completely, he cleared his throat and addressed Lily. "I see no reason you can't be discharged. Your infection is clearing. You just need to have your stitches removed in a week, which your physician in Boston can handle. I'm sure you're anxious to get home for the holidays, so I'll discharge you effective immediately. You can leave as soon as Terri gets your paperwork together." He turned to leave.

"Thank you, Dr. McCranie."

He paused. "How's that?"

"Thank you for fixing my leg."

He seemed confused. "That's my job." He turned to leave. "Have a nice day," he mumbled as he disappeared into the hall.

Susan frowned. "He's full of Christmas cheer."

Lily shrugged. "Well, at least I can go home."

"I suppose we should have told him we aren't leaving until next week."

"It doesn't matter. I can get the stitches out in Boston after New Years Day. I'm ready to get out of this hospital."

CHAPTER TWELVE

Is Mercurial the Right Word?

Caton felt doomed to a life of loss as he lay on his hospital bed. Never before had he been a quitter, but life was getting harder for him every day. He was unprepared to meet the sudden and dramatic memory of Mary's death. He also missed Mariah, who wasn't allowed to be in this portion of the hospital.

Caton's mind was spinning. He had finally settled in his heart that loving another woman was okay for him just when she left him forever. He had no way to find her now she had returned to Boston. Perhaps it was for the better. He wished she had contacted him to say good-bye, but that would have been awkward.

In the solitude of his room, Caton once again bared his soul before God. "Father, what am I going do now?"

Silence.

"Why did You open my heart only to have it shut again?"

Who has shut your heart?

"Well, Lily walked away from me and now she's gone."

Does that change your circumstances?

Caton's forehead furrowed, "Doesn't it?"

I'm not a man that I should lie.

"I'm sorry, Father. I didn't mean to call you a liar."

Be patient. You will see my hand working.

"I hope so," he replied sincerely. "I should go home today."

Silence.

"You'll help me get past this chapter in my life?"

I'll walk with you until the day I take you home. You'll never have to look for me; I'll always be here.

"You're so good to me, Father, and I trust you have great things in store for me."

There is no way to measure how full your life will be. I have many wonderful things prepared for you.

"Father, I don't want to receive from you ungratefully. Take my life and use it as you will."

Mandy entered his room, holding his discharge paperwork. "You're going home, Mr. Harvey. Merry Christmas."

"That's right, this is Christmas Eve! Mariah will be happy to have me at home with her tonight."

Lily found the Crofting to be a comfortable retreat from the hospital. They had full access to the kitchen, but they found the Lodge's restaurant, Rebecca's, to be the best place to eat dinner. Lily eagerly anticipated her evening meal with her mother. Her mind was fraught with her future now that she was no longer employed. She needed to talk about her plans with her mother.

The women sat near a window where they could be continually amazed at the majestic views. They could see White Sands National Park on the desert floor below them, with its bright, white sand winding around the mountains beyond the valley. Compared to the white snow on the mountain, the sand seemed dull.

The town was decorated for Christmas, and everyone in the village seemed devoted to observe the holiday with great enthusiasm. "Cloudcroft certainly has its share of Christmas cheer," Lily remarked.

"Yes, it's interesting to spend the holidays in a place where everyone says 'Merry Christmas' and expects the same in reply."

Lily's eyes darted across the room. "Jayne will be glad to see Rebecca's has a lounge."

Susan shook her head. "There's also a bar on Burro Street that has her name written all over it. When will she be here?"

"Tomorrow morning! I'm excited to see her again."

Their waiter presented the early dining menu. "Hmm, dare we try the Mexican food? This is the Southwest, after all."

Susan considered the question. "What exactly are fajitas?"

"Mother! How can you live your life in such seclusion?" Lily's eyes exploded, "Oh, they're a wonderful symphony of flavors that include beans, avocados, salsa, cheese, and meat." Her smile was satisfying. "I eat them whenever I'm in the Southwest."

Susan replied, "It sounds a little more involved than I'm up for tonight. But the roast duck sounds tempting."

"It does! I've never had duck with strawberry glace. That sounds delicious. I'm so hungry I could eat anything." Lily finally decided on the pistachio trout while Susan ordered the duck. They shared a pleasant meal and sipped their wine while contemplating dessert. "Mother? Have you heard from Ivy lately?"

Susan placed her dessert menu on the table. "Ivy's in Europe. Rome, I think. Or maybe Prague."

"My sister, the world traveler," Lily mumbled.

"She's probably dodging someone she conned. I swear that girl is bound to end up in prison again."

Lily thought of her sister, the hardheaded black sheep of the family who refused to follow the rules. For a few moments, they sat in silence until Lily said, "I miss Father. It's not the same without him."

Susan agreed. "I know. He still seems very real to me, even now."

"Do you still love Father the same way you did when he was alive?"

Susan hesitated. "I'm not sure. We loved each other tremendously, and I miss him dearly. But it's hard to express a romantic love for a spouse who died." She shook her head, "It's hard to explain. I do love him just the same, but I love him differently."

"How long before you decided to date again?"

Susan regarded her question for a moment. "Really, I never decided to date again—life just threw me into the mix. I dated some, but not much." Susan leaned back and changed the subject. "Did you know I started attending a church in Boston?"

Lily's eyebrows rose with interest. "No. Tell me about it."

"We were always members of First Presbyterian Church, but we seldom attended the services."

"I know. I've wondered why we never went."

"All too often, I performed on weekends. We were regular members about the time you were born, but after you get out of the habit of going, not going becomes easier."

"And what made you want to return to church?"

"After your father passed away, some of the ladies in the church started calling on me. We developed a relationship. Something was pulling me closer, I suppose. When you face the death of a loved one, you start thinking about the hereafter."

Lily was silent. God was becoming a frequent topic in her life. Maybe destiny was pushing her forward after all. "Mother, do you believe in miracles?"

"Of course."

"No, I mean do you think miracles occur today?"

"Why do you ask?"

"When I was trapped in my car, I had no hope of rescue, no one knew where I was, and no one knew I was missing. Well, I prayed God would send me some help."

"Did he?"

Lily shrugged. "He must have. I was in a place that couldn't be seen from the highway, and there was no sign of me driving off the road since the snow covered my tracks. Yet, someone found me."

Susan appeared troubled. "Lily, I should have done a better job of taking you to church and teaching you our faith, and in that I failed." Lily started to protest, but her mother lifted a hand. "I know, for the most part I was a good mother, and you had a good home, but when I was a little girl, I used to pray to God often and attend church regularly. Only after I married your father and traveled with the troupe did my church attendance become rare. After your experience, you can only conclude God had a reason for sparing your life. I should've made more of an effort to introduce you to God, so you wouldn't have to ask questions like you're asking now."

Lily leaned toward her with open eyes. "You mean you know the answers to my questions?"

"Do you feel a longing for something you can't find? Like a hunger you can't satisfy?"

"I've never really thought about it, but I think you might be right." Lily thought for a moment. "I think the word *longing* is the best description."

"I believe God created everything and everyone. And why would he do that? Well, I believe he did it for a reason."

"What reason?"

Susan smiled. "I think he did it because he wanted to, just as a man wants to be a father or a woman wants to be a lover."

Lily winced. "I've never thought of God as a lover."

"The idea strikes me also, but it seems appropriate. If he did create us on purpose, then he must have a purpose for us."

"Okay. What's my purpose?"

"I don't know. That's for each person to find out. That's between you and God."

Lily frowned. "Your answers are quite dissatisfying, Mother."

"I know, dear. But how can I answer you? Only God knows what plans he has for your life. But if you ask him, I think he'll answer you." Her eyes narrowed. "Have you ever asked?"

They were interrupted by their waiter. "Excuse me? You have a visitor requesting to join you. Shall I show her to your table?"

Lily turned to see Jayne standing near the entrance, scanning the room. "Yes, please."

"Let the party begin," Susan said with a smile.

Having Jayne spend the holidays with them required no end of adjustments to their expectations for Lily's quiet period of recovery. Jayne hit town with the impact of a hurricane, causing a stir wherever she went. She was arguably the most glamorous woman ever to grace the Village, and the men in town immediately noticed the bombshell. As soon as they saw what was happening, the women immediately stepped closer to their husbands. Jayne had a way about her that created tremors wherever she went—she was impossible to miss.

As Susan had predicted, Jayne quickly discovered the Western Bar on Burro Street and began checking out the local action.

The people of Cloudcroft were unprepared for three attractive blonds to hit town in the same week. Dr. Jason Fox met Jayne at the Western Bar and quickly tried to stake a claim on her, but she was not the type to commit to one man. She did, however, accept his invitation of a night cap at his place, and asked Lily if she wanted to tag along.

Knowing full well what was going to happen once the nightcaps were finished, Lily declined and opted for her own room and a Lifetime movie.

The next morning, Lily's stitches were driving her mad. She continued to ignore her discomfort through lunch, but as the afternoon grew late, she stood and announced she was going to the ER.

"I'll make sure the Fox takes good care of you." Jayne was all smiles.

The emergency room was busier than she expected for a small town. After a lengthy wait, Terri pushed through the door and called out, "Lily?"

"Finally," Jayne moaned. "These magazines are way out of date. That was really sad about the Titanic, eh?"

Lily rolled her eyes. "Canadian humor at its finest."

Terri smiled warmly as if they were old friends. "We need to quit meeting like this." She helped Lily onto a bed and immediately began taking vitals.

"That's for sure," Lily agreed. "This is my last visit. At least I hope so."

"So, what's wrong today?" she asked while scribbling the blood pressure readings on a clipboard.

Lily pulled her sweatpants down to her knees and pointed at the incision. "These stitches are driving me insane."

Terri frowned and examined the wound. "It's certainly inflamed. I'll have Dr. Fox take a look. Looks like your infection is gone." She pulled the curtain for privacy. "Since you're wearing shorts, you can just take off your sweats and relax for a minute."

Jayne sat on the bed next to her. "Maybe we can get the doctor to pay us a house call later."

"You have a one-track mind, Missy."

Jayne tossed her hair. "A girl's gotta have fun. Nothing else to do around here."

The curtain was opened, and Jason Fox flashed his white teeth. "It's so good to see you ladies again." He reached for the glove dispenser and slipped one over his right hand, letting the plastic snap against his hand. He leaned closer to examine the incision. "I think we can take those out. Other than having irritated skin, the wound has closed nicely. I'll grab what I need and be right back." He flashed a second smile, intended for Jayne, and left the curtain open, presumably so she could watch him work.

"Where did they find him?" Lily wondered aloud.

"He's certainly self-impressed," Jayne replied idly.

"Does he not impress you?"

"Oh, I don't care what he does for a living. I'm not looking for a husband. He could be a boring banker or a miserable mechanic It's not about the man, it's about the …"

"I know full well what it's about, Jayne. And you don't have to be so crass."

"But you love me anyway," she teased.

Lily reached for her hand. "I love you like a sister, Jayne. But that doesn't mean I approve of your behavior."

Jayne, no longer listening, was staring across the room. "Look what the cat drug in."

Lily turned and saw him. Dr. McCranie was talking on the phone, referencing a chart. "That's Jack. He's the doctor who stitched up my leg."

"Holy smoking stitches, Batman. He can play doctor with me anytime."

"Easy, Jayne. He doesn't play well with others." She snapped her fingers to get her attention. "He's the one I was telling you about."

"Dr. Jerk McCranie?"

"He's the one."

"I'll bet he's handsome when he smiles."

"We'll never know. He's not the smiling type." They watched him as he became more animated, appearing to be scolding someone. "Looks like he's having a bad day."

"When a man runs his fingers through his hair like that, he's definitely having a bad day."

Lily frowned. "I hate that."

Jayne eyed her curiously. "I thought you didn't like him."

"Well, I hate when anyone has a bad day. I don't have to like him to sympathize."

"Look at his granite jaw," Jayne contemplated. "He's a fine specimen."

Jack McCranie slammed down the phone and breathed deeply. He appeared to be fighting the urge to throw something against the wall.

"Wow, what a temper," Jayne hissed.

In a flash, Dr. Fox returned and began removing Lily's stitches. "So," he asked while snipping, "what plans do you have tonight?"

"Me?" Lily was surprised.

He shook his head. "Sorry, I was talking to Jayne."

Jayne's eyes darkened. "I'm open to suggestions."

"I'm almost done here for the day. Why don't we go up to the ski lodge and have a drink?"

"I could work that into my plans."

"We might be out late," Jason warned.

"Lily knows not to wait up for me."

"There," Jason said as he pulled the last of the stitches from her leg, "as good as new. You're hereby released to roam about the country."

Lily rubbed the incision. "Oh, that's better." Her posture softened. "Thank you, Doctor."

"Don't mention it. But wait 'til you get my bill!" he said, chuckling. "Jayne, would you like a tour of the facility?"

"Would I ever!" she replied. She cast a glance at Lily. "Care to join us?"

"Thank you, no. I'll find my way back to the Crofting." Quietly, she scolded, "Jayne, you're incorrigible." Then she watched as the two sauntered through the double doors and down the hall. She watched for a moment longer and said to no one, "So, I guess I'm done here." Aggravated at the turn of events, she pulled on her sweats and got up to leave, immediately smashing into Dr. McCranie.

"I beg your pardon, Miss DeMar. Are you okay?"

"I'm fine, thank you. Are you well?"

He looked at her for a moment, his eyes searching her face. "Yes, so it would seem."

They faced each other for a second longer, then Jack cleared his throat. "Well, I'd better get back to work, since I seem to be the only one actually working." He glanced around the ER to confirm his accusation. "If you're okay, that is."

"Yes, I'm fine. How's your day?" she asked softly.

He shrugged. "It's the same rat race every day." He looked at his watch.

She nodded politely. "Well, I'll be going."

"I thought you were leaving town?"

"I haven't decided yet. I don't really have a reason to stay." *Lily!* she scolded herself. *What are you doing?*

Jack fidgeted. "Yes, there's very little here. Just mountains and trees. I'm not sure why anyone would be here."

Grumpy Jack jolted her back to her senses. "Well," she replied, "it was nice to meet you." She returned to the Crofting, grateful she wasn't committed to a relationship with a man who was so gloomy. Once back in her room, Lily decided a nap was in order before she and her mother would walk to the Lodge for their evening meal.

A light tap on the open door aroused Lily from her book. She glanced at her watch—seven o'clock sharp. Her mother was prompt—always.

"Lily? Are you ready for dinner?"

"Let me put on my shoes, and I'll be right there." Joining her at the front door, they began the short trek up the snow-covered street to the Lodge.

Susan inhaled deeply. "I love this mountain air. It's so exhilarating!"

"I find it liberating."

"Yes, a very good description, Lily." As they approached the Lodge, she asked "I'm guessing Jayne is gone for the night?"

"I don't expect to see her until tomorrow. She has a new boy toy."

Susan frowned. "I wish Jayne could see how reckless she is. Someday she'll find a man who will do some irreparable harm to her."

"Sometimes it takes a tragedy to end a tragedy, I suppose."

"I'm so glad you didn't find Jason Fox interesting, Lily. He's a train wreck."

"Well, he did a great job removing my stitches," she replied without conviction.

"And why didn't Dr. McCranie remove your stitches?"

"It's first come, first served at the ER, and Fox was the doctor of the day."

"McCranie's an interesting man," Susan continued.

"How so?"

"He seems deeply troubled."

"He always looks like that. Even today. I ran into him as I was leaving, and he still seemed to be a jerk. Some men are just that way, Mom."

They approached Rebecca's, the restaurant in the Lodge. While waiting in the lobby for their table, Susan grabbed Lily's arm and motioned for her to look. "Look who's coming in now." Dr. McCranie walked through the lobby without noticing them, pausing a moment at the host station.

The smiling hostess greeted him. "Good evening, Jack. Headed for the lounge, or would you prefer a table?"

"The lounge, thanks."

"Help yourself."

They watched as he disappeared from view. "I'm guessing he's a regular," Lily suggested.

"That seems to be the case." Susan impatiently glanced at her watch. "I guess we're a few minutes early for our reservation."

Lily found her amusing. "Have you ever been late for a reservation?"

Her mom seemed to appreciate the comment. "Being prompt is a virtue."

Lily started to reply, but she was cut short when Dr. McCranie emerged from the lounge and entered the lobby. Seeing them, he hesitated as if conflicted, politely nodded to them, then headed for the restroom down the hall.

Susan shrugged. "That was odd."

"Did he seem annoyed when he saw us?"

"I'm not sure. He had something on his mind."

"That was quick—he's already returning."

As he entered the lobby, he walked directly to them. "Good evening, ladies. Are you well?"

Susan smiled graciously. "Yes, thank you. And yourself?"

"I'm well." He hovered a second longer, as if struggling to justify approaching them. "I was surprised to see you at the ER. I thought you planned to return to Boston."

Lily thought repeating the same conversation from just a few hours earlier odd. "My mother and I decided to spend a few days enjoying the mountains before returning. We don't have mountains like this in New England."

"Yes, these mountains are rather lofty." His face was emotionless but turned slightly red, as though he was embarrassed by his observation. He pursed his lips together before saying, "I have a table in the lounge if you care to join me."

Susan smiled warmly. "Thank you, but we have a reservation. You're very kind to offer."

He shook his head quickly, and the red tone deepened. "Not at all."

Lily awkwardly added, "I'm not sure I thanked you for taking such good care of me."

"It was my pleasure, Miss DeMar. You had great legs to work on ..." His face burned scarlet. "I mean, your wound was on your leg, and I ..." He shook his head as if angry. "I ..." He swallowed hard. "Please excuse me." He turned and walked toward the lounge.

"Well, that was strange," Susan remarked when he was out of earshot.

"Was he trying to flirt?"

"Yes, I think so." Susan was bewildered.

They watched him enter the lounge, where he paused, seeming to argue with himself. He spun around and returned, catching Lily by surprise. "I know this is highly irregular, but I'd like you to join me for a drink after your dinner. I'll wait in the lounge." Casting a quick glance at Susan, he said, "Ma'am." He then turned quickly and made his way past the host station and out of view.

"Well," Susan remarked after several seconds, "that was unexpected."

Lily agreed. "Completely."

Apparently, you have a date this evening."

"Do I?" She looked at her mother. "I'm still trying to figure out what just happened."

"I'm not certain either"

"Did he really ask me out?"

"Well," Susan mused, touching her chin, "he didn't actually ask you anything. He offered for you to join him, and then didn't give you the opportunity to decline. So, yes. I think he asked you out."

Lily shook her head. "I'm not sure."

"You have to give him points for his confidence. Despite his awkward comment about your legs, he returned and made a rather dashing recovery."

A smile spread slowly across her lips. "Yes, he did."

"And how will you respond?"

Lily thought a second. "I will … join him."

Lily returned to the Crofting shortly after ten o'clock. She found her mother sitting in the common room, reading a novel. She placed the book in her lap as Lily approached. "Well, you're back early. How was your evening?"

Lily shook her head in disbelief. "Surprisingly, I had a good time."

Susan smiled. "Must I beg for details?"

Lily dragged a rocking chair close to her mother, sighing as she sat down. "He's very … mercurial."

Susan's eyes widened. "Is he now? In what sense of the word? Animated? Erratic?"

"As in unpredictable. Or even complex."

"That's a rather unorthodox use of the word, wouldn't you say?"

Lily shook her head. "He's not at all what I expected. At the hospital he was curt, rude, and abrasive. But at the lounge, he was mellow and thoughtful."

"Perhaps he was under the influence?"

Lily considered the suggestion. "Well, he was drinking Scotch. But he didn't seem intoxicated."

"So, your impression has changed?"

Her nose crinkled. "Maybe." Her eyes roamed the ceiling. "Probably. I don't know."

"Well, what is he like? Let's start there."

"He is strong and confident. He has very clear and well thought out opinions. He seems very much an alpha male."

Susan's eyes narrowed. "You just described a wolf."

She slowly shook her head in disagreement. "Not a wolf, but maybe a lion."

"Ah."

Lily rolled her eyes. "And what does that mean?"

Susan shrugged. "Nothing, really."

"Mother! You can't say that and then not follow up on it."

"Very well." She closed her book and ran her fingers over the cover. "He sounds like Rodney."

"What?" She was certainly shocked by the comparison. "Jack's nothing like Rodney."

"Rodney was your husband. You'd know better."

Lily almost seemed to pout. "I hope he's nothing like Rodney." She shook her head. "No, he's not at all. Jack seems to be a very kind man when he's not at work. I saw an entirely different side of him tonight."

Susan nodded. "So, what's next?"

"Well, we are going out tomorrow."

They heard keys rattle softly at the door, and Jayne made a quiet entrance. She looked drained, her hair slightly mussed. "Ah, the welcoming committee awaits my arrival," she said cheerfully.

"Good evening, Jayne," Susan greeted. They didn't have to ask how her date went—she carried the telltale signs. "Come sit with us. You look as though you need to relax for a while."

Jayne smiled broadly. "Jason knows how to show a girl a good time." She took inventory of their mood. "So, what happened? You two are up to something."

"Lily was just telling me about her date."

Jayne clapped her hands and sat on the floor in front of the fire. "Yay! Details. We need details."

Lily stared into the flames. "Well, I joined him after Mom and I ate dinner."

"So, was he your dessert?"

"Jayne!" Lily growled, "behave or I won't tell you anything."

She pouted. "Okay, so start from the beginning."

"I met him in Rebecca's lounge. He had a stack of buffalo wings to the side and a glass of Scotch in front of him."

"Oh, I like him already." She leaned toward the fire with her hands extended to the flames. "Wait. Who is he?"

Lily smiled cautiously. "Jack McCranie."

She was shocked. "Doctor Jerk?"

Lily sighed. "I suppose."

Susan laughed. "You call him Doctor Jerk?"

Jayne shrugged. "He was being a jerk at the ER today. They also call him Doctor Death."

"They?"

"Well, that's what Jason Fox calls him," she explained.

"Whatever." Lily closed her eyes and began recounting the date. "Jack stood when I entered the lounge and greeted me halfway across the room."

"I'm so glad you joined me, Miss DeMar." His facial expression didn't change, and she couldn't tell if he was happy to see her by his tone.

"Thank you for inviting me. And please call me Lily"

He walked ahead and pulled out a chair. "I was just finishing my basket of wings. Would you like to share with me?"

"Thank you, no."

Jack's eyes bore into her own, making it hard for her to hold his gaze. "I'm guessing you drink wine. A dry red, if I wager a guess."

"Yes," she replied cautiously.

He lifted his hand, and the waiter nodded. Within seconds, he placed a glass in front of her and asked, "Would you care for some olives or cheese?"

"Oh, some olives, please."

Jack's expression softened slightly. "I was torn between a Chianti Classico and an Argentinean Malbec."

She sipped casually, focusing her energy on not embarrassing herself. However, the instant the wine touched her lips, she knew what he had ordered. She placed the glass on the table and asked, "Why the Malbec?"

His gaze never wavered. "When I think about you, I can see two possibilities."

"Only two?" She was starting to enjoy his approach.

"I can see the classic, old world, vintage woman, who loves music, art, and wine, hence the Tuscan Chianti."

"But you chose the Malbec."

"I could also see an adventurous woman who loves life and sees love as a journey rather than a destination, and possibly even a lifelong quest."

Lily could feel her face starting to blush. "So, I'm an adventurous Amazonian?"

For the first time he smiled. "In truth, I see both sides equally, and I made a stab in the dark that either choice would be correct."

She sipped the wine again to buy some time before replying. She had never been on a date where she was the object of a man's thoughts. "I think you chose well."

Jayne slapped her on the leg. "I think you chose well? Is that the best you could come up with?"

Lily laughed. "I had no idea what to say. I've never been in that situation before. He was very deliberate and focused, and obviously, I was the center of his attention. He wasn't checking his phone, updating stock prices, telling lame jokes, or talking about himself." She inhaled deeply. "He wanted to talk about me, my music, my hopes, and my dreams."

"How ... what's the right word?" Jayne looked to Susan for support. "Mercurial?"

"Yes! That's the word!" Her eyes narrowed. "So, what's next?"

"We go on a formal date tomorrow night."

Lily knew that something was tugging at her. Something she hadn't expected. Something that ignited and burned deep in her soul.

CHAPTER THIRTEEN

Lizard Rolls and Bear Fat

After a week at home, Caton was growing bored and anxious. He was delighted to be home in time to see Mariah open her Christmas presents, and she was happy to have him there. Obviously, she had missed him, but he hadn't considered how much he had missed her.

Mariah had to make a lot of adjustments while her daddy healed from surgery. Whenever he tried to do something, Mariah would ask him, "Are you still sore, Daddy?"

Mrs. Davis had weathered the days of being alone with Mariah without much difficulty. As with most of their major winter storms, the phone lines went out and the electrical lines were down. Caton had installed an automatic backup generator, powered by a large propane tank.

He didn't have much choice except sit around and get better. He tried reading, but he grew bored after a few days. On Sunday, he dressed for church as usual and surprised Mrs. Davis, who was still in her apron, hovering over the stove. "Where are you going, young man?"

"It's Sunday. Aren't you coming with us?"

"I imagined you wouldn't be up for sitting through a service, not to mention all the hugging that comes with church."

"I have a plan." He unfolded a shoulder sling and pulled his arm through it. "See, now people won't try to hug me." He wore the sling for a moment, then added, "Actually, it feels better to use it."

"You don't suppose that's why the doctor gave one to you?"

He ignored her sarcasm. "Blue Boy leaves in one hour if you want a ride to town."

"I have to assume the doctor released you to drive?"

Caton frowned. "Did anyone tell you I already have a mother?"

"I'm also a mother, and that's what we do. Now, if you'll excuse me, I'll get ready for church."

The service was uneventful, except for his having to repeat the story of his injury to each interested party. A good friend approached him after the service. Caton smiled and held out his left hand. "Hey, Seth, how are Norma and the kids?"

"We're okay." Seth returned the handshake. "Listen, I wanted to know if there's anything I could do for you out at the place. How can I help you?"

Caton thought for a moment. "I can't think of anything. You should take advantage of the slopes and get in some snowboarding."

"That's an excellent idea! I wanted to make sure you were okay." He turned to leave, then changed his mind. "Say, what happened to the woman who went out to visit you and Mariah?"

"You mean Lily?"

"Yeah, that sounds right … Lily. Did everything go okay?"

"Not really. I was trying to rescue Lily when I got hurt. Our visit didn't go very well, and she returned home in a hurry. She's gone from our lives forever, I guess."

"I don't want to get into your personal business, but are you okay?"

Caton was touched. "Thanks for asking. Honestly, I'm a little confused about the whole thing. I thought God told me something, and I messed it up. Now I don't know what's gonna happen."

Seth hesitated. "I don't want to pry, but there's talk of a mystery woman who's living over at the Crofting. I thought maybe she was the same."

Caton's shoulders sagged. "No, Lily left for Albuquerque. I imagine she's in Boston by now."

"Well, I can tell you the woman I heard about was from up north somewhere, and she is dating Dr. Fox. She sounds like the same woman to me." He shifted his weight. "It's not like there's a bunch of blonde northerners running around the Village these days."

Caton was adamant. "It's definitely not Lily. She's got better sense than to chase after a womanizer like Fox." He turned to leave. "Happy New Year!"

"Happy New Year, Caton. Bye-bye, Mariah."

Mariah waved, then turned to chase after her father. Caton almost reached Blue Boy when he heard a woman calling his name. That shrill voice could only belong to one woman.

"Mrs. Poe, did you have a merry Christmas?"

"I suppose so. Did that woman ever make it to your house?"

"Yes, ma'am, she did. And she's already gone home. Thank you for your help."

She scowled at him. "You know it's not proper for a woman to visit a man by herself."

"Yes, ma'am, I do know that. Mrs. Davis was with us the whole time."

"That's not good enough. You should be ashamed of yourself for taking advantage of her."

Mrs. Davis, approaching from behind, said, "Come on, Mariah, let's get into the pick-up." She disappeared leaving Caton to handle Mrs. Poe alone.

"She's already gone home, Mrs. Poe. The incident has come and gone."

"I saw her up at the Lodge the other day."

"I think you saw a different woman. Lily went home to Boston."

April's eyes narrowed. "Nope. It's her."

"Was she with Dr. Fox?"

"Yep!" she said with satisfaction. "That's the one. Why is she still in town?"

"It's a different woman. Lily went home already."

"She still shouldn't have been at your home unsupervised. Who knows what could go on out there?"

Caton wanted to grin at the absurdity of the conversation, but he restrained himself. "Mrs. Poe, I assure you her virtue is still intact."

With those words, she *humphed* and left, having extracted the information she would need tomorrow at the teashop. Caton climbed into Blue Boy and asked, "Shall we have dinner at the Lodge?"

"That'd be nice," Mrs. Davis agreed, "especially since you didn't allow me enough time to prepare an adequate meal before being rushed off to church."

At the Lodge, Susan DeMar sat by herself at a table for two, finishing the last of her cheesecake. A man, his arm in a sling, created quite a commotion as he entered. She grabbed her waiter as he walked past. "Who's that man who just came in, the one with the older lady and the small child?"

The waiter replied, "That's Caton Harvey."

Susan was shocked to see such an agreeable man, smiling and shaking hands. "What happened to him?"

"He was injured in a bad accident south of town just before Christmas." He watched Caton a moment, "It would seem everyone is his friend."

"Yes, it does. Would you do me a favor and come back to my table in a few minutes?"

"Of course." He rushed off to serve another table.

Susan needed to think for a moment. Caton didn't seem to be the man Lily had described. He certainly didn't come across as a callous individual who wouldn't visit an injured friend in the hospital.

And now Lily was spending the day with Jack McCranie, touring the nearby town of Alamogordo. She and Jack seemed mostly compatible after dating every night this week. Should she interfere with Lily's love life? *Of course. After all, I'm her mother.* But she needed more information.

As requested, the waiter returned. "Would you please go to Mr. Harvey's table and ask if I might visit with him for a moment?"

"Shall I say who's asking?"

"No, I'll take care of it."

"Very good." In a flash, the waiter was off. She could see him discretely indicating which woman wanted an audience with him, then he promptly returned. "Mr. Harvey will come to you." Before he finished speaking, Caton was on his feet, walking in her direction. Several other locals shook hands with him as he passed their tables. Finally, he stood in front of Mrs. DeMar.

"Ma'am, I'm Caton Harvey. Is there something I can do for you?"

Looking up, she was greeted by a warm, rugged face with a gentle smile. There was nothing arrogant about him. He searched her face carefully, as if trying to recognize her, but evidently deciding they'd never met.

"Mr. Harvey, it's an honor to meet you. I understand you're the man who rescued the woman on the highway."

His face flashed red. "Yes, ma'am. I helped, but I really didn't do all that much. Other men actually rescued her and took her to the hospital."

"Won't you have a seat?" She pointed to the empty chair. "From what I hear, you played a defining role."

He settled into his chair. "Not really." She could tell he was trying to read her face. "Have we met before? You seem very familiar to me."

"No, this is my first visit to Cloudcroft. Right now, I'm here visiting my daughter and her friend."

His head tilted to the side. She could tell his mind was working overtime. "Please forgive my intrusion, but are you the woman who's dating Dr. Fox?"

Susan's lips pressed thin. "That would be my daughter's friend, Jayne."

Caton's face relaxed. He smiled, obviously relieved. "It's good to meet you ..." He stopped, realizing he didn't know her name.

"Susan."

"Susan." A quiet satisfaction filled his eyes. "A lot of folks had you confused with a friend of mine. I can see why. The two of you could be sisters."

"I think that's a compliment. I wonder who your friend is ..."

"She's from New England, and she's already returned home."

"That seems to make you sad," she prompted.

"Well, I regret she left. We didn't get to say good-bye the way I wanted. In fact, nothing went the way it should have." He shifted nervously. "Is there something I can do for you?"

Susan smiled and, for a moment, she resembled Lily. "I wanted to buy lunch for the man who saved the woman's life."

He shook his head. "No, I can't let you do that. I had very little to do with the rescue."

"If I might ask, how did you injure yourself?"

Obviously, he was tired of telling the story. "Lily's car went off the road and plunged about twenty feet into a ravine. A tree caught and kept it from falling all the way to the bottom. When I got down there and tried to open her door, the car shifted, and I slammed into a tree. A branch pierced through my side and collapsed my lung."

Susan was shocked. "Wow, you're a real hero." She noted her use of the word *hero* made him uncomfortable. "Were you in the hospital long?"

"Almost a full week."

"Do you have a good hospital here?"

"We do, but I was in Lubbock, Texas. They flew me there from the accident. The hospital in Lubbock handles the big cases around here."

"Oh, my. How's the woman?"

"I've had a hard time finding out. I heard they stitched her up, and she's already gone back home." He shrugged sadly. "I'm glad she's okay."

Susan thought for a moment. "Is she a dear friend?"

Caton looked away. "I like to think so." He started to stand. "I'd better return to my family. It was a pleasure speaking with you."

"No, the pleasure is all mine."

As usual, Susan's nose was buried in a book when Lily returned from her day with Jack. "How was Alamogordo?"

"What an incredible difference there is between here and there. We're almost nine thousand feet in elevation here in Cloudcroft. Alamogordo is about five thousand feet. We're just about a mile higher up than they are. And here everything is forest—down there everything is desert. And it's only sixteen miles from here."

Susan smirked. "You seem full of facts tonight. How was the city itself?"

She thought carefully. "There's not much to tell. It has a few stores and a mall, which is very small … the smallest mall I've ever seen, with less than a dozen stores."

"You make it sound rather intriguing." Susan quipped. "What else did you do?"

"We only spent a few minutes in town, then we drove to White Sands National Park, which is awesome. I was standing in a world of snow, but it was almost sixty degrees. I could have worn shorts, while you're up here in the real snow. Jack rented a sled, and we went down some of the taller sand dunes." She pulled at her sweater, making a show of dusting herself off. "I've got about five pounds of white sand in my clothes. Next we drove toward an even smaller town, Tularosa, and toured some wineries and pistachio farms. It was fun."

"It's good to see you smiling."

"Mother, I smile all the time."

"But not because of a man." Mischief crossed her eyes. "You didn't come back engaged?"

Lily smiled at her mother and playfully rolled her eyes. "Not yet. He did ask me to stay in this area for a while. He wants to try us out to see we fit, as he put it."

"Is that too fast?" Susan asked carefully.

Scrunching her nose, Lily considered her response. "I'm not sure. I mean, it's only been a few dates in less than a week." She got up and pulled her nightgown from the bureau. "I enjoyed his company."

"But?"

She exhaled sharply and sat on the bed. "He always orders for me at the restaurants."

Susan put the book in her lap. "That's odd. You always seemed to enjoy a man who will take charge. But now you've found him, and you hesitate."

"Yes ..." Lily paused. "I'm so complicated. I do enjoy a man who knows what I want and will be 'the man.' But he seems to be 'the man' incessantly. I do like it, but I don't want just that. Am I making sense?"

"You also want to have some choice in what's happening."

"I always dreamed of finding a strong man—the take charge type—but now that doesn't seem as incredible as I imagined."

Susan smiled. "Be careful what you wish for—you may get it?"

Lily grunted. "Something like that. I'm very traditional, but I think he's from the eighteenth century. On the plus side, he's not trying to get me to jump in bed with him. He seems to respect my desires to take it slow."

Susan smiled at her. "You were always very conservative. I like that about you."

Lily shrugged. "I don't know, it's just—it seems a man won't respect you if you give him too much too soon."

Susan's eyes lifted. "When is it not too soon?"

"Well, for me, after the wedding." She pointed a finger at her mother. "You're the one who taught me to be virtuous."

"Yes, I did. You don't regret that, do you?"

"Not at all. I'm worth waiting for," she said with a shy smile.

"Yes, you are. You're committed to those values?"

"What are you asking, Mother?"

"It's been a long time since you were married. Perhaps you miss the romance."

Lily nodded. "Of course I do! But I don't think that's a good reason to move too fast." She turned away. "I do think about it."

Susan smiled. "It would be hard not to give in, especially after being a married woman."

Lily sighed. "Rodney was no great lover. He was only concerned about himself. I don't really have a lot of experience. And our time together was rather ... disappointing. I was hoping for more. Perhaps it turned me off from wanting to try again."

"How tragic. There's nothing like being married to a man who's passionately in love with you. Do you think Dr. McCranie could be such a man?"

"He certainly seems very interested in me." Lily went to wash her face. "I'm really starting to like him more each day. I might even fall in love if given enough time."

"What a thing to say, Lily."

She threw a hand towel at her mother in playful protest. "Stop it." She sat on the edge of the bed. "You and I both know you can't truly love someone until you get to know them."

"Do you think you're heading that direction with Jack?"

"Possibly. He and I need to discuss a few things before I allow myself to get involved."

"Such as?"

"You know, while we've been talking about this, I keep thinking that when he's ordering for me at restaurants, he is projecting how I belong to him—that I'm his property."

"That's certainly one way of looking at it."

Lily rolled her eyes. "One way, Mother? I suppose you have an observation?"

"I don't disagree with you. Some women really like such qualities in a man. In fact, *you* like that in a man, Lily. Rodney was very similar, if you remember."

Lily raised her hand. "We're not going to discuss Rodney." Her hand returned to her lap and she breathed deeply. "Okay, I do like strong men. I always have. But if my man is going to order my meals, I want him to know what I like to eat, not what he wants me to like."

Susan smiled warmly. "Which seems more than fair. In fact, you should bring it up."

"Of course. Thank you, Mother." She blew a kiss to her affectionately.

Susan picked up her book again. "I met a friend of yours today."

"A friend of mine? Who?"

"Caton Harvey."

Lily nearly fell off the bed. "Why are you telling me this?"

"Because there's more to his story than you know."

Lily's face turned scarlet, and her eyes flared. "Why are you doing this? Why now? I've moved on. He had his chance and rejected me. I'm interested in Jack."

Susan pretended to read. Lily changed into her nightgown and sat on the bed to brush her hair. "So, what did he tell you?"

Susan put her book down. "Did you know Caton was there on the highway the day you were rescued?"

She frowned in thought. "No, I don't think he was."

"It's true. I asked him myself."

A frantic look crossed her face, "Mother! You didn't!"

She lifted a hand to calm her. "He didn't know who I was. His arm was in a sling, and I asked him what had happened."

Lily stopped brushing her hair and sat still until her mother started talking again.

"Apparently, he regrets letting you go, and he chased after you. He's the one who found your car."

Her knees felt weak. "Oh, my ..." Then she shook her head in protest. "But that doesn't excuse his refusal to visit me at the hospital."

"There's more."

"Of course there is," Lily said reluctantly.

"Do you remember one of the rescuers had to be flown to Lubbock because he was injured?"

As realization came to her, she exclaimed, "Mother—it's not true, is it?"

"He's the one who saved your life and almost lost his in the effort."

Lily was silent.

Susan told her how Caton had been injured trying to stop the car from falling. When she told the part about his emergency surgery and recovery in Lubbock, Lily nearly cried.

"Oh, no, what have I done? How could I be so wrong?" She felt sick. "And that's why he didn't visit me?" She reached for a tissue. "Oh! And he was probably wondering why I didn't visit him at the hospital." Her face clouded as she pressed her lips tightly together.

Susan pulled Lily's brush from her limp hands. Softly, she began to stroke Lily's hair. "When I met him, I saw a real man. There is nothing pretentious about him. He's kind and considerate, a man who knows what he believes. I saw a man who has been through the fire and slain the dragon. He regrets letting you go. Moreover, he thinks you're already gone, which is why he hasn't come to visit you. He doesn't even know you're here."

Lily collapsed into her mother's arms and cried.

Caton sat in his garden, braced against the cold wind. Winter always served as a time to focus on indoor projects; however, his doctor had, in no uncertain terms, ordered him to take a rest and allow his body to heal. Caton concluded that forcing himself not to be active was as stressful as being active. He was confused and disappointed. He was certain God had promised him a relationship with Lily. As God can't be wrong, Caton thought he must have misinterpreted what God was telling him.

"Father, what did I misunderstand?"

Silence.

"I really thought You placed us in each other's lives. Was I wrong?"

The cold forced him to get up and walk around in small circles. A thick layer of snow blanketed the meadow and the forest surrounding him. What had he done wrong?

Who said anything was wrong?

"I did. It seems I misunderstood you."

My timing is perfect.

"Then what are you planning? I would appreciate knowing."

Silence.

Caton looked down. Who was he to tell God what to do? "You're right. I don't really need to know everything, no matter how much I want to know."

Trust me.

"I'm learning to trust you."

Returning to the house, he embraced its warmth, but the house felt too small. He needed to do something. He went to see about Mariah. She hadn't been feeling well—Mrs. Davis suspected she might have an ear infection. She was taking a nap, so he decided not to disturb her. He found Mrs. Davis in the utility room, folding freshly washed sheets. She ran him off because he was upsetting her ability to concentrate. Finally, he decided to drive into town to check on his work crew. He promised to be gone for only a few hours, but Mrs. Davis, quickly preparing a grocery list, insisted he take his time.

Finding his crew eating lunch at the Pine Stump Café, he sat down to join them. They ate in silence for a moment, then Vinney pointed out the window. "Man, have ya'll seen the woman who's been running around town?"

Caton nodded. "You mean the blonde?"

"Yeah, she's a knockout, isn't she?"

Jerry asked, "How old do you suppose she is?"

"I spoke to her once down at the Lodge," Caton volunteered. "and she looked to be between forty and forty-five, give or take a few years.".

"Shoot, that ain't the woman I saw. This one is in her twenties," Vinney insisted. "And man, is she a looker."

Caton shook his head. "No, that's not right. I talked to her for several minutes, and she wasn't in her twenties. I can see how you'd make that mistake; she's a beautiful woman."

"Nothin' doin', boss." Vinney defended himself. "This woman is young and pretty. She has shoulder-length blond hair and a great figure."

"She's shapely too," Jerry observed, "not that I noticed."

Caton laughed. "You better watch yourself, or I'll tell Joyce that you're moon-eyed over another woman."

Jerry fought back, "Well, if you tell on me, you'll have to tell Shelley that Kenny was eyeing another blonde."

Kenny straightened in his chair. "You two leave me out of this. My wife gets upset about such things. So, if that doctor wants to date a younger woman, then leave me out of it."

"If you'd ever seen her, you wouldn't be able to get her out of your mind." Vinney stated. "I just saw them going into the Pizza Palace."

Jerry continued, "She has a really pretty name also … what was it? It makes her sound rich or something."

"Susan?" Caton offered.

Vinney shook his head, "That's her mother. This one's named … I can't remember."

Caton searched his memory. "Susan said her friend's name was Jayne."

Vinney nodded. "Yep, that's her friend. But I'm talking about Susan's daughter. I can't remember her name, but I do know she's from Boston."

Caton eyed them warily. "You boys trying to pull my leg? That sounds like Lily."

"Yep, Lily! That's her name." Vinney was satisfied.

Caton was on edge. "What? Do you mean Lily is her name?"

"Just that. Her name is Lily."

"Not Susan?"

Vinney wagged a finger at him. "Nope. Susan is her mother. Lily's the one with the doctor."

Caton was growing agitated. "It can't be the same Lily. She went home to Boston."

"I'm telling you, it's the same woman."

Jerry's eyes were wide with caution. "Vinney, let's just let it go."

Caton was trying to make sense of the news. Finally, he said, "It can't be Lily because she stayed a few days in the hospital and then went home."

Vinney wagged his finger again. "It is her. She ended up with an infection of some kind—almost got amputated—and stayed in the hospital for several days. Then, when she was released, she stuck around so she could hook up with the doctor."

Caton was desperate. "You're talking about the woman in the accident?"

This time a nod. "Yep, that's her. The woman who you got hurt trying to help. Now ain't that just like a woman? You try to help them, and what do they do? They put you in the hospital."

Dismayed, Caton mentally checked out. He found himself stumbling out of the café and into the street. A fog bank settled over his mind. If Vinney was right, then Lily was still in Cloudcroft and ... dating a doctor? How could this be? In a numbed stupor, he marched to the Pizza Palace and jerked open the door.

Lily endured a sleepless night after her mother delivered the news about Caton. She never anticipated that she had misunderstood what happened to him. He almost died trying to save her? That knowledge tugged deeply at her heart.

What about Jack? She and Jack were really hitting it off. She fully intended on setting some ground rules with him about their relationship, which is why they were having lunch today.

Now she was sitting in the Pizza Palace with a man she wanted to know better, wondering why her head was spinning.

Jack's gray eyes probed her face. After a moment, he leaned forward. "Lily, is everything okay? You seem a little on edge."

She nodded. "I'm preoccupied. That's all."

"Is there anything I can do?"

She shook her head. "I need to sort out my thoughts."

"You look miserable. Is it anything I've done?"

"Not really."

Jack didn't seem to miss the implication. "What do you mean by 'not really'?" His deep voice bore the weight of authority.

She waved him off. "It's just ..." she hesitated. "I found out what happened to the man who was injured trying to rescue me. You know, the one who was flown to Lubbock?"

"What about him?"

"Did you know he's the one I came to visit?"

Jack seemed confused. "Well, I knew you came to visit someone, but you seemed reluctant to talk about it. I didn't think it was my business. This is the first time you've mentioned him specifically. Who is he?"

"Caton Harvey."

Jack's eyes narrowed. "Caton is the man you came to visit? He was the one injured rescuing you that night? They flew him directly to Lubbock."

Tears filled Lily's eyes. "I know that now, but I just found out last night. All this time, I thought he rejected me, basically dismissing me from his life. And then I find out he almost died and was lying in intensive care thinking I was the one who left him." She reached for a napkin to blot her tears. "And now I know I'm the one who messed things up."

Jack rubbed his eyes. "And then I came along."

She softened some. "Yes, you came along. And actually, I came here to discuss how much I was looking forward to getting to know you better."

Jack's face didn't reveal his thoughts. "Lily, I'm sorry for the confusion, but this doesn't change how I feel about you."

His words made her tears flow again. *Oh, why is this happening?* She closed her eyes and pressed the napkin hard against them. She felt Jack's strong hands reaching for her fingers.

"Look at me," he said. "Come on, look at me. That's better." He smiled and spoke slowly, deliberately. "We'll figure this out. You and I have a good thing going. I have to get back to work soon, but why don't we get together this afternoon? I'll pick you up, and we can have a quiet evening. Yep, that's what you need. A quiet evening." His voice was soothing her troubled soul, causing her pain to diminish. "We won't go out at all. I'll fire up the grill. I have some salmon in the freezer, and we can have a quiet meal, just the two of us. I'll pick you up at five."

Why was she susceptible to his voice? She found so much comfort in his words—and his smile. She was a huge fan of his handsome smile. And he was smiling at her right now. "I can't wait to see your home," she replied hopefully.

His eyes were probing her face again. "You understand my cabin is very humble? It's rather rustic …"

She watched him carefully. "But?"

"Well, it's not finished." He threw his hands in the air as if exasperated. "I work on it as I get the time. So far, I've only finished what I absolutely had to finish to live in it. My kitchen is complete—and the living room. Well, actually, they're one room … they just blend together. My bedroom floor still needs hardwood, and my bathroom is barely functional. I have a toilet and a shower, but no tile work or anything."

Lily enjoyed listening to Jack talk about his home. Seeing him animated about any subject was a rare occurrence. Suddenly, a man threw the front door open. His frame filled the opening, as if he were a marshal looking for an outlaw. Lily noticed Jack's face, then followed his gaze. "Oh, my …" she murmured.

Standing in the door, Caton's eyes found hers. Lily saw the confusion on his face and knew how he must be feeling. He was at a loss.

He marched straight to their table. "Lily?"

Shock was controlling her reaction. "Caton, what are you doing here?"

"It's good to see you too."

Embarrassment quickly followed shock. "I … uh …" She had no idea what to say.

Jack stood. "Caton, perhaps you could give Lily a moment?"

Caton barely noticed him. "Lily? I had no idea you were in town …" He blinked hard. "What … how …"

"Caton," Lily started. "I just found out about your being injured—last night. Believe me, I don't know what to say. But, I'm here with Jack. Maybe we can talk this afternoon?"

Caton looked hard into Lily's eyes, pleading for an explanation, but his confusion clouded his ability to think. Every person in the Pizza Palace was gawking at them. Lily could hardly breathe. Finally, he muttered, "I just need to think." He turned robotically and made his way back through the door.

"Oh, my," Lily repeated. She glanced at Jack, whose face seemed harder than normal. His fists were clenched.

"I have to get back to work," Jack said carefully. He reached for her hand. "Look, I know this seems bad, but we'll figure it out. Give him some time to get his head around what happened, okay?"

Lily shook her head. A cauldron of emotions, she couldn't decide which one to experience first.

"The poor man looked like he'd seen a ghost, for heaven's sake." The idea brought more tears. "Oh, Jack. What have I done?"

Lily stormed into her suite at the Crofting and saw her mother across the room.

Following a rather animated rendition of the event, Susan commented, "Sounds like I missed quite a show."

"Quite a show? Mother, I've never been so humiliated in my life."

Susan reached for Lily's hands. "I can only imagine how horrible it must have been."

Lily shook her head. "Horrible hardly covers it. Caton, looked ... betrayed." The words were hard to say. "He had a hollow, haunted look. And, I wouldn't talk to him. No, I *couldn't* talk to him." She looked at the ceiling. "What was I supposed to say? It was an impossible situation. Clearly, he didn't know I was in town. He must think I'm a horrible person." The tears began again. "Maybe I am." She began to sob. "This is all my fault."

Susan embraced her. "It'll be okay, Lily. I know the situation seems impossible now, but everything will work out. How did Jack respond?"

Thinking of Jack seemed to suppress the tears. "He was very gracious. He had no idea what to do or say. We were all at a loss. This will be one of the worst memories of my life."

Caton drove aimlessly down James Canyon Highway, winding his way past Peñasco, then finding himself in the high desert, heading toward Texas and the Guadalupe Mountains on Cornucopia Canyon Road. His mind was numb—he couldn't think or feel.

Finally, after an hour of pointless wandering, he asked, "What's happening, Father?"

You're running away.

"Can you blame me?"

Silence.

"How am I supposed to react? I felt so stupid standing there. It's obvious she has no interest in me. And now she must think I'm a huge loser."

Silence.

"And how am I supposed to compete with Dr. McCranie? Look at the man! He's Captain Awesome, and I'm the idiot who didn't even know Lily was still in town. It's all my fault."

Silence.

Caton stopped driving in the middle of a gravel road. A bitter realization flooded over him. "Well, I guess I deserve it. I was the one who rejected her, causing her to drive off in a storm." He opened his door and stood in the road. "What am I supposed to do?" He picked up a rock and hurled it into the vast Chihuahua Desert. "What am I supposed to do?" He picked up another rock and threw it farther. "WHAT AM I SUPPOSED TO DO?" he yelled, then spun on his heels, kicking at another rock. He found rocks everywhere, and he began kicking and throwing them until a small dust cloud hovered over him. He stopped to catch his breath. "What am I supposed to do now?" he asked, his voice small.

Go to her.

"Isn't it too late? She's probably shacked up with that doctor now."

Silence.

Caton collapsed to a sitting position on the road and hung his head between his knees. "Is it too late?"

Go to her.

"Should I?"

Go to her.

"Yes, I'll go to her. Is it that simple?"

Trust me.

"Okay." He was starting to feel strength again. "I can do this." He stood and dusted his pants, creating another cloud of white dust. "I'll stop and buy flowers. Flowers always help, right?"

Just go to her. That's all you need to do.

"I can stop and pick up flowers at the roadside stand."

Trust me.

"Yes! Thank you, Father!"

Lily thumbed through a magazine while Jayne filed her fingernails. "If I don't find someone who does nails, I'll have to rip mine off and go natural," she complained.

Lily was feeling sour. "And no one wants 'natural' Jayne. The earth would spin off its axis."

"Ouch!" Jayne snapped back. "And no one wants to be with Pouty Lily. She's mean."

Lily crossed her arms and settled deeper into the couch. "This is a horrible day. What else could possibly go wrong?"

The doorbell rang. The women looked at each other. Lily stared at Jayne, who pointed to the fingernail polish in her hands. "Don't look at me, eh? I'm busy making myself prettier, not uglier, like some people."

Lily rolled her eyes in disgust. "Fine." The bell rang again. "Keep your shirt on," she mumbled, turning the knob. She couldn't have been more shocked to see Caton standing in the entry, one hand behind his back, the other about to press the doorbell again. "Caton?"

Caton's smile was rugged and unrefined. "Hello!" His voice was cheerful.

"Um, hello," Lily was too surprised to say more.

"So, who is it, eh?" Jayne yelled from the couch.

Lily turned, "It's Caton Harvey."

"No way! I wanna look at him." Jayne scrambled to her feet. "What does he want?"

"I don't know." She turned to Caton as if he was supposed to answer Jayne's question automatically.

His smile was still genuine. "I was in town and wanted to bring you these." He pulled his hand from behind his back and held out a bouquet of lilies.

Lily squealed "Ugh!" and slammed the door on him. She spun around and pressed her back to the door.

Jayne stared at her as if she was sprouting bananas from her ears. "What on earth?"

"He brought flowers." Her eyes were wide and her breath short.

Jayne was still confused. "He was probably looking for a different reaction."

Panic filled her eyes as she slowly sank to the floor, her back still pressed against the door. "You don't understand. He brought lilies."

Jayne threw her hands in the air. "You're absolutely right. This is totally uncalled for. Who does he think he is? I'll grab the knife. There's a shovel out back. We can make it quick."

"You still don't understand. I'm deathly allergic to lilies. If I breathed any of the pollen, I would have full-blown anaphylactic shock, and I'd be back at the ER."

"Lily! You just slammed the door on a man who was bringing you flowers. He was probably here to apologize."

"But he could have killed me." She was frantic. "It's really weird. I'm deathly allergic to my namesake.

"We?" Jayne shook her head. "You'd better hurry 'cause he's starting his truck."

"Oh, Jayne ..." She was frantic. "Don't let him leave! Tell him something."

"What am I supposed to do? Should I tell him to run, because his psycho girlfriend's head is spinning in a circle?"

"Oh, please hurry! He'll leave!"

"Fine, get out of the way."

Lily rolled to the side and allowed Jayne enough room to squeeze past. She could hear Jayne shouting in the driveway and tried to make out the words. Finally, she felt a push on the door, but she was still leaning against it.

"Lily! Let me in!"

She rolled to her knees and opened the door a crack.

"It's a little cold out here, Lily." Jayne was aggravated. "Let. Me. In."

"Are you alone?"

"Yes!"

Lily opened the door to Jayne, scowling at her. "What's the matter with you?"

"Did you say anything to him?"

"He was gone like a flash." She was exasperated. "And why not? You were completely insane. I've never seen you like that before."

"Oh, Jayne," she whimpered. "What have I done? Things keep getting worse." She banged her head against the door. "Do you still have that shovel?"

"Yes."

"Hit me with it. Please?"

Caton, staring sullenly into the fireplace, stewed over the turn of events. He couldn't imagine what went wrong.

Mariah sat in her father's lap, playing with a doll. "Daddy, see my doll?"

Caton hardly noticed her. "Uh-huh. It's pretty."

Mariah repeated. "See my doll, Daddy?"

Caton barked at her. "Yes, Mariah! I see the doll. It's pretty."

Mariah face first registered shock, then gave way to fear. She started to cry. Immediately Caton felt remorse for his harsh tone. "I'm sorry, Mariah. I was wrong to speak to you like that. Will you forgive me?"

She stopped crying and watched him with large, wide eyes. "Uh-huh." She held up the doll. "It's Mommy."

He looked at it and said, "Mariah, Mommy had brown hair. This one has blond hair."

"Mommy has blond hair."

"No." He picked up a photo of Mary on the table next to his chair. "See? Here's Mommy. She has brown hair."

Mariah was getting angry with him. "No! Not that Mommy. The other one."

"What other Mommy? You only have one."

"Mommy on the phone."

"Lily?"

Mariah nodded. "Mommy."

Caton didn't know what to say. Mrs. Davis stepped in and took her hand. "It's bedtime for our little angel. Say nighty-night to Daddy."

Mrs. Davis left with Mariah, leaving Caton to brood by the fire.

In a few minutes, Mrs. Davis brought a tea serving and set it on the table. "How about a hot cup of tea?"

He looked up. "No thanks. I'd rather have coffee."

Mrs. Davis extended the tray again. "What you need is tea." Her voice bore a measure of finality.

Scowling, he reluctantly reached for the cup and sipped. Surprised, he said, "This is coffee."

"I figured you might want something besides tea tonight."

He blinked at her. "But—you said it was tea."

"Sometimes what you think you're getting and what you actually get are two different things."

"Huh?"

She frowned at him. "Caton, sometimes I wonder about you."

"Well, I ..." He didn't know what to say, so he stopped trying.

"You're moping around like you've ruined everything."

"That's because I have ruined everything."

"Nonsense, dear. It might not have gone the way you wanted, but you got your point across."

"What point?"

"That you're back."

He looked down, contemplating her words.

"So, what?" she continued. "You might have embarrassed her a little, and you might have made her a little mad, but you did let her know that you still care about her."

"Go on ..." he prompted.

"So now you need to figure out your next move."

"Which is?"

"My goodness. This needs to be your idea, not mine. I'm taking my tea to my room. You can talk it over with God."

He watched her leave, then turned back to the fire. Flames consumed the logs, turning them to ash.

Your frustration is consuming you.

"What else can I do? I really messed things up."

Things aren't as bad as you imagine.

"I want to believe you, but you should have seen her face. She was horrified to see me."

The phone rang. "Who would be calling this late at night?" he grumbled.

An unfamiliar female voice said, "May I speak with Caton Harvey?"

"Listen, it's a little late for a telemarketer. Have a good night."

"Caton! I'm not trying to sell you something. Hello?"

He glowered. "I'm still here."

"My name is Jayne Hamilton. I'm Lily DeMar's friend."

"Oh?"

"Yes. Listen, things didn't go well today, and Lily wants to explain what happened. However, she wants to do it in person. Can you meet her tomorrow for coffee?"

He exhaled slowly. "I don't know."

"Caton? She doesn't know I'm calling you. She's up in her room crying from embarrassment. She was supposed to have a date with Jerk, er, Jack McCranie tonight, but she was too upset to leave the house. I know how confused you must be, but let me tell you, this situation is not impossible."

"I can't imagine how." He was sounding grumpy.

"Please, come to town tomorrow and talk to her. That's eight o'clock at the Village Teashop. Please? Once she explains, you'll understand, and all will be well."

When Caton arrived at the Village Teashop in Cloudcroft the next morning, he immediately noticed a tall, platinum blonde peeking out from the doorway. At first, he thought she was Lily, and his breath quickened, but as he exited his truck, he saw she was taller than Lily and stretched her sweater a little tighter. She had to be Jayne. Scowling, he slammed his pickup door. What was he doing? This entire situation was ridiculous.

Jayne, suspecting he was wavering, opened the door and gestured for him to come in.

"Confound it," he mumbled.

Jayne's eyes seemed to be frisking him for hidden weapons. "You have to be Caton," she said with a tone of satisfaction. "I didn't realize you were so tall."

"Jayne, I presume." He was in no mood for jokes.

"Please come in. Mrs. Poe has a table for you in the back."

His eyes grew large. "Don't tell me you included April Poe in this matter." He was already irritated, and now he was hovering just below angry.

As if on cue, he heard her shrill voice. "Caton Harvey! So good to see you. Come in and sit down. I have a table in the back all prepared."

"Thank you, Mrs. Poe." This day was deteriorating with each passing second. He maneuvered past several tables to the back of the building. He expected to find Lily sitting at the table and was surprised to see he was alone. "So?" He turned to Jayne and waited.

She was still looking him over with probing eyes. "I can see why this was such a fuss," she said to no one in particular. "Lily's on her way. I'll be clear with you—she doesn't know you're here." She smiled flippantly. "This was all my idea. You two had such a bad day yesterday, and I want you to have a chance to start over."

Caton's anger flared. "Look, I don't think this is a good idea …"

"Shh." Jayne lifted a finger to his lips and offered a devil-may-care smile. "This will work. Just let it happen. Take a seat, and we'll get started soon, eh?" When he didn't move, she placed both hands on his shoulders and pressed him into a chair. "There. Comfy?" She patted him on the cheek. "Now, don't move. I'll be right back. Coffee or tea?"

Caton frowned. "Neither for me."

"Coffee it is. And we'd better make it decaf." She nodded, then moved to the counter.

Inside he was stewing. What had he gotten himself into now? Just as he was about to get to his feet and walk out, he heard April Poe shout, "Joe? You can't sit back there. Caton Harvey is trying to make up with that Yankee woman from Boston. You have to sit here by the counter."

"Oh, no." Again he started to stand, but Jayne returned with his coffee and a fried pie.

"Here you go," she said cheerfully. "I started to bring you a muffin, but when I saw you were wearing mountain man clothes, I decided you'd rather have something fried. They were all out of lizard rolls and bear fat, so I brought you the next best thing."

He couldn't tell if she was trying to be funny or insulting. Perhaps both. Had she tarried a moment, he would have asked, but she was gone in a flash, positioning herself near the door. The bell on the door rang, and he turned to see Lily standing at the front. Her silhouette caused him to swallow hard. She and Jayne seemed to be fussing, until Jayne grabbed her by the hand and forcefully pulled her to his table. He rose and clumsily offered her a chair.

"Good morning." She greeted him with what appeared to be a forced smile.

"Good morning." He didn't know what else to say or do, so he sipped his coffee loudly. He could feel his ears turning red. He was about to speak when Jayne returned with a tea serving for Lily.

"All right, you two." Her tone was stern. "Things are not as bad as they seem. You need to talk and get everything straightened out. Now, I'm going to be sitting nearby, so don't either of you think about leaving." She made a fist and punched her hand. "I dated my fair share of linemen, and I know how to tackle." She slowly backed away, leaving them alone.

Caton cleared his throat. "I'm not sure if this is insulting or amusing."

A thin smile crept across her lips. "I'm leaning toward embarrassing."

"Suits me." He dared to cast a glance at her and saw her cheeks were flushed,. She was beautiful. Her hair was soft and flowing, her lips were full and distracting. He shook his head and sighed. "I'm really glad to see you again, even under these circumstances."

She seemed to wilt at his words. "I owe you such an explanation," she said softly. "And I have no idea how to start."

"Well, let me start. I immediately regretted letting you drive away that morning. I felt as though my whole world was falling apart when you were there, but the moment you left, I knew what I was losing." His smile was delicate. "I was so afraid to open my heart. I thought I was betraying my wife. Now I know I can start over." He looked into her eyes. "I can love again. I can open my heart again. But, I didn't know until you drove away. And then ..." He closed his eyes and stopped mid-sentence.

Lily leaned forward. "And then?"

He shook his head. "I don't have the proper words. I can't do this."

Lily's shoulders sank. She nodded reluctantly. "No, you can't."

They heard Jayne say, "Oy vey" from a nearby table, but ignored her.

"You can't do this," Lily continued. "Not without my explanation." She pressed her lips together, searching for the right words. Finally, she said, "I was so heartbroken when you let me go. When I woke up in the hospital, and you weren't there, I thought you really were done with me. All I had at that point was a grumpy doctor and a broken heart. But Jack was a doctor who ..." She heard Jayne coughing loudly and stopped talking. She inhaled deeply and frowned. "You weren't there. Now I know why. I had no idea you were injured as well. That's why I didn't check on you, and that's why you didn't check on me. We were both expecting the other to do something." She reached for his hand and squeezed his fingers tightly. "We really missed a great opportunity for something great."

He nodded slowly. "We've had a rough go of it. But when you're paddling in white water and you lose your paddle, you don't jump out of the canoe."

She waited for him to finish his thought, but when he said nothing else, she replied. "Okay. Well, I'm sorry things didn't work out for us. I'm so glad I got to meet you and Mariah. She's a sweet girl. I'm going to be staying around this area for a while longer. Jack McCranie and I are dating, and I want to see where that takes me."

Caton was dumbstruck. In the distance he could hear Jayne's voice uttering curses. Was she breaking up with him? How could she? They weren't even together? He glanced at Jayne, who was shooting daggers at Lily with her eyes.

Lily placed her napkin across her plate and stood with determination. "Caton? I wish you well, and I'll always think fondly of you." She turned, leaving him staring after her, confusion slathered on his face.

Jayne intercepted her. "Lily? What are you doing?"

"Let me go, Jayne." She forced her way past her friend and threaded her way around the counter. Placing a hand on the door, she turned to look back, then stepped into the crisp, winter air.

CHAPTER FOURTEEN

DUELING BOYFRIENDS

Jayne spun in a full circle, torn between chasing after Lily or throwing a bucket of cold water on Caton. She turned to him and yelled, "Do something!"

As he watched the door close, Caton felt his own heart starting to close as all his hopes faded into shadows. Despair was heavy on his tongue, and heartache seeped into his stomach, as though he'd been punched. He couldn't breathe. He couldn't move. Something was strapping him to his chair.

Reaching for his cup, he carefully took a sip, but then spewed the liquid across the table. He had grabbed Lily's tea by mistake. Tea!

Fire flashed in his eyes as he stood up, tossing his napkin aside and pushing past Jayne, who was still gawking at him. Dashing from the store, he caught up with Lily as she rounded the corner. He reached for her arm and spun her around.

"What in the ..." Lily cried out.

"We're not doing this," he said flatly.

Lily turned to look at Jayne, who stood in the doorway watching. "What? What Mrs. Davis said, 'sometimes we don't get what we're expecting, but it doesn't mean we should stop trying.'"

She blinked at him. "Mrs. Davis said that?"

Warmth radiated from his smile. "Something like that. Anyway, I came here to get you back, and that's not what happened, but I'm not going to quit without a fight. You're the best thing that's happened to me in years, and I'm not letting you go. Not only for me, but for Mariah also. And for you," he added.

Lily glanced from him to Jayne and back again. "Well, I ..."

"Look, I don't know if I love you yet, and I don't know how you feel about me. However, I'm thinking you and I are meant to be together. I also know you're dating Jack." He nodded to her. "Fine. That's all fine." He placed his hands on her shoulders. "Keep on dating him. In fact, I insist you do." He leaned toward her and made sure she could see his eyes. "But I'll be pursuing you as well."

Lily's face was red. He wasn't sure if it was from the cold or a reaction to him. "I, uh …"

"So, tomorrow afternoon at two, you and I are going out. Dress warmly and wear some shoes that will allow you to walk in the snow. I'll pick you up at the Crofting." He smiled broadly, then turned and left her standing there. He didn't look back.

After Caton left, Jayne approached Lily, who was still standing in shock—her feet rooted in place. "What a way to start your morning, eh?"

Lily turned angry eyes to Jayne "You and I are not friends at this moment. You tricked me into coming here, and then you steamrolled me into the most awkward conversation I've ever had. What were you thinking?"

Jayne began twisting a strand of her hair. "I think my plan worked out just fine," she replied innocently.

"Ugh" was the most civil response available to Lily.

Jayne reached for her hand. "Come on. Let me make it up to you with some tea."

Lily resisted. "I don't want any tea."

"But I need to apologize to you. And that requires tea or wine." She looked at her watch. "Unless you're in a book club, it's way too early for wine—unless you're French. And the last I checked, you shave your legs, so it has to be tea."

A crack on her lips suggested that Lily might smile.

"What if I throw in a scone?" Jayne continued. "An apology scone is always a good gauge of true regret." She tilted her head. "And, we have two men to talk about. They need to be sorted and discussed at length." She reached for Lily's hand again.

"I could go for a scone," Lily almost whispered, allowing Jayne to lead her back to the corner table.

"You told me Caton was rugged, but you failed to tell me he is rugged hot! He's got a very natural kind of handsome that sneaks up on you when you're not looking."

Lily bit into her scone, comparing it to Mrs. Davis's crumpets. "But Caton isn't handsome because of his looks. It's just part of who he is."

"I know, right? He's really hard to describe." Jayne spooned sugar into her tea. "But Jack—he's handsome too. And I mean underwear model handsome."

Lily sighed.

"But Caton has a very genuine smile."

"Caton never stops smiling, I think. Even when he's upset, his eyes still reflect a hidden smile. He's a good-hearted man."

Jayne sat straighter. "But Jack never smiles. He's super serious, a real take-charge kind of man."

"Oh, he does smile," Lily corrected her.

"When? I've never witnessed it."

Lily thought. "He smiles when he's at home, relaxed. Not at work."

Jayne frowned. "You've never been to his house."

"Well, I mean relaxed. Not at work."

"No, you mean when he's sitting in a lounge with a glass of Scotch," Jayne countered.

"Jayne! That's not at all what I mean." Lily shifted in her chair.

Jayne sipped her tea, waiting for Lily to speak. She could see Lily's mind was just about to enter a high-speed wobble. She thought it best to let it happen now rather than later. She watched Lily tap her spoon on her teacup, a sure sign her thoughts were in overdrive. From a lifetime of friendship, Jayne knew what Lily liked about Jack.

Jack was a man's man. He was a former Army surgeon, who had served in wartime. He was highly educated, brilliant, and confident. Jayne suspected the man knew how to kiss a woman in a way that would make her heart skip.

But Jack never smiled. Jayne recognized a form of darkness living in his heart that stole any joy he might have possessed in the past, a claw that held him in its clutches with unyielding strength. Jack had the kind of history people whisper about. He was broken. But was he fixable?

Jayne knew Lily's mind was spinning each of those facts into probable outcomes, trying to decide if he could be fixed.

On the opposite scale, Caton was a genuine soul. He had faced the darkness, but he was still alive. The problem with Caton, though—he didn't know he was still alive. He had lived in pain for so long he had accepted it. However, once Lily stirred his soul, he revived, making him more desirable than he would ever realize.

Caton's chief failure was allowing Lily to leave Glenfield when she'd offered her friendship to him. Rejection of that nature shakes a woman to the core, causing self-doubt. The pain is hard to overcome. Could she forgive him and trust he won't bail on her again? Talk about taking a risk!

"What a problem, eh?"

"What's that?"

"Just a few weeks ago you had no one in your life and no prospects on the horizon. Now you have two desirable men at your disposal. You get to choose which man will be your lover."

Lily frowned. "Oh, Jayne, don't be crass."

"Crass?" Jayne was slightly offended. "Think again. I'm not talking sex—well, not really. I'm talking about being your emotional lover, the man who will hold you when you're old, who will hug your grandchildren and brush your dentures when your arthritis kicks in. That man, my dear, is a lover."

Lily adjusted a strand of hair that had strayed from its designated place. "I'm overwhelmed. Either of those men would be the top of any list. I wouldn't even have to think about them."

"But?"

"But, those two are the list. They are the choices. I have two impossible men from which to select. And they are both totally awesome."

"I know, right!" Jayne's eyes were on fire. "You can't go wrong with either of them."

The thought cast a cloud over her head. "I know."

"Do you want my opinion?"

Lily shook her head. "I'll pass."

"Fine, but you have to own your mistake," Jayne said, pouting.

Lily reluctantly acquiesced. "Okay. What do you think?"

"You have to ask yourself one question." Jayne was suddenly serious. "Which man makes your heart sing?"

Jayne considered her answer. "They both do, but they play different songs."

"Which song do you want to hear for the rest of your life?"

Again she hesitated. "I like both of them. I can close my eyes and listen to either song for the rest of my life."

"Then you know how to do a tiebreaker?"

Lily groaned. "Please don't say anything about cage fighting."

Jayne clapped her hands. "What a fun idea! I can see it now. They would both be wearing T-shirts that get ripped off, and they would both be barefoot, and their jeans …" Lily's eyes warned her to remain focused. "Fine. Here's your tiebreaker. Which one reminds you of Rodney?"

Lily winced as if slapped. "Why do you have to do that? Why do you have to be mean?"

Jayne backed off. "Hey, you know better," she replied softly. "And you know I'm right."

Sorrow filled Lily's eyes. "I know."

Lily found Jack's cabin in the woods to be charming. The home was modest, but it had a rustic charisma that made her feel like she was standing by a mountain stream on a frosty morning. As Jack warned her, the cabin was not finished, but the parts he had completed demonstrated his work in progress would eventually be a masterpiece. He handed her a glass of wine, then led her on the "fifty-cent tour."

The cabin had three bedrooms with two baths. The upstairs was the master suit, roomy and comfortable. She could see the cabin would make a wonderful home if Jack ever found the time to work on it.

"Such is the life of a small-town doctor," he said casually. "We work insane hours and our days off include babies and kidney stones. There's not much time left for construction projects." He led her back downstairs and pointed to the bedroom on the left. "This is my main guest room. It's big enough to have a bedroom set and a small sitting area. I designed this for my mom. She's getting older and likes to have a quiet place where she can sit and read, or post pictures of Grumpy Cat on Facebook. The problem is, it's not finished."

"It seems you haven't finished anything yet."

He smirked. "You're right, of course. I fully expect my mom to visit sometime soon. She wanted to come for Christmas, but her sister fell and broke a hip, forcing her to stay at home for the holidays. I'm sure she'll come with short notice, and I'll have to scramble to make everything work."

Lily laughed. "And where will she sleep?"

"Ah, you've diagnosed my problem. I don't even have a bed she can sleep on. When the time comes, I'll be in full panic mode."

"So, why don't you prepare for her arrival?"

His lips curled. "That would be way too easy. I prefer to procrastinate and then panic." He pointed to her glass. "More wine?"

"Yes, please."

"Oh, and I need to check those salmon fillets on the grill." He seemed torn which to do first.

"I'll get the wine—you get the grill." She gazed into his face. "Can I pour you something?"

"I have a Scotch already started. I think I left the glass on the counter." He pointed to the kitchen. "I'll be right back."

Lily watched him disappear into the snowy back yard. He had such a strong presence about him. When he looked at her, she felt her stomach draw into a knot. She could fall in love with him, effortlessly.

She found his Scotch on the counter—his glass was empty. She reached for the bottle and poured a proper two-finger serving. Examining the label, she immediately recognized Jack's taste in Scotch was pricy. Her father once stocked the same bottle, a twenty-five-year-old Laphroaig, in his own cabinet. She allowed herself to imagine her father and Jack as great friends, sitting on the back porch with cigars and after-dinner cognacs, discussing horse racing and politics. The notion warmed her, making her smile. Would Caton sit on the back porch and smoke cigars with her father? Somehow, the idea didn't connect with her.

Lily chastised herself for thinking about Caton while she was with Jack, making a mental note not to compare the two men … at least not while in their company. She reached for the wine and refilled her glass. By force of habit, she examined the label and was shocked to see the vintage was in a language she didn't recognize. Examining the fine print on the back label, she finally found a description in small letters that made her do a double take. The wine was from Turkey. *Really? Who drinks Turkish wine? Who is Jack McCranie?* She was intrigued.

While she mused, Jack entered the house, holding a platter of fish and looking apologetic.

"I'm afraid I have overcooked the salmon," he confessed. "I'm not very gifted when it comes to seafood. My true gifting is red meat and racks of ribs."

"Let's see." Lily offered. "Fork?"

"Fork? Oh, you mean utensils. Top drawer next to the stove."

"Set it down, and I'll take a look." She used the fork to lift a flake of pink meat. Perfect. "It looks fine to me."

The table was loaded with saws, hammers, a drill, and a layer of dust, so they sat at the bar to eat. Lily was impressed that he had prepared a Caesar salad and sautéed asparagus tips in advance. Once the salmon was ready, he had the meal ready in less than three minutes.

"Do you eat like this all the time?"

Jack waved at the sautéed asparagus. "Of course. Now you know the real reason I haven't finished my house. I'm too busy playing chef."

Lily giggled. "This is quite good."

The corners of his eyes smiled, but his lips hardly moved. "I know how to make five or six dishes, and all of them I learned, so I could impress a woman."

Another woman? Lily wasn't expecting him to go there. "An ex?" she asked cautiously.

Jack grimaced. "Ex-girlfriend. She was a surgical nurse where I served my internship. I really wanted her to fall in love with me."

"What happened?"

He nodded slowly. "We hit it off okay at first. But when you work the crazy hours of an intern, you don't have much free time. We dated off and on for about a year."

"And then?"

"She married a pharmacist."

"Ouch. I guess that ended your relationship," Lily said awkwardly, for lack of better response.

"Rather soundly. That's when I accepted a commission in the Army. She said I wasn't serious enough. She preferred a man who takes himself seriously."

Lily almost choked on her wine. "What? How's that possible?"

Darkness flooded his eyes. "I used to be rather cavalier."

The idea made her smile. "Cavalier? That's hard to imagine."

He nodded. "Oh, I know what you're thinking. But I was cavalier in an ungracious way. I thought I knew it all, and I was untouchable. She said I didn't take my profession seriously. And I didn't consider how others were affected by my decisions." He pressed his fork into a crouton, crushing it. "I was self-centered and a bit jocular."

Lily was confused. "I can't see you being jocular."

Jack smiled. "Well, I was. But my humor was always at someone else's expense."

"Ah." Lily put down her fork, her curiosity building. "Why are you telling me this?"

"Because I know I come across rather hard. Some people call me Dr. Death—they don't know I hear them." His mouth lifted into a smile. "But there's another side to me, and I want you to see both sides."

Lily was touched. "I see." She watched him carefully. Was this his effort at being transparent and open? "Well, I'm not one to judge too quickly. I look beyond the surface."

"I know." His gray eyes were burning into her face now. She needed to look away but was powerless to do so.

Jack sighed. "That's what I knew about you from the first time I saw you. I knew you were an incredible woman. I was interested in you from the very start."

Her eyes narrowed. "But you were so short and fierce."

"Yes, that." He sipped his Scotch. "That's my Achilles' heel. I found myself interested in you as they wheeled you into the ER. However, I can't date a patient. Therefore, I tried to make you reject me, so I wouldn't be so conflicted. It's my defense mechanism."

Lily had no response. She simply stared at him, trying to read his stony face. Now, in a relaxed environment, she could see he was smiling, even though his face didn't respond. "A defense mechanism? It's effective."

He frowned. "Yes. I'm sorry."

Lily's heart swelled. "Well, let's not be difficult anymore."

"Deal." He held out his hand and initiated a handshake. Changing the subject, he said, "I wish I had a clean couch for you to sit on. I'm afraid this is the best I can offer."

Lily glanced around. "Where do you sit when you're here alone?"

"I usually eat at the Lodge, come home, turn on the TV in my bedroom, and fall asleep watching *M.A.S.H.*"

The idea of him watching old reruns made her laugh. "That's not what I expected."

"What did you expect?" His eyes probed hers.

"That you came home and sat behind a desk, reviewing patient files and charting healthcare strategies."

He shook his head. "Maybe if I was still at Parkland Hospital in Dallas, but there isn't much of a need for that here." He looked out the window and sighed. "I'm barely a doctor anymore. I'm trying hard not to be a veterinarian."

She knew he was trying to joke, but it was an awkward attempt. "Well, I'm sure you'll find your place."

"Perhaps." He held up a finger and motioned for her to be silent. "Can you hear that?"

She listened intently. "No. What do you hear?"

"Nothing." He gazed at her intensely. "Not yet. The house is silent. However, soon I hope there'll be children running up and down the stairs, and dogs barking, and piano practice, and family movie nights."

She winced when he mentioned having children and immediately felt a stab of panic, knowing she couldn't conceive. She swallowed and decided she wasn't up for that conversation just yet. Besides, she rationalized, there was no reason adoption wasn't a consideration, should she decide to pursue a permanent relationship with Jack. She looked around the room. "You can hear all of that? Impressive."

"I want a family someday. I want to have children and grandchildren. I have a legacy but no one to leave it to. I want those things, and this is the closest I've come to having them." He refilled his Scotch. "Back when I was a mover and shaker, I didn't have time for a family. Now I'm no longer a world-class surgeon, and I can focus on having a family." His smile warmed his face. "And a dog. I want a dog that will catch Frisbees and play fetch."

Lily watched him for a moment. *Who is this incredible man? Why hasn't he been snatched up?* "I like that dream. It sounds nice."

His eyes focused on her again. "That's the future."

"Oh" was all she managed to say. Everything he said made her heart seem full. She knew he was laying out a plan for their lives, a plan she could get excited about. She deeply desired to have a man who wanted a family, and she knew without doubt Jack would be an excellent father. She could see him throwing baseballs and baiting hooks. She could see him coming home to her every night, and she would be happy to make him happy.

His gaze returned to her face, but his eyes suddenly shifted, harder than before. "What happened today at the tea shop?"

Lily felt her blood turn cold, as if he had doused her with ice water. Why did he have to take her on such a roller coaster ride? "The tea shop?"

His eyes bore into hers. "I understand you met Caton Harvey there this morning." He read her face for a moment and answered her unasked question. "It's a small town. Nothing happens that doesn't get reported, especially when April Poe is involved."

"Ah." She hesitated. "Well, Caton and I did meet for coffee. We needed to talk about what happened between us."

His eyes were burning into her soul. "Good." He nodded. "That's good. How did it go?"

Lily was growing uncomfortable under his blazing glare. "I told him I was dating you, and I wanted to see what happens between us."

He watched her expression for a moment. He seemed to be x-raying her mind again. "But?"

She sighed. Why was he being difficult when she had been having such an enjoyable conversation with him? "But Caton told me he was not going to let me go."

"And?"

Really, was he going to get out the thumbscrews? "And we have a date tomorrow."

Sparks flared from his eyes. "This is how you want things to be?"

Lily wasn't in the mood to be bullied, and she was hovering just beyond anger that he was ruining her pleasant evening. "Until now, I wasn't sure I would go out with him."

"Meaning what?"

Lily stood and leaned toward him. "It means I'm free to date anyone I want."

He watched her for a moment, then softened, clearly backing down. "Okay."

"Okay?" She wanted to be clear.

"Of course, you can date anyone." His words were flat.

"But?"

He finished his whiskey in one swallow. "Isn't he the reason you were in that car wreck? Isn't he the one who hurt you?"

She tried to read his eyes and measure the meaning behind his words. "That's true, to a certain degree."

Jack rose from his chair. "But that's where I come in." His voice was calm, and his tone rich. Lily began to relax. "That's how destiny brought us together."

She blinked at him, trying to dismiss the spell his voice was casting over her. "Back to destiny?"

He smiled. "Wouldn't that be a great title for our story? Destiny brought you to the mountains and then brought us together. Just like a tapestry. Our lives were woven together, and now we are here, sharing this moment."

Lily didn't know how to respond. His mercurial shift from hot to cold was confusing her. When he was hot, he was ... well, hot. "So, this is our destiny moment?"

"Yes, can't you see?" He reached for her hand and held it close to his chest, causing her mind to spin. "You aren't meant to be with Caton. You're meant to be with me."

"Well, I ..."

He pulled her close to him, and she allowed him to wrap his arms around her. She leaned into his chest and felt his voice vibrating in her soul. How long had her heart ached to feel the warmth and security of a man's embrace? She looked into his eyes, her lips parted.

"And this is the part of our story where we kiss for the first time." She could see the desire in his eyes and hear his hunger for her in his voice. He wanted her—now was their moment.

He leaned down to kiss her, but his words struck her as odd. She pulled away. "Don't fight it, Lily," he coaxed, pulling her back in. "You know this feels right."

But it didn't. Not yet. She wasn't ready to give herself to him. She knew if she kissed him, more would follow, and she would be defenseless to stop. Blinking hard, she pushed away from his chest, creating a sliver of space between them. "Jack, I ..."

She saw the flame ignite in his eyes. He didn't release her. "You know this feels good."

She could smell his intoxicating eagerness. "Yes," she conceded, "it does."

"And you know you want me to hold you tight."

"Yes, I do," she whispered and closed her eyes.

"Then why don't you relax and let it happen?"

His words were dissolving her resistance. She wanted to release herself, to melt into him, to become part of him. She felt his strong hands gently caressing her back, calling to her. She could feel his body against hers, inviting her to explore him. It had been so long since …

His hand strayed farther down, and she instinctively flinched. She realized something was whispering in her heart, something she couldn't identify, something she'd been ignoring. She closed her eyes, summoned her strength and pushed away again, creating more distance. "Jack, I can't. Not yet."

His grip relaxed, but he didn't release her. "Is it him?"

She didn't respond at first. "I don't know. Maybe." She pushed farther away from him. "I can't explain. Caton holds a place in my heart. There's something between the two of us. And I can't surrender myself to you, not until I know for sure Caton and I have no future." Her heart was racing, and she felt flushed. "And not without a ring. And that's non-negotiable. Got it?"

Anger flashed across his face. "Then why are you leading me on?"

"What?" Now her tone was shifting.

"You came here to mock me?"

"What?" She didn't know what he was talking about, and she wasn't going to accept his accusation. "Jack, I like you. I want to know if you and I can work. But you're not an easy man. In fact, you're a difficult man. And I want to know if the spark I feel with you will become an eternal flame."

His eyes were pleading with her, but his voice was strong. "Caton had his chance. Now it's our time. Remember, he rejected you once. He'll do it again."

His words were like a bucket of cold water in her face. "So, what are you saying?"

"I'm saying he isn't the right man for you. You want to be with me. You know I'll never reject you. Look in my eyes and tell me you don't see my desire for you.

She couldn't risk looking him in the eyes. She was too vulnerable at the moment.

"No, you don't want to be hurt again. Let me love you. Let me hold you. Let me make you happy."

Lily knew this was too much pressure for a relationship that was only a few weeks old. Her mind was exploding. She needed some space and time.

Jack saw her resistance. "But you still want him?"

"I don't know what I want, Jack."

"But you obviously don't want me." And just like that, he was pouting.

"Jack, don't overreact."

"Overreact? I'm trying to protect you. You aren't right for him. He's not right for you. You don't need to confuse yourself any more. Just let him go."

Lily was tired of the pressure, and she felt something rising in her soul. As she began to speak, her voice grew louder and bolder. "You know what? I'm not a big fan of being told what to do. I'm the one who has a choice to make, not you. I'm the one who has to decide between two incredible men, not you. And I want to have time to let the right decision form. Why does it have to happen tonight? You and I aren't anything. Not yet. We're only dating. We barely know each other. We're not in a position to declare ourselves a couple. So, back off and give me the space I need to find out if we can be a couple. Do you really want me to always doubt us? Well, until I can figure that out we're're nothing more than a date. Got it?" She was shaking, partially from anger and partially from the adrenaline rush.

Confusion flashed over Jack's face. He obviously didn't know how to respond. He was silent for a moment. "I want you to choose me."

"Jack!" She was exasperated. "Aren't you listening to me? I am not ready to make that kind of decision. I need space."

He pressed his body closer to her. "I know what you want. And I am ready to give it to you."

She shook her head in disbelief. "Believe it or not, Jack …" She deliberately relaxed her tone. "I had a good time tonight. I enjoyed discovering more about you, and I like you." She looked at her watch. "Oh, my gosh!"

"What?"

"It's past midnight."

He smiled at her. "See? Time flies when we're together."

"I'll say." She looked at the counter. Her bottle of wine was empty, as was Jack's bottle of Scotch. She was glad to be walking those few blocks to the Crofting rather than driving. She looked for her purse. "I have to get back home."

"Don't rush off."

"Jack," she smiled warmly. "I have to go. I have another date tomorrow." She immediately regretted her words.

He flinched as if she had slapped her. "Are you really going out with him?"

"You know I am."

"I ..." his face contorted. "I don't like it."

"Trust me, Jack. This is the way it has to be." She smiled and turned the doorknob. "I really did enjoy the evening."

"I take it your night was a big hit." Susan was smearing cold cream on her face as Lily settled into a chair, sighing in exasperation.

"Then I must have given you the wrong impression," Lily complained. "Why are men so dense?"

"Do you remember the Sunday school story about how God cursed Eve in the Garden of Eden? This is what he had in mind."

"That helps a lot. Thanks."

Susan turned her attention to her daughter. "Want to talk about it?"

"I had a nice time. He cooked a perfect meal of salmon and asparagus. He served a perfect wine—from Turkey, by the way."

"Turkish wine?" Susan shrugged. "Why not?"

"Dinner was wonderful. I really liked the wine. He'll have a perfect house someday. He even shared with me his vision of the perfect future, complete with kids and a dog that catches Frisbees."

"Yes, I can see where everything went wrong."

"I was just coming to that." Lily began changing into her flannel nightgown. "I was really enjoying the evening, and then he asked me about Jayne's little stunt at the tea shop."

"Ah, word gets out fast. See? I knew I should have lunch at the hospital dining room more often."

Lily pointed her finger. "Exactly. So, Jack wanted to know if I let Caton down easy, and then got agitated when I explained I was going to continue dating him. Them. Both, that is."

"He didn't like that?" She let a *tsk* escape. "That's hard to imagine."

Lily lifted her hands in surrender. "I know. But he forced the issue, demanding an answer. I wasn't sure I was going out with Caton at all until Jack tried to paint me into a corner." She started washing her face. "Am I missing something?"

Susan began smoothing lotion on her legs. "I doubt it. It's a small town, and there's not much competition here. Then a sophisticated, beautiful woman mysteriously arrives. Jack probably fell hard for you. Before he came to Cloudcroft, he was exposed to a broader worldview, and he might find women who don't have much world knowledge to be less engaging. He's a very intelligent, driven man. Wouldn't you find it hard to be with a man who had never seen Europe?"

Lily blinked at her. "Not so much. Caton doesn't have much traveling experience, and I like him fine."

"But Caton's not an average mountain man, is he?"

"Hardly."

"Anyway, you're an exciting woman, and you show up in a place where nothing exciting happens. Jack may feel pressured to grab you before you get away."

"Okay, that makes sense."

"You do realize I'm only guessing."

Lily dried her face and sat on her bed. "It does fit. He seems afraid that if I date Caton, I'll lose interest in him."

"That might happen."

"Well, it will happen for one of them."

"But it doesn't have to happen tonight." Susan flipped the lights and climbed into bed. "I was starting to think you might not come home tonight."

Lily sighed deeply. "Nope, I'm here."

"Jack is a very handsome man."

"No kidding. I find it hard to concentrate around him. He makes me remember my married days."

"Because he reminds you of Rodney?"

"Mother! That's not what I mean and you know it. You and Jayne seem to take great delight in how much Jack reminds you of Rodney."

"Sorry, I misunderstood you." She rolled over. "Good night."

Lily had to borrow her mother's boots, but she managed to find the proper clothing Caton prescribed for their date. "I wonder what we're gonna do that requires me to be outside?"

Jayne was excited. "Maybe he knows of some snow cave, and he's going to drag you by the hair into the cave and ..."

"Jayne, please. I don't need any hair pulling today."

She shook her head dismissively. "You don't know what you're missing. But to each her own." She fussed with Lily's hair for a moment. "There. You look fantastic. Almost as nice as me, but not quite."

"A girl can dream, though. Someday I'll be as pretty as you."

"That's the spirit." Jayne pinched her on the cheek. "Now try to come home without any makeup on. That'll be a story worth telling."

A knock on the door announced Caton's arrival. Lily reached to her hair. "How do I look?"

Jayne rolled her eyes. "Really?"

She grimaced. "I'm just nervous. You know this is our first actual date."

"So you've said. Five times."

The knock came again.

"Are you going to answer that? We know he'll drive away after a few minutes. Remember?"

Lily winced. "Okay. Here I go." She opened the door with a smile. "Good afternoon."

Caton stood smiling in the doorway. "Lily, you're so beautiful." He held his hand behind his back. "I didn't have much luck with flowers last time, but I thought I'd try again." He revealed his hand and was holding a white scarf with a lily embroidered on it.

She gasped and received his gift graciously. "This is very nice, Caton. Thank you. Would you care to come in and say hello?"

"Maybe for a moment. We do have plans, you know," he added with a lighthearted grin.

He entered the room, reminding her of an elk scouting the landscape. When he saw Jayne, he nodded appreciatively. "Jayne, it's good to see you again."

"Likewise." Jayne eyed him carefully. "You definitely look like you're dressed to explore a snow cave."

"I reserve spelunking for second dates as a general rule," he quipped.

The kitchen door opened, and Susan entered, carrying a teacup and saucer. "Mr. Harvey, welcome to our temporary home. Would you care for some tea?"

"None for me, thanks."

Lily stepped forward and said, "Caton Harvey, I'd like to introduce you to Mrs. DeMar, my mother. Mother, Caton Harvey of Glenfield."

Leaning toward her, he said, "How do you do? I believe your name is Susan?"

Lily blinked at him. "You two have met?"

"I met Susan, but didn't make the connection," he replied.

Susan smiled. "Yes, Susan. You have a good memory."

"No, I just remember pretty faces. There aren't a lot of those around here … until lately, that is." He turned to Lily. "Well, if you're ready to roll, we have a date to commence."

"As you please, sir." She placed her hand in his arm and walked with him to his pickup. They made small talk as Caton drove to the edge of town and turned on Sunspot Highway.

"I've been here before," she observed.

"This is the road to Glenfield." He drove another half mile, then pulled onto a wide shoulder that became a parking area. After parking, he pointed to a small wooden box sitting on the console between them. "Open the box, if you please."

The blue bow on the box released easily as she pulled on it. Inside, she found a pair of gloves and a knit cap. "Caton, they're a matched set to my scarf!"

"I hope you like them."

She was touched. "I do. They're simply wonderful. Shall I put them on?"

"That's why I bought them for you. I figured you didn't have much cold weather gear with you." He reached and adjusted her knit cap. "There. Perfect."

"Thank you." She was all smiles.

"This place has magnificent views. Come with me." He held out his hand, which she accepted with a grin.

"Where are we going?"

"Over the river and through the woods."

She giggled. "Ah! Grandmother's house!"

"We're almost there."

They walked through the trees for a short distance. "Do they always shovel snow on these mountain trails?"

"No, never. But I thought you might enjoy the walk better if the snow had been removed."

"Wait? You shoveled that much snow?" She turned and looked back. "That's a lot!"

He shrugged. "It'll be worth the effort. Come on, just a little farther." He continued to hold her hand as they walked down the path. "I hope you enjoy simple meals. This is a hard time of the year to prepare a fancy outdoor feast."

As they stepped into a clearing, Lily saw that Caton had prepared an elaborate date. He had cleared an area of snow and built a fire, already burning red hot, including two folding chairs and a large picnic basket. "Oh, my!" Lily gasped.

"This will be a short evening. It's not very cold right now, but it will be once the sun goes down. I figure we have an hour before we'll have to return to town."

"This is marvelous!"

He escorted her to a chair, then reached into the picnic basket. "Would you care for some hot chocolate? Or would you prefer coffee or tea?"

"Hot chocolate, please." She tried to peek into the basket. "Did you bring all three?"

He smiled sheepishly. "I wanted to cover my bases."

Caton pulled out a thermos and poured the dark liquid into her mug, then sprinkled a few miniature marshmallows on top.

She sipped carefully. "Oh, this is delicious!"

"It's Mrs. Davis's recipe. She has a special mix that she puts together every winter. I was hoping you'd like it."

"So far, I like everything Mrs. Davis does."

"Yep, I'm a blessed man to have her in my life." He reached into the basket again. "Marshmallow or hotdog?"

She laughed and crinkled her nose. "I would rather have a hot dog at the moment."

"Okay. I have everyday dogs or bratwurst. Do you have a preference?"

"Oh! I'd love to have a brat. I used to eat those with my dad when he took me to see the Red Sox play."

"Oh, no!" Caton was suddenly serious. "I could never date a Red Sox fan."

Lily rolled her eyes. "Let me guess. A Rangers fan?"

"Guilty. Rangers and Astros."

"This may be the end for us," she teased.

He finished rustling through the basket and stuck a bratwurst on a stick for her. She immediately stuck it into the fire.

"I see you've done this before."

"It's been years." She winked at him. "Is this where you take all of your dates?"

His face slightly contorted, but he shook his head. "Gosh, this is the first date I've been on in more than ten years."

A shadow flickered across her face. "Oh, I'm sorry! I forgot … Mary …"

"No problem," he interrupted. "Don't think twice about it." His smile didn't change. "I love the view from this lookout. My crew built a house just around the bend on the highway. I'd come here because I could get a cell phone signal, and I could order materials. I spent so much time here that I eventually came here just for lunch. I've never really shared this place with anyone."

"Thank you for sharing it with me."

"I'm hoping for a really nice sunset."

"Oh, it's already happening. This is just wonderful." She emptied her cup. "May I have more cocoa?"

"I brought plenty." He refilled her cup. "So, do you think you'll be in this area long?"

She shrugged. "I'm not sure. I'm a classical violinist. I'm not sure Cloudcroft needs one of those."

He sat quietly for a moment. "I'm not really sure what I'm doing here, other than trying to get to know you better." He glanced at her expression and must have misread her face, for he stammered and said, "No, what I mean is, I'm so out of practice, and I don't know what I'm doing. With dating, I mean."

Lily nodded softly. "You're doing fine."

"Thanks. Anyway, I know I'm not supposed to ask you to marry me or anything on our first date, but I'm the kind of man who likes to have a plan. I like to think things through. Sometimes it gets me into trouble, which is what led to you driving away and off the mountain." He chuckled, causing her to join in. "I want you to know I'm not looking for entertainment. I have a warm home and a beautiful daughter, and I have plenty to do. But I am looking for a future." He placed another log on the fire, and they watched as sparks flew into the air. "The only reason I want to date you is to find out if we have a future. In other words, I'm into courting and not dating. If you determine we're not a good match, then I'll bow out politely, and you won't be troubled with me again. No hard feelings." He glanced at her. "Am I talking too much?"

"Go on. I'm listening." She continued to turn her bratwurst as she sipped her hot chocolate. Caton's own brat was turning golden brown, while hers was turning mostly black.

"Look, I'm not pressing you for an answer today," Caton continued, "but I want you to approach our relationship as if you're interviewing me for the role of a husband. I want you to evaluate me and decide if I'm the right man for you, because that's what I'm doing with you."

Her head shot up at his frank assessment, but she smiled. "I suppose our situation is a bit odd. Normally, if a man starts talking marriage on a first date, then I'm getting nervous. But, I suppose this isn't really our first date. I think we can use unconventional rules for an unconventional situation."

"Thank you." He rose from his chair and examined their meal. "I think we can call these done." The way he said "done" caused her to giggle again. She had reduced her bratwurst to a black piece of jerky. He reached into the basket and retrieved two buns. "I hope you don't mind if I handle your bun …" His face turned beet red, and his embarrassment was obvious. Lily, unable to help herself, began laughing, more from his reaction than the words themselves.

"I think it's too late for you to ask. You've already staked my brat with your hand, so I can let you touch my bread." Her efforts to be delicate only caused them to laugh again. Caton placed the brats on the buns and spread mustard on both servings. "What you didn't know before we started is part of the fun of cooking for your date. See? I cooked yours, and you cooked mine."

She was confused. "What're you talking about?"

"This is all part of the interview process. I wanted to see if you can cook, so I had you roast my bratwurst." With a wink, he handed her the one he cooked, which was golden brown.

She laughed. "The brat I cooked is burnt, Caton. You can't possibly eat it."

"Watch me." He lifted the bun to his lips and made a show of biting through the tough brat and deliberately chewing. After a few seconds he said, "I have to admit, you're not doing so well on this part of the interview."

She laughed. "But mine is delicious."

When they finished their meal, Caton placed more wood on the fire and asked, "It's a bit cold, do you need a blanket?"

She nodded. "Yes, please"

He pulled a small lap blanket from the basket and proceeded to tuck her in to her chair. "There. Comfy?"

"I am!" She smiled broadly. "What else do you have stashed away in that magical basket?"

"Marshmallows?"

Her eyes lit up. "Oh, yes, please! I love roasting marshmallows. Are we making s'mores?"

"Of course." He placed one on her stick. "Let's hope you're better at this than with brats."

She cringed. "I can't believe you ate that thing. I hope you don't get sick."

"Nonsense. It was fine." Then he pretended to be dying, making her laugh again.

She roasted a few more marshmallows, setting them all on fire. Caton made a production out of eating them and pretending to throw up each time. As the hour passed, the colors of the sun set the surrounding mountain peaks on fire, bathing them in warm shades of burnt orange, with accents of red and yellow. The view was glorious, and the evening was every bit as wonderful as she hoped. Caton was warm and engaging as he told stories about mountain folk he knew and funny things Mariah had said. Before she knew, dusk was approaching, and the temperature was dropping fast. Caton was worried she was getting too cold, but with the fire and the blanket, she was comfortable. She wanted to stay and enjoy the evening, but she realized she was going to need a restroom before long, so she reluctantly surrendered to the inevitable and allowed Caton to pack up their camp.

Lily couldn't express how much she enjoyed their date and how much she was looking forward to their next adventure, whatever that turned out to be. Knowing she was planning to spend the following evening with Jack,

Caton asked for the following day. She happily agreed, almost floating through the door and back to the welcome committee at the Crofting.

The next evening, Jack McCranie picked up Lily at seven. After driving her through the Mescalero Indian Reservation, he took her for a late dinner at Casa Blanca, a Mexican restaurant in the nearby town of Ruidoso. Once they were seated, Jack waved off the menus and told the waiter to bring them two top-shelf margaritas.

"The special today is the habañero fajitas." Jack hesitated and glanced at Lily. "How are you with spicy food?"

She shrugged. "I don't know. It's not really something I eat very often. Sometimes I like spicy Thai, but I don't know about habañero …"

He raised his hands. "I'm sure you can handle it." He turned to the waiter. "Very well. That's what we'll have. Oh, and sopapillas for dessert."

Once the waiter was gone, Lily pensively stirred her margarita. She had yet to talk with Jack about limitations, and they were unlikely to be interrupted tonight. She cleared her throat. "Uh, Jack? I have something I want to talk about."

"Okay, shoot." His steel grey eyes shot into hers.

Returning his gaze, she found herself irritated by him. She felt he was trying to intimidate her.

"Umm, what if I'm not in the mood for fajitas?"

"Excuse me?" He clearly didn't follow her.

"It's just—you ordered without consulting me, and I might have wanted something different. You never gave me the chance to decide."

His eyes seemed to flare, but not from anger. "You don't like fajitas?"

She pressed her lips together. "That's not what I'm talking about. I like fajitas. A lot, in fact. But I also like enchiladas."

His forehead creased. "Do you want me to change your order?"

She shook her head. "No. Not really. What I'm saying is, while I'm flattered you assume to order for me, there's a certain amount of autonomy I'd like to claim."

His head tilted as he processed her words. "You don't want me to order for you?"

She exhaled through her nose. "Yes." She shook her head. "No. That's not what I mean. I'm just saying, sure, you can order for me. That's fine. But is there a reason you can't consult me before you do?"

His eyes bore witness to his confusion. "But then I'm not ordering for you …"

Lily fought hard not to roll her eyes. "All I'm saying is, I want you to consider what I might want before assuming you know."

He wasn't getting it. "I do consider what you want. That's how I order for you."

Lily blinked several times, trying to understand him. "Okay. Explain that."

"I considered you and your personality when I ordered. You are an adventurous woman who loves trying new things, and you have a certain zest about you. You have a refined background, so you already know you like traditional meals such as steak and lobster. You also have a satisfied emotional balance."

"What does that mean?"

"It means, you'd love the fajitas more than the enchiladas."

She blinked again, this time trying to decide if he was being sweet or stifling. "I still don't understand you."

He shrugged. "You're more of a chicken and seafood type of woman, and less of a beef and potato eater. Am I wrong?"

She nodded. "Yes, I do like those things, but I also like steaks and French fries."

He considered her for a moment. "Very well. I guess it won't hurt to ask before I order for you."

She wasn't sure they'd gained any ground in this conversation. She'd have to wait and see. She continued to watch him while he stared at her. His eyes were looking at her, but they appeared to be seeing something else. Holding his spoon between his fingers, he lightly tapped the back of his other hand.

"What are you thinking about?" she asked.

His eyes focused on her. "Hmmm," he replied. His stone face revealing nothing of his thoughts. "I was just thinking about your date with Caton."

That was unexpected. "What about it?" She slowly felt her stomach start to sink.

He swallowed. "Do you intend to keep dating him?"

She looked at him for a moment before answering. "Is that a problem?"

His jaw seemed harder than ever. "I don't understand why you're not deciding."

"You don't understand?" she repeated coolly.

"Yes. Why don't you make a decision?"

She leaned forward. "Why should I?"

His lips twitched. "It's not fair for us. You keep dragging this out. And I'm left wondering what's happening."

"And that's not convenient for you?"

He smiled. "See? You do understand."

She shook her head. "No, I don't. There's no reason why I have to declare my devotion to either of you just yet. I hardly know Caton, and I know even less about you. And you expect me to just drop Caton because you want me to?"

"I didn't say that."

"That's what it sounds like to me." Her voice had an edge.

"Look, you and I both know I'm the best choice for you. Just let him down—easy of course—and then we can move on."

Lily was at a loss and rubbed her eyes in dismay. "Let him down easy, huh?"

"Well, I don't want you to hurt him. I just want us to settle in."

Her eyes pressed closed. "You're already tired of trying to win me over?"

"Come on," he smiled again. "You and I are a perfect match. Tell me one thing that's wrong about us."

"Jack, don't you understand? That's what I'm trying to figure out. I want to get to know you well enough to know if we *are* a good fit."

"All right," he said flatly. "If Caton didn't exist, would you go out with me?"

She hesitated. "Yes."

"And would I be a man you would fall in love with?"

"Maybe."

His smile broadened. "There you have it. What more do you need?"

She was slightly miffed. "The same is true for Caton. If you didn't exist, I could just as easily fall in love with him." She sipped her margarita. "And right now, he's starting to look even better."

"Meaning?"

"Meaning that I don't appreciate you trying to force my hand. We've only known each other for a few weeks and already you're drawing a line in the sand."

His voice was stronger. "Lily, that man had his chance, and he blew it. Now is our time. You and I *are* a perfect match. We fit together."

She didn't respond, mostly due to the sensation of banging her head against a concrete wall.

"We have so many common traits. We both know and have experienced a wide array of cultures. Has Caton ever traveled out of New Mexico?"

"He has family in Texas."

"Big whoop!" He continued, "I know how to travel through Europe, and even Africa and the Middle East. Does he?"

"He's never had the opportunity."

"Did he go to college?"

"Yes."

"And what did he study?"

"I'm not sure."

"But you know I studied medicine."

She was unimpressed with his argument. "Jack ..."

"I'm just trying to point out you have no future with him."

"But I do with you?"

He smiled again. "See? That's not so hard to understand."

She shook her head. This wasn't going to work. And she still had to finish a date she no longer wanted to be on. "You just don't get it."

He leaned forward and almost glared at her. "No, I *do* understand—all too well, in fact. Caton invited you into his life, and then, when you were vulnerable to him, he tossed you out like last week's trash. You deserve better."

"That's not exactly what happened."

"Well, it ends now."

Her eyebrows shot up, as did the tone of her voice. "Excuse me?"

"You just need to accept he's wrong for you. I want you to stop allowing him to distract you."

"Meaning?"

"Meaning, I want you to end it with him. I can offer you a great future. And I can relocate anywhere you want to go. You can't play your music here, but we can move to a place where you can. I want to move to a bigger town, anyway."

She considered that but didn't respond.

"Is he willing to put everything aside and pursue your dreams?"

Lily looked down. "How do you know he isn't?"

Jack looked around as if sharing a secret with her. "Because he buried his dead wife at that monstrous house of his," he whispered. "Do you really think he would move away?"

"I haven't considered it."

"Well, I have. And I want it to end. You're mine, and that's all there is to it."

Before she could reply, the waiter returned with a sizzling skillet of fajitas and placed it gingerly between them. "Careful, don't burn yourselves."

"It may be too late," she replied coolly.

The waiter didn't understand her but smiled politely. "Can I get you anything else?"

"That'll be all," Jack dismissed him. "Hey, this smells great."

"It smells very spicy too."

"Just like you." He winked at her.

"Jack, I don't want to do this," she said regretfully.

"We can order something else, if you like. After all, you do like enchiladas."

She exhaled loudly. "No, Jack. I don't want you to dictate to me what I can do and what I can't. The way you're pressuring me screams at me to run away from you."

"Well, that would be a mistake." He reached for a tortilla and began assembling his fajita. "You'd better get started."

She shook her head. "I've lost my appetite."

"What? So soon? We just got started."

"Jack, I just can't do this. For some reason, I was determined to see if we could find enough common ground to make this work, but I can't handle you being this dominant. And if it's a problem now, it'll be much worse in the future. Some women appreciate a strong hand. I also find a strong man to be attractive, but you're pushing me further than I want to go. I think it's best we go back home."

"Nonsense. You're just being emotional."

Jayne was still awake when Lily stumbled home at almost two in the morning. As soon as she saw Lily's expression, she asked, "Care for a glass of wine?"

"Ugh. Yes." Lily looked at her watch. "No, actually. Wow, I'm tired."

"Yep. You're not built for these late hours, are you?" Jayne was nibbling on a platter of grapes.

"Why are you still up?" Lily asked casually.

"Just got home."

Lily could tell by looking at Jayne's hair that she'd had a busy date. She chose not to address the topic and instead reached for a grape. "Are all men dense?"

"No, some of 'em are flat-out stupid." Jayne sipped her wine. "Which one is Jack? Oh, wait? Who did you go out with tonight? It's hard to keep up with, eh?" She winked.

Lily smiled. "Well, after tonight, I'm down to just Caton."

"I see." Jayne plucked a grape from the cluster and examined it. "What happened?"

Lily rolled her eyes. "He refused to let me date anyone else."

"So?"

"So, that started a looooong discussion." Lily opened her purse. "I know I have antacids somewhere."

"You're all messed up," Jayne laughed softly. "Dating doesn't agree with you."

"Habañero fajitas don't agree with me either." She found a roll of antacids and popped two tablets in her mouth. "I love Mexican food, but habañeros are just evil."

"Some like it hot."

Lily looked at her. "I told Jack to take a hike."

"Really? That doesn't seem likely."

She rubbed her eyes. "Why not?"

"Because he's Rodney Part II ... your kryptonite. You like that kind of man."

"And what kind is that?"

"The kind who don't smile and like to tell you what to do." Her tone was conversational.

"You know, I was just a kid when I met Rodney. He was sophisticated and powerful. I admit I liked that. But I'm hardly the same person now."

Jayne shrugged in agreement. "Okay. Maybe that's why you're having so much trouble with Jack."

Lily's eyes narrowed. "Umm, what?"

"He has that sizzling look about him, and he's a man every woman notices. Every woman," she repeated. "But, looks aren't enough for you. And neither is power or wealth. Otherwise, you'd hook up with him and be happy."

Lily's exhaustion was overwhelming her. "Why can't I be happy with Jack? I really want to like him. I want to fall in love with him."

Jayne shook her head. "Nope, that's not who you are. You want a soulmate, not a marriage partner. You want the man who'll make you smile. You want a man who cares about you as much as you care about him."

She sighed. "And is that wrong?"

"Oh, sweetie, of course not! We're all different. We all want something different from life. I'm happy with a man who knows how to get busy. To me, the proof is in the pudding, and the rest is just nonsense I ignore. I don't need an emotional connection to fulfill me. Your mom likes a man who's sophisticated and philosophical. You want a man who has an old soul and a young smile."

"And Jack isn't that man, is he?"

She shook her head. "Jack's a good man. He's a little overbearing, but he's not ever going to be anything different than what you see. He's type A, strong and confident, but he's not going to be the tender man who shares emotionally intimate moments with you."

"He's not Caton?"

Jayne smiled. "Caton is a once-in-a-lifetime find. He is a rugged man. He's the one who makes you smile and warms your heart. At the same time, he'd get tangled up in a fistfight if someone insulted you. He's wine and roses, leather and gunpowder. He's dancing and walking and sweat and salt."

"Then why can't I just commit to him?"

Jayne considered that. "Well, he hurt you. If he did it once, he could do it again."

Lily chewed a grape. "Is that what I think?"

"Probably." She drank more wine. "Can you get past it?"

Her forehead wrinkled. "Maybe I already have."

"So, what did you tell Doctor Death?"

"Don't call him that, Jayne. He's a good man. I didn't really tell him anything. We argued, and I finally got out of his truck angry at him. He's so bull-headed."

"That's who he is." She emptied her glass. "Don't ever expect him to be different. You can't change him. If you choose Jack, that's who you'll get, so make the choice with your eyes wide open."

"Yeah," Lily mumbled. "I'm too tired to think about it now, but for some reason, I won't say no to him. Something in me wants him. But tonight, I'm mad at him."

"You've got to choose which of those two incredible men you want— then don't look back. Regret is a marriage killer. Once you decide, then let it go."

Lily leaned forward and kissed her on top of her head. "Good night, Jayne. I love you."

"Sweet dreams, O Confused One."

The ringing phone woke her up before the sun crested the eastern horizon. Lily groaned as she recognized the number displayed on her cell. Was she still mad? She was too sleepy to know for sure. "Hello?" Her voice was still asleep.

"Lily, I'm so sorry to wake you." Jack's deep voice sounded strained, regretful. "But I need your help."

"Ugh." She was still trying to wake up. "Help? What?"

"My mother is coming to visit."

She could hear the stress in his voice. "Uh … okay?"

"And I don't have a place for her to sleep."

Lily wrinkled her forehead. She was starting to remember his circumstances despite the fog in her brain. "She can have my bed if you let me go back to sleep."

"I'm sorry I woke you, but I really do need your help." He was starting to sound desperate.

"Jack, none of this is making any sense."

He sighed with exasperation. "Look, I know I was a little overbearing last night." His voice was softer.

She opened her eyes. "Yes, you were." She was too sleepy to be gentle.

"I know I have my issues. And I know I can come across a bit sharp on occasion." His voice trailed off, but Lily remained silent, waiting for him to apologize without her requesting one. Finally, he said, "And I was sharp with you."

If this was his display of sorrow, then it wasn't going to work. "Jack? This could have waited until the sun came up."

"It's been a long time since I was in a relationship with a woman, especially a woman I was interested in … as I am with you."

"Jack, please. You aren't making any sense. What does that mean, 'I am with you'?"

He inhaled deeply. She could tell he was struggling. "Okay. I'm saying I'm interested in you. I'm interested in us. In us being a … couple." He exhaled. "I want to start over. I'm ready to talk to you and to open myself up to you."

Lily sat up and leaned against her pillow. "Go on."

"I was wrong to speak to you the way I did last night." His voice was tight. "And I apologize."

Lily grinned softly. "That wasn't so hard, was it?"

He was silent for a moment. "Lily, I just apologized to you, and you make fun of me?" The edge was back in his voice.

She was alarmed. "No, that's not what I mean. Look, I only wanted you to recognize what you did wrong and to say you were sorry. Which you did. And I accept your apology."

He sounded frustrated. "Thank you. And now we're back on good terms?"

Her eyes closed again. "Yes, I suppose so."

"Good, because I need your help. My mother's coming."

She forgot that part of the conversation. "And how can I help? You know I can't swing a hammer."

"Well, I need a woman." He was sounding gruff again, which amused Lily. Did he always sound gruff when he was asking for help?

"Are you asking me to marry you?" She grinned. *There, that should put him off balance.*

"What? No!" he said way too quickly.

"Okay, Jack." Her tone should help him de-escalate.

"I don't have any furniture for her in her bedroom."

Realization dawned. "Ah, yes, you *are* in a pickle." Her good humor was starting to return.

"I know." He still sounded panicked. "Can you help me?"

"Jack," she pleaded, "I don't know what you want from me. Please just say it."

"Will you go with me to El Paso, where I can buy some furniture? I need a woman's touch."

Lily didn't laugh aloud, but she couldn't hide the amusement in her voice. "Okay, Jack. I'll go. When?"

"Can we leave within the hour?"

It was her turn to be on edge. "What? Are you kidding me? What time is it?"

"It's already five. It will be almost eight by the time we get there. I've already called Jason Fox to cover the ER for me today. He owes me one from Christmas."

"Ugh, Jack." Lily suddenly felt exhausted again.

"Lily? Please? We'll have some great time to drive and talk." He was almost begging. "And you can ask me anything you want." The pain in his voice was obvious, but was it pain from asking for help, or from being willing to talk? "Plus, I'll buy you breakfast at this Mom-and-Pop dive in Alamogordo. They have homemade tortillas and really good carne asada."

Feigning anger, she asked, "What did you call me?"

"That's not what I said." The edge was back in his voice. He didn't like being teased.

"Very well, Jack. I'll get ready, but you have to provide breakfast within the hour."

"I'll be there in fifteen minutes."

Lily rushed through a shower and pulled her hair into a ponytail. When Jack arrived, she was mostly put together, save her mascara, which she could apply on the road.

When they stopped for breakfast, Jack asked her if she'd like to try something new. He took her to a local taco shop, Amigo's Bakery. She enjoyed the red chili burrito. Jack tempted her to try his own selctions, the green chili, beef, and potato burrito, and a brisket burrito. When she relented, she discovered another passion. Mexican food breakfasts are better than pancakes and waffles. Period.

Their drive was pleasant, and Lily enjoyed the casual time she spent chatting with Jack about unimportant things. She was able to squeeze out of him a few interesting stories about his time in the Army. She watched him as they drove and kept thinking, *See? This is good? We're able to be casual and not be fussy. There really is a warm side to Jack.*

El Paso was a mad house, and traffic was extraordinarily heavy due to accidents on Interstate 10. She cringed at several near misses, hardly believing Jack could drive his large pick-up and pull a trailer through the chaos. She had never seen drivers behave the way they did in El Paso. They all seemed to drive with the aggressive passion so prevalent in Mexico. Jack turned from the highway and took her on Transmountain, a bypass that went over the top of the mountains. When they reached the top of the pass, he pulled over and allowed her a minute to stand in awe at the mass of humanity spread out below them.

The El Paso area was a thriving population of eight hundred thousand people, but on the south side of the Rio Grande River, which flowed along the very edge of downtown, Ciudad Juarez was bulging with two million plus residents. Houses and streets spread across her view from horizon to horizon, and the air pollution that hung over the two cities was alarming. How could more than three million people live in this congested desert valley? The concept made her value the tranquility found in the quaint mountain village of Cloudcroft. She yearned to be back among the peaceful pines and quaking aspens that made the Village so beautiful. She realized she was even beginning to think of Cloudcroft as home. The idea caused her to smile.

Jack took her to several outlet furniture stores along the interstate, but Lily didn't find anything that suited her, much to his chagrin. Being frugal, she insisted on the best deal possible. After several fruitless searches, they decided to try the east side of El Paso. She was astounded that El Paso came complete with towering skyscrapers and charming, old town districts.

Later that afternoon, Jack pulled into a smaller store. Lily found a bedroom set, and they loaded the trailer with furniture designed for both comfort and appeal.

"Man, look at the time. My mother will arrive in a few hours, and we're nowhere near Cloudcroft."

"Yow! That doesn't give us much time to put things together. We still need to buy sheets and towels, and some wall décor."

"Man, I didn't even think of all that stuff." He grinned. "I'm very glad you came along."

She laughed. "Did you think she was just gonna flop on a mattress and be happy? Of course, we have to buy the rest of the stuff. Now find a Bed Bath and Beyond, and I'll take care of everything." She patted him on the leg. When she did so, she felt an odd kinship with him that made her smile. Sure, last night Jack made her madder than she'd been in years, but the issue was now behind them. Their day trip to El Paso made her see him in a different way. He was relaxed, he laughed, and his eyes smiled in a way that made her blush. He was incredibly handsome, and when he smiled, he was the most gorgeous man she'd ever seen. But, could she be happy with him?

Just as she was about to answer that question, she remembered she had completely forgotten her date with Caton. Checking her watch, she mentally calculated the time required to drive back to the mountains. She had an hour and a half to shop for the remaining items and get back home. For a moment, she thought she could pull it off, but would she really want to go on a date looking like she did? Her hair was in a ponytail, and she was wearing minimal make up. Her heart sank as she faced her situation.

Five minutes earlier, she was thinking about how happy she was spending the day with Jack, and now she was distraught about not looking nice enough for Caton. What a confusing world! Well, one thing was certain: they would have to get their shopping done quickly, then, hopefully, Jack would get her home without further delay.

"Oh, man!" Jack was disgusted. "I can't believe our freakin' luck!"

"What happened?" Lily was confused at his sudden outburst. They had been discussing Lily's life in London when Jack broke off into a stream of profanities.

"They're closing Highway 54—that's what happened!" Venom dripped from his words.

"What does that mean?"

"Argh!" Jack was visibly distraught. "The blasted White Sands Missile Range is shutting down the highway." When he saw her confusion, he elaborated. "Sometimes they test fire some weapon, or missile, or whatever, and they close the highways when they do because the blasted highway runs right through the testing range."

"How long?"

"That sign back there said expect up to two-hour delays."

"But … two hours?" *What about my date with Caton?*

He heard the stress in her voice. "Are you okay?"

How could she tell him that she was in a hurry to go on a date with his competition? That struck her as cruel. "I, uh, didn't expect to be gone all day."

He closed his eyes, as if trying to calm down. "I knew something like this would happen. Two hours! We could be home in just over an hour! This is setting us back three hours. Really!" He slapped the top of his steering wheel, causing Lily to jump in her seat. "Of all the freakin' luck!" his voice was just short of breaking. "Of all the days for them to shut the highway down!" He was seething.

"Is there another route?" she asked hopefully.

"No!" He inhaled sharply. "They've closed every road." He slapped the steering wheel again. "This is freakin' awful."

"It's too bad we can't just cut across the desert," Lily moaned. This was not happy news for her, but she had no steering wheel to pound.

He was silent for a moment, and then turned to her. His eyes narrowed. "Well, there's one remote option. But it's not the best one. And it would only save us forty minutes, at the most."

"Go on."

"We could leave the highway at Oro Grande and take the back roads up to Bug Scuffle, and then on to Timberon, and then to Cloudcroft."

"Butt Scuffle?"

He laughed. "Bug. Bug Scuffle. It's a hunting camp in the foothills, just below Timberon." His eyes smiled briefly. "I'm game if you are."

"Let's do it." She glanced at her watch. There was barely enough time for her to get back, change, and go out again. She rolled her eyes. At what point did her life suddenly become so congested?

Jack drove another mile and turned onto an unmarked dirt road that didn't look promising. After a brief, bumpy jaunt, they turned onto a larger, graveled road, and Lily began to feel confident that Jack knew what he was doing. "I've only been this way once, but really, it's not hard to figure out. There are only so many options. Eventually, we'll get where we're going."

He smiled broadly at her. "I hope you're up for an adventure. There's no telling what we're in for."

Lily didn't share Jack's optimism, and the farther they drove from the highway, the more she was regretting the decision to deviate from the known path. She tried to console herself. *Oh, well, it's the road not taken. And we're taking it. Robert Frost would be proud.*

Despite her reservations, the mountains in the near distance grew larger, and the dusty road proved to be taking them in the right direction. "I can't believe how much empty desert we're traveling through," she observed.

"We are miles and miles from any other person," he explained. "There was a ranch house a few miles back, but we're alone. Just you and me." He had a devilish, mischievous look in his eyes. "We're making fairly good time, but the road will get rough until we get to the hunting camp." He thought for a moment, then pursed his lips together, as if calculating the odds of drawing an inside straight in a poker game. "There's a short cut bypassing Bug Scuffle. It would save us twenty miles, or so."

Lily shook her head. "I don't know." She tried to sound cheerful. "I'm curious to see this Bug Scuffle. It sounds like a once-in-a-lifetime treat."

Jack looked at her. "No, this will be best. We'll bypass the camp and go straight for the cut-off to Timberon. Trust me."

Lily forced a smile. "I don't really have much choice, do I?"

He cast a curious frown at her but continued driving. He found the fork in the road he was looking for and pulled off the main gravel road onto the less-traveled ranch road. Rocks and washed-out places slowed their progress immediately. As they drove slowly through the sagebrush and cactus, the trailer groaned in protest as they pounded along the rugged terrain.

"Jack, I'm not sure about this." She was trying to sound calm.

"I know this looks bad, but I've driven this road before."

"Road?"

"Well, it's a ranch road. And it's not well traveled, but it will save us twenty miles of desert driving."

"I don't think this road was intended for pulling trailers." She pulled out her cell phone. Predictably, there was no coverage. *Just like the horror movie.* She continued to check every few minutes, but she knew she wasn't going to find a signal for many more miles.

The road became rougher and almost impassable, as Jack weaved around large rocks and washed-out ruts. Immediately, the pickup was bouncing roughly and squeaking as the frame twisted and contorted to accommodate the path. As they crested the top of a short, rocky hill, Jack, unable to see where he was going, missed the curve. The front end of his pickup slipped off a small boulder, and they smashed against some smaller rocks, bouncing hard. The loud scraping of metal on jagged edge caused Lily to scream. "Oh, Jack, this can't be right!"

"Trust me, baby. I really have been here before." He was sounding more confident than his face appeared. His lips were set hard against each other.

"But were you pulling a trailer?"

"Fair point." He shifted into reverse and slowly backed down the hill. "Ah, there's the path. See?" He turned onto the road and began driving forward.

"What's that smell?" Lily asked.

He grimaced. "That's engine oil."

"And it's not good, is it?"

"Odds are" was all he said as he found a flat place near a dry gully. "I'll check." He jumped from the cab and bent low to see underneath. The string of profanity that followed told Lily all she needed to know. They weren't going any further.

"We busted the oil pan," he growled between choice words. "I must have hit a rock back there and punctured it."

"Wow, a rock. Imagine that." Lily was more sarcastic than she intended to be.

Jack shot her a dirty look. "What's that?" His words were a challenge to be quiet. She waved casually at him and chose not to respond. Instead she asked, "So, I'm guessing you can't fix it?"

He spat. "No, I can't freakin' fix it, Lily." The anger in his words betrayed his fear.

Angry or not, Lily was not going to allow him to speak to her so harshly. "That's enough of that, Jack. We may be in trouble, but there's no reason to act childishly."

His eyes flared at her, and for a moment, she feared he would slap her. "I'm fully aware of our situation, thank you very much. And I'll act however I please."

Lily closed her eyes and laid her head on the back of her seat. How much worse could this situation get? And then realization dawned on her. "We're stuck here until someone finds us, aren't we?"

He spat again. "Probably." He closed his eyes and frowned. "Yes." Anger was visible in his features, and his body language told Lily he was just short of a full meltdown. He turned and walked into the desert a short distance, then picked up a rock and threw it with a loud yell. She had never heard anyone use such profanity in all her years. As she watched him come apart, fear began to settle into her heart. What would he do next?

To his credit, after a minute of venting his anger, he settled down and almost seemed at peace when he returned to her. She sat in the cab and watched as he leaned into the open door. "Feeling better?" she asked hopefully.

"Sorry." Shame settled into his eyes. "I can't believe this is happening."

Lily was forcing herself to remain calm. "Well, now what?"

"I can't fix this," he said quietly. "I can't fix anything." He seemed to be talking to no one in particular.

"What about Bug Scuffle?"

"It's a good fifteen miles away." He glanced at the sky. "We're less than an hour from sunset."

"We can walk in the dark, can't we?" She was trying hard to find a workable solution.

"Lily?" His voice was condescending. "This desert is full of snakes, spiders, coyotes, mountain lions, scorpions, and cactus. Not to mention aggressive bees. Do you really want to walk in the dark for fifteen miles? We don't even know for sure we will find anyone when we get there."

"Fine," she surrendered to his point. "So, where does that leave us?"

"That leaves us right here until someone finds us. Do you understand?"

"Got it." Jack was becoming difficult to appreciate. She decided to try some humor. "Well, we have a bed in the trailer! We can set it up and spend the ..." but once his eyes met hers, she knew he was not in a mood for the bright side of anything.

"I'll set up a temporary camp. Go around and pick up anything that'll burn, and we'll get a fire going while we still have daylight."

Lily had never been so miserable. She collected firewood for the better part of an hour, dragging limbs and roots to their new camp. Jack dug in his toolbox until he found a hatchet. "There's bottled water in a box in the back of the cab. And I have a few MREs in the box. Why don't you get them out and set them by those rocks. We can sit on them."

"The MREs or the rocks?" She tried to smile, but Jack shut her down quickly. She sighed in frustration. "MREs are Army food, right?"

"Yep. Meals Ready to Eat."

"Well," she said cheerfully. "At least we won't be hungry."

For the first time he smirked. "Wait until you eat one, and then tell me that."

"I don't seem to have a better offer." And then she frowned. For she did have a better offer. In about an hour, Caton was going to arrive at the Crofting and expect her to join him for a night of ice-skating and dominoes with Susan and Jayne. Figuring they were probably bored with Village life, he suggested they do something fun together.

She watched Jack reduce her pile of branches and roots into manageable chunks of firewood. The air was cool, but Jack was starting to sweat. She'd never thought of him as a hands-on kind of man. Watching him swing the hatchet made her think of him in a positive light again, which was important, for his current attitude was certainly unpleasant.

As dusk settled in, Jack built a fire. Lily could feel the flames bring a small measure of cheer back into her life. Having accomplished that task seemed to make Jack less hostile, and he began sorting through the MREs. After a few moments, he calmly announced, "Well, I have good news and bad news." He looked at her and allowed her to choose. "Okay. The good news ... this package is chili-mac."

"And the bad news?"

"I have three packages of chicken a la king."

"And this is bad news?"

"I see you've never had an MRE with chicken a la king."

She grimaced. "I've never had one period. And now I'm worried."

He smiled. "Well, these will make you super-constipated, which leads me to another element of good news."

"Constipation is good news?"

"We're running low on tissue."

"What?" And then she understood. "Oh. You've got to be kidding."

They were sitting in front of the fire, staring into the flames. Jack gathered the trash from the MREs and burned as much as possible, throwing the rest into the back of his pickup. He opened one of the packages of bedding and handed her a blanket, which she carefully wrapped around herself. Jack opened a second package and unfolded a blanket for himself, making Lily grateful they'd found a two-for-the-price-of-one sale on bedding. Otherwise, they would be huddling under one blanket. Sometimes huddling in front of a fire leads to lowered inhibitions, a situation she didn't want to contemplate.

"I wish I had my violin," she mused.

"That'd be nice," he agreed. "But you know what I do have?" He jumped up and searched through the compartment between the seats in his pickup. He smiled widely, revealing a bottle of whiskey. "Care for a slug?"

"I think I'll pass. I'm more of a wine girl, thanks."

Jack shrugged and pulled the cork. "Here's to an unexpected journey." He lifted the bottle to his lips.

This is going to be a long night. An hour into the darkness, Lily hadn't moved much, except in her futile effort to find a more comfortable rock. She watched as Jack descended into the depths of his bottle, each small sip contributing to the larger effect. She noticed his tongue was heavier, and his mood was lifting. Maybe her mother was right when she said that Jack's moods were dependent upon the amount he was drinking … or had Jayne said that?

Jack tried to get her to drink with him, but she steadfastly refused. The longer they sat and engaged in meaningless chatter, the faster his mood shifted. At first, the whiskey made him happy, then turned him dark. She knew intuitively he was the kind of man who became sullen and offended when fully intoxicated, and she dearly hoped he would stop drinking before he reached that state. Maybe he would stop at happy, but she could tell by watching him he was an experienced drinker. Maybe a more serious conversation would help him stabilize.

"So, what do you find to be the biggest difference between practicing medicine in a big city like Dallas and a small town?"

When he looked at her, she saw frustration in his eyes. Oops, bad topic choice. His lids were dull and thick. "The biggest difference? There's nothing to compare them to. They are entirely separate worlds. They don't even have the same sun."

The same sun? Wow, either he was becoming philosophical, or he had drunk more than she realized. "Yes, life in a small town seems different."

"Oh, does it? And how long have you been in a small town to actually notice? Hmmm?"

Great. It's too late. He's already obnoxious. "This is my first lengthy stay in a non-urban setting."

"Well, let me tell you ..." His words were slurred. "Life is better when you're on top. And being here is not the top. It's the bottom. Being here is the lowest level possible for a world class surgeon." He spoke slowly, enunciating carefully.

"Oh, I don't know," she said trying to remain positive, "Cloudcroft is really pretty."

"Who gives a flying rip about how pretty it is? This small town blows. The people pretend they like you, but they only want your money. They always smile when you come in, but they smile bigger when you leave."

"I find most people here to be agreeable and friendly."

"Really?" His voice bore the weight of a challenge. "And how many locals do you really know?"

"Well," she said, "I do know April Poe."

"Ha! The town gossip? Her tongue is so long she can lick the egg beaters in the kitchen from her living room sofa."

"Wow, that's very descriptive."

He shook his head disapprovingly. "Don't patronize me. I know you're soft-stepping around me. Maybe I scare you a little?"

"Yes," she replied softly, "maybe you do."

"But I'll bet Caton Harvey doesn't scare you."

"No," she agreed, "Caton doesn't scare me."

"Well, he's not the man for you. And you have to know that by now. He's the one who jerked you around and hurt you."

"Funny," she said, "you're the first person I've heard speak lowly of him."

"Me? I like him too. He's a real peach of a guy. He's just not good enough for you. You deserve better."

"And you're better?" His attitude was wearing her patience thin.

"I didn't say that." He twisted the cap off his bottle. "In fact, I'd say I'm not. As far as I know, he's never killed anyone. Does that make him better than me?"

Lily cocked her head sideways. "What does that mean? Who have you killed?" A cold finger ran down her spine at the thought of what he meant.

He must have read her face. "Oh, you can relax. I'm not talking about that kind of killing. But do you know how doctors sometimes kill people? We have trouble sleeping at night because of our former patients." For a moment he stared at her, and then a tear traced down his granite jaw. His lips tightened as he stared at the fire. He was sliding deeper into whatever depression the alcohol was nurturing.

Her heart began to sink, as she realized he was speaking from a deep-seated, haunting pain. "Do you want to talk about it?"

CHAPTER FIFTEEN

Black Hawk Down

Jack was obviously in pain, both emotionally and mentally. He sat unmoving for a moment, at war within himself. His fingers traced the neck of the bottle, caressing it. He inhaled sharply and closed his eyes, exhaling slowly, as if practicing a relaxation method. While he remained silent, Lily could see he was gaining control of whatever demon was tormenting him. Finally, he replied. His voice was so tender her heart bled. "You can't imagine how painful this is for me." He pressed his eyes with his fingers as if he could switch off the memory haunting him.

"Jack, it's okay," she said softly. "We don't have to do this."

He shook his head vigorously, and in his drunken state, he seemed a bit more animated. He swallowed. "No, I have to do this. I can't live like this anymore." When he looked at her, she could see that his eyes were wet, making her heart hurt. "Please let me tell you this, and for heaven's sake, don't interrupt me. This is hard enough without distractions."

Lily nodded. "Okay." She settled on the ground and leaned against a large rock. "I'm here for you."

He didn't seem to hear her. His eyes were staring thousands of miles away from the desert surrounding them. He pressed his lips together and spoke, his voice so low she could barely hear him. "You know I was an Army surgeon during my last deployment in Afghanistan. I specialized in trauma, and I was gifted with emergencies. The more traumatic the situation, the better I functioned. When most people panicked at the sight of blood, I felt my nerves relax and my senses sharpen. I could focus like a laser on the problem." He grimaced and his shoulders sagged. "Or at least that used to be who I was. I haven't been that man in a long time." He removed the cap from the bottle and sipped carefully.

Lily wanted to let him know she was so sorry for his pain, but she remained still.

When he continued, he sounded defeated and hollow. "When I left the Army, I took a position at Parkland Hospital in Dallas, where I was an attending trauma surgeon." He shook his head as if he couldn't believe what was happening to him. "The stories you heard about me are true," he said flatly. "I had to leave Parkland because I simply couldn't function there any longer. I was already starting to slip before I took the job, but I ignored it and tried to convince myself I would get better with time." He stared into the flames and spat with anger. "But it was a lie." He wiped his lip with the back of his hand. "I lost the edge. I lost my nerve."

He lifted the bottle to his lips. "One night a gang banger was brought in by ambulance. He'd sustained multiple stab wounds in his throat. The angle of the cuts resulted in internal injuries to the artery that were all but impossible to fix. He shouldn't have even made it to the ER, but those paramedics did incredible work. Every time he was moved or shifted, the bleeding would start again. From the surface, the wounds looked like they could be managed with simple pressure bandages. But what we didn't know was the internal injury to the artery resulted in a steady but completely unnoticed blood loss." He took another swig from the bottle. His hands— and his voice—were trembling.

Jack cleared this throat and continued, "I knew I wasn't able to face the situation. My hands were already shaking, and my pulse was racing when we got him into the OR. I was fighting a panic attack, but I ignored it, and I ignored the voice in my head, screaming at me to hand off this patient to another surgeon.

"He was already in massive shock, but I steadied my nerves and started working." Jack clenched his teeth and closed his eyes again. "When I removed the pressure bandages, his artery started shooting blood into my face. Normally, that's when I focus on the job and find myself centered. But ..." he said, looking at his feet. "I panicked. I watched the blood for ten full seconds while the surgical staff tried to jump-start me into action. When I finally engaged the situation, I realized the angles of the cuts on his artery were almost impossible to reach—I couldn't get any clamps on the bleeder. We had to hold pressure farther down on his artery while we wiped it down, trying to dry it off and get a visual of the laceration. From there I should have been able to ligate the artery back together." Again he took a drink. "That is a difficult procedure under ideal conditions, but I wasn't really in the game. As he lost more blood, his pulse increased. I couldn't seem to get enough suction to see what I was doing. The situation was spiraling out of control, and I couldn't get ahead of it. That's when my panic overwhelmed me. I backed away from the patient and simply sank with my back against the wall." He stopped talking and shook his head bitterly.

After several minutes of silence, Lily asked, "But you weren't the only surgeon in the OR, right?"

He looked at her with dark eyes and took a long pull from the bottle. "I had a surgical intern with me. He was a first-year intern, and he had no idea how to perform such an involved procedure. It was over in less than a minute." His voice was cold. "We couldn't get enough blood back into him. His heart seized, and the intern couldn't both revive the patient and repair the artery." Jack's voice was rising. He was in visible distress. "And I was leaning against the wall watching it happen. The surgical nurse was pulling on my arm, trying to get me to stand, and the intern was screaming at me for help."

He looked up at the stars, and his tone changed again. He was angry. "The hospital convened a review panel, but I quit before they could fire me. Losing a patient happens to every surgeon. However, I didn't lose him while fighting for his life. I lost him because I lost myself. And no hospital will hire a surgeon who's lost his nerve." He held up the bottle and examined it carefully. "I descended into a drunken state for the next three months—those days are a blur—but my mother checked me into rehab, where I spent the next forty-five days admitting I was an alcoholic and making amends."

He seemed to be talking to the bottle now. "I wasn't really an alcoholic. I never have been. I just turned to liquor to silence the pain. Once I got back on my feet, I was able to put the bottle down. It doesn't call to me. I don't crave alcohol." He sealed the bottle and placed it at his feet. "I was no longer a top-notch surgeon. The only hospitals interested in me are these small, podunk towns that don't perform anything other than minor procedures, like the one you had." He rolled his head in a circle as if relieving stress. "Well, now you know my secret."

Lily stared at him for a moment with tender eyes. Her heart was melting from the pain he was experiencing, but she suppressed the desire to take him into her arms and hold him. She watched him staring into the flames, lost in his own horror. He was a broken man, but was the brokenness permanent? She didn't know what to say to him, or if she even should say anything. Instead, she reached for a piece of wood and leaned forward to drop it into the fire. The wood landed hard and shot sparks into the air. Jack's sagging shoulders stiffened when she stirred the fire. His lips tightened. Something was still not right with him. He said something about already starting to slip before he took the job at Parkland.

"Jack?" she asked, but he didn't look up. "Jack? Hello?" She snapped her fingers, but he didn't respond. He stared into the fire as if it was speaking to him. Lily considered what he told her a few minutes before. He was an Army surgeon, and then he was suddenly working at Parkland in Dallas. Something had happened to cause him to fall apart in Dallas, something that happened before he left the Army. "Jack?" she called to him again, but he seemed unable to hear her. On a whim, she called out, "Captain McCranie!" When she did, his mind snapped back to the moment, and he stared at her.

"What did you say?" he seemed confused.

She exhaled, slightly alarmed by his tone. "Where are you, Jack? You obviously aren't here."

His forehead wrinkled. "What do you mean?"

Lily hesitated. Did she really want to know what was happening to him? Already he had unburdened his soul to her, but he didn't seem relieved by it. He was still in distress. There was more to his story. "Jack, what happened in the war?"

He flinched as if slapped. For a moment his lips moved, but no words came forth. Whatever demon he was fighting in Dallas had nothing on the torment suddenly overwhelming him from the war. Finally, he spoke. "I'm not sure I'm drunk enough to tell that story." He shifted his position and shook his head slowly. "Then again, maybe I am. But let's be sure."

He drank again, though seeming revolted by the burning whiskey. "You know, the shrink I saw at Parkland told me I could get my job back if I would tell him this story." His voice was starting to drag. "But you know what? It was more a matter that I couldn't tell him, rather than I wouldn't tell him. I wanted to tell somebody, but I just didn't have the strength. Maybe tonight?" He looked up into the stars. "Maybe I can release this burden tonight?" He seemed to be praying, but Lily wasn't sure.

"It's okay, Jack" she encouraged him. "We have all night. What else is there to do?"

He smirked. "Right." He looked at her through hard eyes. "Nothing else is happening tonight, so I might as well as get hammered enough to talk." He shook his head again as if trying to sweep away cobwebs. "I wouldn't be much fun in this condition anyway." He laughed as if he was being funny.

Lily watched him laugh and realized Jayne was right. Jack rarely laughed, and he hardly smiled. Why was she drawn to such men? He seemed to live behind emotional walls in a highly defended fortress. She watched him now as he was descending into drunkenness, and only then did he allow himself any emotions.

Caton was the one exception to the type of men she pursued. His smile was always ready, and his face was warm and inviting. Caton was always trying. She smiled at the memory of the flowers he brought her. How could he know she was deathly allergic to lilies? Caton was not an aggressively decisive man, but he was a man full of life, despite the injuries from his past. He had faced his own horrors and could still smile. Jack? Well, Jack was a different type of man. She missed seeing him smile and laugh, but now, watching him do just that, she found him less attractive.

She watched Jack place the bottle on the ground and slowly stand. He was definitely drunk, which didn't win him any points with her. He was surprisingly nimble, even in that state, but his motions were slightly delayed and a bit exaggerated. He stooped to pick up more wood and almost lost his balance. Turning, he dropped an armful of mesquite into the fire, sending sparks flying wildly into the darkness. His eyes bore into the sparks with anger. "THERE!" he shouted. "Can anyone see that fire?" He slowly sank back into his sitting position and placed the bottle in his lap.

Lily was embarrassed for him. Pity was starting to replace affection. "Jack?" She waited until he looked at her. "Do you mind if I have a drink?"

He watched her carefully and smirked. "I know you only want to take the bottle." He lifted it from his lap and tossed it in her direction. It landed in the sand just in front of her. "I don't need it anymore. I'm drunk enough to talk now. Do you still want to hear my sad story? How I'm all eleven up and three down?"

She nodded. "If you want to talk, I do, but I don't know what eleven up means."

"It means I'm eight up." He looked at her with a smirk. "It's an Army thing. It means I'm not standard—messed up." He pressed his lips together and rolled his head in a full circle. "I was a trauma surgeon in the Army." The quirky smile escaped him. "But you already know that part." He wiped his mouth with his sleeve. "Do you have any chewing tobacco? No, I didn't think so. When I drink, I like to smoke cigars and chew tobacco—a disgusting habit." He winked at her. "You're seeing a whole different version of me tonight." He shrugged. "Oh, well, might as well get it over with.

"I needed to go from the hospital in Bagram to Kandahar, and I was catching a lift in a helicopter. A patrol had gone into the mountains. They were ambushed and shot up pretty bad. Our bird was diverted to help pick up the rest of the patrol. Fortunately, the chopper was attached to the hospital in Kandahar and was equipped with some medical gear.

"They told us their medic had been hit. When we arrived, we saw the entire squad had been killed, except for the medic, who was leaning against a boulder. I jumped out and assessed him. He had taken two rounds in his legs and one in his shoulder. I applied a CAT to his leg and dressed his wounds. Other than losing blood, he would be fine."

"What's a CAT?" Lily asked.

"Hmm?" He looked at her as if he had forgotten she was there. "Oh, it's a tourniquet. I carried a few in my pockets all the time. You never know when you might need a tourniquet. So, the crew started loading bodies into the chopper while I was prepping the medic for the flight.

"You have to be really careful to make sure the wounded stay warm. They've lost blood and once they get into the air, their body temperature drops. So, I strapped the medic to a board and wrapped him tightly in a blanket. About that time, an RPG exploded just behind us. We loaded the medic and as I was climbing on board, I saw that I'd left my med kit lying on the ground. No big deal, right? We were on our way to the CaSH, where we had plenty of gear." He stretched as if trying to relax.

Lily took advantage of his pause and asked, "What's a CaSH?"

"Combat Surgical Hospital," he explained with careful, deliberate words. "Normally, the MEDEVAC would fly the wounded to an aid station, but the CaSH was closer. As we were lifting off, an RPG hit the chopper. Compton, the pilot, was able to get the bird off the ground and gain enough elevation that we weren't taking any more rounds, but we were hit hard. We flew maybe ten kilometers into the mountains before we started losing altitude. When we went down, we went down hard. I knew Compton was trying to set down in a small clearing near a little stone hut, but he was losing control. We ended up slamming into the house."

"Oh, my gosh!" Lily exclaimed.

He ignored her outburst. When he continued, his voice was steady, and his mind seemed to be clearing. "I blacked out when we hit. When I came to, there were bodies everywhere. The chopper had collapsed the house on impact, and then rolled free. As I came around, I could hear Compton calling out to me. He was still buckled into his seat, but his chair had been thrown from the chopper in the roll. Both of his legs were nearly severed just below his knees. I made my way to him. I had two CATs in my pocket and managed to get one on each leg, high up on his thighs.

"I began assessing the men. Everyone in the crew died, but the medic was not any worse off than before. He was strapped onto the litter, which must have protected him when we rolled.

"When I assessed myself, I could see discoloration in my abdomen, and I knew I had probably ruptured my spleen, but for the moment, I was operating on adrenalin. I got the medic out of the wreckage and dragged him near the pilot, who was now unconscious. Jack picked up a stick and poked the fire, sending more sparks into the air. His posture became smaller and his voice softened. "Then I turned my attention to the house, or what was left of it. Already night was falling, and my visibility was diminished.

"From what I could tell, the family was eating when we crashed into them. They appeared to be sitting on the floor when the walls collapsed. Everyone was dead, except for a small boy. I found him near the back door. He was unscratched, but he was blocked off from his family by the rubble. I was able to get him uncovered and removed from the house." Jack closed his eyes and inhaled sharply. "He was a brave boy, about eight or nine years old. Of course, he didn't speak English. After a while, I was able to determine that his name was Aamir.

"I knew the chopper would act like a Taliban magnet. So, Aamir and I set up camp in a small, wooded area not too far away from the crash site. It took us forever to get everyone relocated to a covered position. Aamir helped me build a fire to keep my patients warm, and he and I sat and waited for help to come. By now, it was dark, which meant the search and rescue would be even harder. I had no ability to communicate with anyone, and only God knew where the flare gun ended up. My plan was to build up the fire once I heard the choppers, so they could find us. It was risky, so I decided to wait until the last minute. I kept just enough of a fire going to keep Compton warm. I didn't want to risk any neck injuries, so I left him strapped in his seat.

"By this time, it was getting cold. I took off my BDU top and wrapped it around the pilot. I still had my T-shirt on underneath, but the temperature was dropping. I added a little more wood to the fire, and we settled in for the night. My abdomen was aching, and I was starting to realize just how injured I was.

"About an hour later, Aamir tugged on my arm and pointed into the darkness, whispering something. I could tell he was scared. I don't know what he saw, but he was unhappy. Suddenly, the air ripped apart as an RPG exploded just behind us. It smashed into the brush and showered us with debris ..."

"Oh my gosh!" Lily exclaimed again.

"Yeah," Jack agreed. He shook his head. "In my efforts to keep everyone warm, I had built up the fire enough for the Taliban to find us. I had no idea how many were attacking, but it didn't really matter. I threw Aamir to the ground, and then knocked Compton over so he wasn't such an easy target. The only weapon I had in my immediate grasp was my Beretta. I had a vague idea where the round came from, so I returned a few shots with the pistol, just to let them know I was armed. And then we waited. I don't know if they were reloading or retreating, or how many there were. I kept my head down behind the woodpile and prayed for help. Since the Army didn't know if we survived, they would send a CSAR team of pararescuers, but where were they?

"I glanced around to check on Aamir, but the way he was lying looked odd. I low-crawled to him, and when I got close, I could see what was wrong. The RPG blast sent shrapnel flying. A shard of wood from a tree had landed near us, and when I threw him to the ground, he landed on it, puncturing his neck." Jack's voice broke for the first time. He shook his head in disbelief. "It was my fault ..." His hands went to his face." I was the one who threw him to the ground." His arms were shaking as he relived the moment.

"Oh, Jack," Lily whispered. She started to move to him, but he threw up his hand to stop her. She returned to her position. "I'm so sorry," she pleaded.

"Believe it or not, it gets worse." His lips pressed together, and he swallowed. He couldn't look her in the eyes—instead, he looked into the flames. He sniffled once and continued. "That massive splinter punctured his neck and compressed the carotid artery. As long as I could keep him still and keep the splinter from moving, he was going to be okay. But I had nothing to secure the wood to his neck, and the pressure from the artery was pushing the shard out of his neck. I'd used my last roll of gauze in packing the wound on Compton's shoulder, and I had nothing other than my own clothing close by. I pulled off my T-shirt and my belt and made a rather pitiful bandage that wasn't going to work for long. But, until I addressed the threat from the enemy, I didn't have the freedom to search the area for better supplies.

"Then I heard movement—the sound of branches breaking. He was on us before I realized he was so close." Jack was shaking as if experiencing an adrenalin rush, and his voice was strained. "It happened so fast. He appeared out of nowhere and threw himself into me. We landed hard on the ground, and then we were rolling and fighting. I lost the pistol somewhere in the dark. The fighter shifted his weight, and I caught the reflection of the fire in his knife blade. I was lying on the ground, and he was straddled across me, ready to drive the knife into my chest. I had my hands around his arms, and I lifted my hips as high as I could to buck him off balance. I was able to roll him to the side and get to my feet. He was trying to stand, so I launched myself forward and plow-drove him into the dirt. I felt something hard under my knee, and realized it was my pistol. I lifted the gun just as he was rolling over, ready to thrust. I shot him four times in the chest. He had a blank look on his face as he realized what happened.

"It wasn't anything like the movies. He didn't just collapse and die. He glared at me and stumbled forward, even more intent on killing me. I put two more rounds in his chest; I know they were lethal hits. Finally, he pitched forward, landing on top of Aamir ..." Jack cleared his throat and looked at his shoes.

Lily was dumbstruck. She was watching Jack tell his story, and she could see the pain he was experiencing, but she had no idea what to say or do. When Jack continued, his voice bore witness to his distress.

"I rolled him off Aamir, and I could see the shrapnel had moved. The T-shirt was completely soaked through. I dragged him closer to the fire so I could see his wound. I removed the packing and the wood fell out of the wound. I had no choice but to stop the bleeding or he was going to die. I shoved my finger into the cut and felt the artery pulsing. I pressed on it and was able to stop the blood flow. But, I had nothing to clamp it with.

As long as I could hold pressure on the artery, he was fine. If I let go, he was going to bleed out."

"Oh, my." Lily was near tears. "It's similar to what happened in Parkland—with the gang banger."

His face was grim. "Yeah." He looked up to the stars. "I could hear the choppers in the far distance, but they weren't close enough. I knew if I could build up the fire, they could find us, but I couldn't let go of Aamir's wound. Slowly, the sounds of the chopper faded into the distance, and we were alone again. With what little light I had, I could see that the bruise on my abdomen was serious. In the struggle, I made the internal bleeding worse. I knew I needed surgery to fix my injuries, but there was no way that was going to happen anytime soon. So I settled in to wait.

"Aamir was so brave. He knew he was seriously injured, but he never cried or moved. He just lay still while I held pressure on his wound. He must have been in terrible pain. I know I was pressing on the nerves at the same time I was pressing on his artery. But he just watched me as I watched him. His dark eyes were at peace—he was going to be okay.

"We stayed like that for another hour. Neither of us moved. I was losing feeling in my fingers, but we were doing okay. However, the pain in my abdomen was growing to the point I was distracted. I could see the blood was causing my stomach to distend, and I was growing light-headed. I knew I couldn't stay conscious much longer. And then I started to drift."

"Oh, no!" Lily whispered.

Jack pressed his lips together and seemed to fight tears. He looked into the sky as if searching for strength. "I could feel myself go before I passed out. I felt the weightlessness in my body, and then the throbbing blackness overwhelmed me. I tried bunching my stomach muscles to force the blood to my head, but my wounds were too severe for that to work. I tried breathing deeper, but the more I fought against it, the more it fought me. Realizing I was only delaying the inevitable, I tried to position my body in a way where my fingers would stay lodged in his wound ..." His voice cracked again, and he gasped deeply. "But, it didn't work. As soon as I passed out, he started bleeding again." Jack was trembling as his voice turned to sobs, his chest was heaving deeply. "When I woke up ..." He gasped again and wiped his sleeve across his nose. "When I woke up, he was already c-cold." He cried openly, unable to suppress the pain any longer.

Between sobs, he muttered, "I must have been out for an hour or more. He still had a peaceful look on his face," he said pitifully.

Lily moved beside him and wrapped her arms around his neck. He leaned into her and wept inconsolably.

At first light, Lily found Jack sitting by the fire, poking it with a stick. She was tired and stiff, and her clothes felt damp and uncomfortable. She found her rock near the fire and sat down. "Good morning," she said, her voice lacking enthusiasm.

"Morning," he replied stiffly, rolling his neck back and forth.

"Did you get any sleep?"

He shook his head. "No, I was afraid to go to sleep." His voice was weary. "How about you?"

Lily bunched her shoulders together. "I might have dozed off for a minute, but I'm not sure I can call it sleep. I wish I had a cup of coffee."

"If wishes were horses then beggars could ride," he replied solemnly.

"I beg your pardon?"

He shook his head in defeat. "A saying my Chief Surgeon used to tell me. Basically, it means you're out of luck."

"I see." His attitude was beginning to irritate her. "I guess we should talk."

"Probably should." He was short with her.

"Look, Jack, I'm not sure what happened last night …"

"Don't worry about it," he interrupted. "It won't happen again."

Lily hesitated patiently. "What? What won't happen again?"

He exhaled slowly. "Lily? I know I'm broken. My life is pretty screwed up. You're better off without me."

She closed her eyes. "Whatever is happening to you can be fixed. Isn't that called being shell-shocked?"

He smirked. "Back in World War II they called it shell-shock. Now we call it PTSD."

"PTSD?"

"Post Traumatic Stress Disorder."

"And it's treatable?"

"Yes." He was not as agitated.

"Will you be seeking help for it?"

He exhaled through his teeth. "Yes. I know the VA clinic can help me. And I know plenty of therapists who can treat me."

Lily nodded. "Good. How can I help you?"

He licked his lips and closed his eyes. "This is the part of the story I've been dreading." He rolled his head in a large circle. "You can let me go."

"Jack!" she protested. "Be serious."

He held up a hand to silence her. "I'm no good to you in this condition. It wouldn't be fair to try and have a relationship with you until I get back on my feet. My PTSD is one issue. My alcohol abuse is another." He frowned. "I'll always be an alcoholic. Maybe now I can be honest and admit it." He ran his fingers through his hair. "I'm just not in a place where I can deal with all of those issues and have a girlfriend." He was emotionless again. His words were matter of fact. "It'll take at least a year before I should even consider having a girlfriend."

Lily struggled within herself. She knew what he said was true. She had thought about their situation over the course of the night and had come to the same conclusion. "I know this is hard, but I agree with you. You can't emotionally invest in me right now, and I think it would be unfair of me to ask you to do so. We should both agree that we are not going to pursue our relationship any further."

"Good. I'm tapping out." He seemed relieved. "Thank you for not making this any harder than it has to be. I thought all night about how to release you without hurting your feelings." His tone was softer. Lily now realized that his gruff demeanor was simply a symptom of his stress.

She didn't know what to say. The whole situation was awkward, and they still had to be together until they got back home. Finally, she said, "Everything is going to be okay."

"And you understand I'm releasing you, right?"

She didn't know what he meant and felt her ire growing. "I'm sorry?"

"You and Caton." He shrugged in resignation. "You belong together."

"Oh." She only thought it was awkward a moment ago.

"I'm serious." He smiled roughly. "I'm not the right man for you. When we get back, I want you to contact Caton and make nice with him." When she didn't respond, he continued. "It's okay. Really ..." he insisted. "You and I could make it work, but not for a long time ..."

Lily held up her hand. "I get it!"

He smiled warmly. "See? It's already on your face. You know I'm right. You and I can be friends. I'll get the help I need, and you can go fall in love. We have different paths to walk—our destinations are different."

She looked into his eyes. "Thank you, Jack."

He blushed. "No, thank you. And I'm serious. Thank you. My shrink in Dallas never could get me tell him about Aamir. For some reason, I was able to tell you. Already, I feel a tremendous pressure lifted from me."

"Yes, I can see it in your eyes."

He nodded. "Do you know the other reason you and I wouldn't work?" he asked with a wry smile.

"Dare I ask?"

"I'm not really into blondes. I'm more of brunette kind of guy."

"Jack! That's not nice."

"Another reason not to go out with me." He looked across the horizon. "Are you ready to go?"

"Yes, why?"

"I can see some headlights coming down the road. We're about to be rescued."

CHAPTER SIXTEEN

Caton Went a Courtin'

By the time Lily made it back to the Crofting, she had been missing for more than fifteen hours. Local authorities would not take a missing persons report until she had been gone for a full day, so no major effort had been launched to find her.

Caton had arrived on time for his date with Lily. He drank tea with Susan while patiently waiting for Lily to return from El Paso with her other suitor. Jayne flitted in and out, making herself busy until Lily arrived. When Lily failed to return, Caton suspected they were caught in the road closures and explained to Susan how they were a common occurrence on the highways. He also explained that cell phones don't work well in that part of the desert.

As the evening grew late, they began to worry. Caton called the sheriff's office, but no accidents had been reported. Jayne didn't help matters by suggesting that Lily must have decided to spend some personal time with Jack—time that would keep them out all night. Susan didn't think that was the case, though she didn't dismiss the idea entirely. Still, Lily was the type who would call her mother and tell her not to worry if she was going to deviate from the plan. Caton held out hope they were simply broken down, and she hadn't intentionally blown off their date.

At midnight, Caton wanted to launch a search party, but Susan insisted he wait until morning. Reluctantly, he acquiesced to her suggestion and returned to Glenfield. Once the sun was up, he risked a call to the Crofting and discovered Susan hadn't slept either. He jumped into Blue Boy and raced to town, ready to start a one-man search party. They were immensely relieved when Lily finally found a cell signal strong enough to establish contact. All was well.

Lily was exhausted from her ordeal, but she was more hungry than tired. Susan went to work preparing a meal for her daughter, insisting Caton share breakfast with them. She set the table while Lily talked to Caton over a cup of coffee. "I don't think coffee has ever tasted so good."

Caton was relieved beyond measure. "I was so worried about you—both of you. I knew something must have gone wrong."

"It was a long night," she whispered, her exhaustion evident.

Susan set a platter of scrambled eggs, bacon and toasted English muffins on the table. "You need a hearty breakfast, so eat up." Lily didn't need further instructions.

"How's Jack?" Caton asked.

"He had a worse night than I did. I imagine he's sleeping it off right now and will probably be out for a while." Between bites, she described how they ended up stranded in the desert. Once she finished her meal, she gave a short explanation of her difficult night, being cautious not to share anything that would embarrass Jack.

"Oh, that's too bad," Susan replied. "Post Traumatic Stress Disorder is a serious issue. Is there help available locally?"

"Jack told me the Veteran's Clinic can treat PTSD. Apparently, the problem is far-reaching." She looked to Caton. "Is it true you were about to come looking for us?"

He smiled. "I was worried. These mountains and desert can be unforgiving."

"How well I know, but all is well for the moment." She yawned. "I'm sorry I missed our date. I was very sad when I realized game night was going on without me."

Jayne stumbled into the room. "I'm *so* not a morning person." She looked at Lily. "Oh, you're home, eh?"

"We were just talking about missing game night." Lily lifted her foot and pushed out a chair for her without getting up.

"It wasn't the same without you, Lily. I think Jayne cheats." Caton winked at her.

Susan laughed. "Jayne is a master cheater! You have to keep both eyes open when you play with her. She doesn't follow the rules."

Jayne was still grumpy. "I was only worried about Lily."

"Yeah," Caton chimed in. "We need to make sure Lily doesn't make any more trouble. She seems prone to accidents."

Lily rolled her eyes. "Only here in New Mexico ... since I met you."

"Oh, so I'm the problem?"

Lily touched his hand warmly. "Yes, you're a big problem." She smiled and caught his eyes. "Jack and I are no longer seeing each other."

Caton watched her carefully. "So," he asked slowly. "You're saying you're down to me?"

Her face turned red. "I think so. If you're still interested."

He stood and looked down at Lily and said, "Lillian DeMar, with your permission, we could begin the formal courting process."

She blushed and self-consciously touched her hair. "It would be an honor."

"Great! Now pack your bags, and I'll prepare the guest house for you."

Lily hesitated until Caton continued. "All three of you are invited to spend as much time as my guests as you might wish."

Jayne lifted a hand and asked, "Wait, would we have our own rooms?"

Caton laughed, "Of course, Jayne. There's plenty of room."

"Oh, thank goodness," Susan lifted her hands in victory.

When they arrived at Glenfield, Lily proudly introduced Susan and Jayne to Ruth Davis, who was bursting with enthusiasm to be their hostess. She excitedly declared she had both ovens working overtime as she prepared a feast for her honored guests.

Susan and Jayne took a moment to carry their bags into the guest house while Mrs. Davis followed them, telling them about the house and where to find whatever they might need.

Mariah busied herself picking blossoms from a trailing vine growing along the edge of the garden. She called to her father for help, but before he could get to her, Lily knelt next to her and plucked the small, yellow flower. Handing it to Mariah, she said, "I think this pretty, just like you." She glanced up at Caton and saw he was gaping at her.

"Are you okay?"

He closed his mouth, his head tilted, his eyes narrowing. "Yes, I'm fine. It's just … I've seen this before … in my dreams."

A blush spread across her cheeks. "I remember you telling me that!" She stood. "Is it exact?"

He squinted in disbelief. "Kind of. Except, in my dream you were wearing a black formal."

Lily shyly met his gaze and asked, "So, what happens next?"

He swallowed. "We take one step at a time toward our marriage."

Her face was rosy when she replied, "Isn't that a little fast? You haven't asked me to marry you yet." She grinned. "That's a big step you're missing."

"Maybe, but we'll take that one step at a time also."

Susan and Jayne joined them, and they ventured further into the garden. There had been no snow since the blizzard, so the garden was starting to clear wherever the sunlight reached the ground, allowing them to appreciate the potential of such a garden in the spring. They concluded their garden tour and returned to the parlor of the big house. Lily smiled when she saw Jayne and Susan both gasp in admiration at the proud glory of the home Caton had built. Jayne embarrassed Lily by continually asking if Caton had a brother. "Are you sure you're not a twin? 'Cause if you were, that'd be great."

Lily excitedly turned to Caton, placing both hands on his shoulders. "Do we have time to tour the house before dinner? I really want them to see your home."

"I don't see why not," Caton replied.

The ladies journeyed through the bedrooms and into the great room where Caton added a log to the fire, inviting them to sit and enjoy themselves. Lily noticed that Susan was delighted to see the library, and Jayne walked with Lily as they examined the artwork hung across the room.

To Lily's delight, Caton led the tour up the stairs to the master suite where Caton endured another series of compliments and astonished gasps. Lily's face burned scarlet when Jayne saw the granite shower and shamelessly announced, "I'm gonna invite all my friends over to take a shower. There's room enough for everyone!" When Caton opened the door to his gazebo, Lily noticed he'd cleared the snow off the path, and she could see the hot tub, ready to go. Jayne offered a few observations about where her shower party could go when they were ready for an outdoor adventure.

When they returned to the bedroom, Lily took special note of the painting on the wall, *Campaspe*, by Tomasz Rut. She was somewhat taken aback by the art. Caton noticed her awkward glance and commented, "I bought the painting the moment I laid eyes on it. I thought I was seeing Mary in it, and I still do."

Lily nodded, not intimidated by his mention of Mary. "From the photos I've seen of her, I can see Mary in the painting as well."

Caton turned to the group, "I think Mrs. Davis is waiting on us downstairs. Shall we join her in the dining room? I hope everyone likes a home-cooked meal of elk and wild onion." The ladies shared guarded glances, not sure whether he was joking.

Caton sat at the head of the table and savored the moment with his guests. He hadn't realized how empty the house had been until it was full of smiles and excited chatter. Now he couldn't imagine it without them. After saying grace, he picked up a platter of meat and passed it to Lily. "I grow vegetables in the summer for canning and pickling. I also have cherries growing down by the entrance." Pointing to the opposite end of the meadow, he said, "I have a few apple trees for some good pies." He was proud of his accomplishments and happy to answer his guests' many questions. At the end of the meal, Mrs. Davis proudly set a steaming cobbler in a cast iron skillet on the table and smiled as the women gasped in awe.

"What is it?" Susan asked.

"That is Mrs. Davis's famous blackberry cobbler."

Lily was excited. "I've never tried blackberry cobbler before."

Caton lowered his head and said, "You'll be severely disappointed if you try it."

Mrs. Davis slapped his hand. "Now you better behave. You'll run our guests off before they have a chance to enjoy themselves."

Caton submitted to her playful scolding. He stole a glance at Lily, who looked away, allowing him to search her face. She was elegant and graceful, and Caton felt a burning deep in his chest as he watched her speak softly to Mariah. Could happiness be this close at hand? "Thank you, Father," he whispered. "You're so good to us."

Trust me.

Caton nodded in acknowledgement of his Father's voice.

Be patient.

"What do you mean?" Caton asked silently. But he failed to receive a reply. With a burdened heart, he excused himself and stepped into the great room. Leaning against the fireplace, he felt the heat radiate against his face.

"Father, I'm so confused. Lily's not a believer. She says she isn't offended by you, just that she doesn't know you. I feel you've brought her into my life, and you've destined us to be together, but how can I marry someone who doesn't share the same beliefs? Your Word cautions against being unequally yoked."

Trust me.

"Father, I do trust you. But isn't it irresponsible of me to fall in love with a woman who doesn't share my values and worldview?"

My son, be patient. You won't wed her tomorrow, or next month. Be patient. Allow her some time to process what's happening. For everything, there's a season. This is her season for examination and reflection. Allow me to work it out. Trust me.

A sense of peace swelled in his heart. "Thank you, Father."

Returning to his guests, he began to tell stories of Mariah when she was a baby, his eyes sparkling as he remembered her as an infant.

When they finished their dessert, Caton rose quickly to his feet and held out a hand to Lily. "If you'd like, I would enjoy a stroll in the garden."

Jayne, bristling with excitement, winked and said, "Maybe if I come along, we can make doubly sure Caton doesn't get too frisky."

Caton responded, "Jayne, you're always welcome, but bear in mind, it's cold outside—too cold for much frolicking." He added with a smile, "I think she'll be perfectly safe with me."

"That's too bad," Jayne whispered loudly enough to be heard by all.

Lily's smile was forced, but not unfriendly. "Dearest Jayne, kindly put a sock in it, eh?"

The air was crisp. Lily could see her breath carry in the still air. She exhaled slowly and watched as the vapors slowly dissipated. Caton watched her for a moment, then said, "Mariah loves to do that."

"She's a wonderful little girl."

"She's special." He glanced back at the house. "Do you suppose anyone will accompany us?"

"No, I think we're alone tonight."

"Good," he said with satisfaction. "There's some business you and I need to address." He held his arm to her, and she placed her gloved hand into the crook of his elbow. They ambled along the pathway, chatting randomly about the stars and the possibility of more snow. Finally, Caton stopped and face Lily. "I should apologize for embarrassing you at the Pizza Palace. I was out of line."

"I don't mind, but at first, I was shocked," she admitted.

"And now?" he prompted.

"And now I think you were simply reacting to an unexpected situation. We all were."

They continued along the path around the fountain. He paused, clearly having something on his mind. He started and stopped several times before figuring out how to express his thoughts. "Lily, despite the risk of being too forward ..." He grinned sheepishly. "... and too fast, I want to be perfectly clear with you. I believe God has brought us together. I don't really know how this works, but I'm excited to have you, all of you, staying in the guest house."

Lily grinned. "Aren't you glad you didn't call it the 'mother-in-law house'?"

He smirked. "That'd be a bit awkward." He looked into her eyes, and she allowed him to look. "Maybe I can change the name later."

She blushed, and they continued walking. Suddenly, they found themselves at the gate to the cemetery. Lily felt anxious, not knowing what to say. Caton paused. "Lily, this is a little hard for me. I don't know how to merge my past with my future."

She was soft in reply. "Caton, please understand, I don't want to replace Mary or have you ignore her memory. She was a special part of your life. I'm not intimidated by Mary or by your love for her. That's your past, and I don't want you to dismiss it." She placed a hand on his arm. "We'll figure it out."

Caton nodded. "I can promise you this, I'll make a bucketful of mistakes."

"Then I'll make them with you," she replied softly.

He lifted her gloved hand and kissed it, smiling awkwardly. Together, they turned and continued down the path toward the stream. At the top of the small bridge, Caton paused and turned to face her. "I once knew a couple from Colorado. They were Christians, and while they were dating, they vowed not to kiss, and they limited how much they touched each other until the day they wed, save holding hands. I always liked the respect they had for each other." He inhaled deeply, as if gathering strength. "I've made many mistakes in my past, but I want to make our relationship special." He shifted his weight, trying to focus his thoughts. "I know it's old-fashioned, but I want us to be really careful. It's been a long time since I've had ... uh—" he stammered and cleared his throat, "well, physical contact ... with a woman, that is." His face turned read. "Gah! With anyone!" He chuckled when she rolled her eyes and laughed. "And I, well ..." He looked up in exasperation, and she patiently watched him with a knowing grin.

She placed a hand on his chest. "I know. And it's hard to talk about things like this when we don't know each other very well. But, I have the same struggles. It's been years for me too. So relax and just say what you're thinking. It's okay." She nodded to show her support.

He smiled shyly. "I'm not good at this, even under perfect conditions." He swallowed. "Okay, I'll start over." He cleared his throat. "I don't exactly trust myself. I'm so excited about the prospect of opening that door again. And I'm coming from the point of view, 'thou shalt not' to 'thou shalt, but not just yet.'" He smiled. "You know what I mean?"

She grinned. "Go on. You're doing fine."

"So, how about we make a pact? You and me? Let's swear to avoid sexual contact until we're married. And in order to accomplish this, let's swear not to kiss."

Her forehead crinkled. "At all? Or on the lips?"

He looked up, as if seeking inspiration, then tilted his head and sighed. "How about this? Our lips shall never touch until we've said our vows." He was unsuccessful in his effort not to be shy. "I might kiss you on the cheek once in a while."

Lily grinned. "I look forward to it." She paused, then said. "This is a weird conversation."

He agreed. "Isn't it, though? I've never done this before. But I want to do everything right, and this will protect both of us."

Warmth flooded over her, and peace filled her heart. "Thank you." She leaned closer to him.

"Are you cold?"

"Actually, I feel warm." She touched her nose and giggled. "But my face is numb."

"Let's start back to the house. It's been a long day. Besides, I don't want Jayne to think you were indecent out here."

She stopped walking. "Caton? Jayne can be a bit ... overwhelming at times, but she's a dear friend of mine ..."

He stopped her. "Your friends are my friends."

"Thank you." She wasn't through with her warning. *I only hope she's well behaved out here. I wish I could trust her.* "But, she can be ..."

"She can be what?"

"A bit of a tease."

"Ah."

She frowned. "Well, more of a wanton vixen."

Not sure how to react, he said, "She is quite playful."

She laughed at herself. "Actually, more like a femme fatale. Quite dangerous, in fact."

"Okay." He thought a few seconds. "Why do you mention this?"

She paused. "I just want you to know. Better safe than sorry." She offered him an apologetic smile. "Okay, now I'm cold." Returning her hand to his arm, she stood closer to him.

They walked even more slowly, neither of them wanting to give up their first walk together.

"Caton?"

"Yes, Lily?"

"Say something soft and sweet to me."

"Custard pie," he replied.

She laughed until she cried.

THEN CAME GRACE: A GLENFIELD EXTRA

CHAPTER ONE

DRESSING BARBIES & GOING TO CHURCH

The crisp, clean night air was laden with scents of mountain pine as the moon slowly drifted over Glenfield. A tendril of smoke wandered lazily from the chimney, hinting that the magnificent house was full of warmth and love.

Caton's boots crunched in the snow as he returned from lighting the fireplace in the guest house. Pausing a moment, he peered in the large windows into the majesty of the great room, where Susan and Jayne curiously explored the hidden treasures found in the room. He searched eagerly, but he couldn't see Lily. His heart skipped when she rose from her seat and faced the fire. He savored the moment, willing his eyes and mind to record every minute of his time with her. So much had happened in the last few weeks, and he needed to wrap his mind around the changes since the day Mariah accidentally dialed Lily and called her Mommy.

Caton watched as Lily paused near the mantle to examine its knickknacks, scattered carelessly and collecting dust, then exited the room. "Thank you, Father. For the first time in many years, I feel peace. I believe you've healed me." He resumed his slow walk back; it was Mariah's bedtime.

In her room, Mariah had a vast number of dolls spread in front of her. She had undressed all of them and now was struggling to put the long slender boots back on her favorite Barbie. It wasn't going very well. She looked up and saw Lily standing in her door. "Mommy!" she exclaimed.

Lily's heart gushed with warmth by Mariah's insistence she was her mother, but she was determined to respect Caton's constant correction that her name was Lily, not Mommy.

"You can call me Lily."

"Mommy," she replied, grinning.

"Lily. Can you say Lily?"

"Uh-huh. See my baby?"

She sat in the floor next to Mariah and picked up some clothes, "Are you trying to dress your baby?"

"Uh-huh. See, here is her boot." She held a plastic pink boot in her hand.

"Oh, that's pretty. Can I help you dress the baby?"

"Uh-huh."

Lily picked up the doll and made short work of getting the doll presentable. No sooner had she returned the doll to Mariah, than she started undressing the doll again. Patting Mariah on the head, Lily examined her room carefully. Caton—Mrs. Davis—had created a wonderful bedroom for her. Mariah's bed had a pink comforter and a dresser with pink flowers painted across the drawers. Her room was large enough to double as a playroom, and, from the looks of things, Mariah never suffered from a lack of toys.

Lily closed her eyes and mentally inserted herself into Mariah's life, wondering what being a mother would be like. If she couldn't have children herself, she considered herself lucky to find a ready-made family. Her heart was light and free while contemplating the prospect. She felt at home.

Mrs. Davis popped her head into the room and announced, "Mariah, it's time to get ready for bed." She then busied herself, helping Mariah pull off her clothes, put on her pajamas, and brush her hair. She glanced over at Lily. "Are you enjoying yourself, dear?"

"Yes, thank you."

Without looking up, she continued. "Caton is so pleased to have you back in his life. Things were miserable around here when he thought you had left for good."

"It's crazy," Lily replied. "All that time, I thought he said his goodbyes the day I left."

"Oh, you should have seen him. He was frustrated at himself for letting you go. Within the hour, he was trailing after you."

Lily nodded. "And I didn't know he played such a large part in my rescue."

"He tells me God showed him where to find you."

She considered the idea. "Wow! That's amazing!"

"Caton said your car couldn't be seen from the highway. If he hadn't been guided by the Almighty ... well, he's sure you would have died."

She grimaced. "I should thank him."

"Thank who, dear? Caton or God?"

She stammered for a moment, temporarily caught off guard. "I suppose I should thank both of them."

Mrs. Davis patted her on the hand. "There you go. You know, faith is a large part of this household."

"Yes, I'm beginning to see that."

Mrs. Davis had Mariah ready for bed and tucked her in tightly. "Your father will be here in a minute to say your prayers." Mariah nodded and looked at Lily. "Good night, Mommy."

Lily said, "Good night, Mariah. Remember, my name is Lily."

She stepped aside as Caton entered the room and stood next to Mariah's bed. "Say your prayers, Baby Doll."

Mariah softly thanked God for the trees and the snow. Then she thanked him for her babies and her daddy. She peeked at Lily and said, "Thank you for Mommy, amen."

Caton grinned at her. "You refuse to call her Lily, don't you?"

Mariah smiled at him and nodded.

"Actually, you should call her Miss DeMar. All children should refer to adults respectfully, right?"

Mariah nodded.

Caton prayed over her, and she said "amen" with her father—a practiced event.

Feeling like an eavesdropper, Lily stepped out and returned to the great room, where she found her mother and Jayne filtering through the books. "He has a remarkable collection. Here's a copy of *Pilgrim's Progress*." Susan looked for the copyright date. "From 1853."

"He certainly does have a nice assortment," Jayne said, ignoring Susan's find. She picked up a leather-bound book with raised bands and marbled paper cover boards. "Look, here's a first edition of *Pride and Prejudice*."

Susan crowded her. "You're kidding, what year?"

Jayne opened the book reverently. "1833."

"But that's not when *Pride and Prejudice* was first published," Lily argued. "It was before Jayne Austen died in the early 1800s."

"Look!" Susan was pointing at a boxed set, "There it is."

"What?" They pressed in to see.

"This is how they published the very first edition, in three volumes. Let's see," she gingerly opened one book, "in 1813."

Lily asked, "Where did he get that?"

Jayne placed a finger on her chin. "Now comes a harder question, why would a man have a book by Jayne Austen in his library?"

Lily laughed at her. "Stop it. It's perfectly masculine to have *Pride and Prejudice* in his library." After a dubious stare from Jayne, she amended, "Besides, if you must know, he bought the book for Mary years ago."

Jayne placed the book on the shelf. She picked up another. "*The Complete Tales and Poems of Edgar Allan Poe*. Who is this man?"

"What do you mean?" asked Susan.

"Well, he's a rugged mountain man who hunts elk and builds houses. He's nobody's doormat. He stood up to Doctor Death and won the lady. Yet, he's a gentle father and an excellent host. He's a religious man, but not arrogant. And he stocks his library with things other than girly magazines and books about cars. Heck, just the fact that he has a library is remarkable. I've never seen anyone like him. He probably fights off bears with his bare hands."

Susan smiled, "You should have met my husband. In many ways, he's like Caton, but in a business kind of way. He was gentle, but not a pushover—passionate, but still masculine. I think the best way to describe Caton is to say that he's a real man. He appears to be everything a real man should be."

Jayne considered the idea for a moment and shook her head, clearly dismissing the notion. "In my mind, a real man is one who is a good lover."

Susan nodded. "Sure, but there's so much more. The real man is a good lover because he's a combination of all the other things, not because of the way he performs. The way he loves a woman is a consummation of all his other attributes."

Jayne almost appeared sour. "Gee, Lily, I'm jealous. I see the way he looks at you with desire, but then he's restrained by discipline. I want that—someday."

She took a book to the fireplace and sat on the recliner across the room, out of earshot.

Susan looked to Lily. "I like Caton. You've found a man who deserves you."

Lily nodded. "I like him too. You know, he hasn't asked me what happened between Jack and me when we were stranded in the desert. I wonder if he cares."

"Oh, he cares," Susan said carefully, "but he respects you too much to ask."

Lily hadn't had much time to process what happened in the desert, and suddenly, tears began to well in her eyes. "Momma, I was so scared when Jack got drunk and started talking crazy. I thought he was going to snap and kill us both."

Susan wrapped her arms around her daughter and whispered softly, "I know. Psychotic episodes can be scary, but God was protecting you."

She held her mother tightly. "I was so sad. He was in such distress, but I had no idea how to help him." Her voice cracked. "I really thought he might do something violent."

"Thank God things turned out the way they did. Jack's PTSD issues are significant, and he might even be suffering from flashbacks in his sleep. Until he gets the help he needs …" She paused. "Well, he shouldn't start a relationship until he gets that help. Fortunately, PTSD is treatable and curable. If he'll get the help, he'll be fine. And, thank God, you have Caton in your life. A lot of women don't have a safe man who can protect them. All too often, their men are the ones hurting them."

Lily pulled away from her mother. She glanced at Jayne, who was reading by the fire. "I know what you mean. She's"—indicating Jayne with her eyes—"had a lot of bad men in her life. I think that's why she's so difficult."

"There's a lot of pain in her heart."

"I think that's why I care for her so much. I need her and she needs me." Lily wiped her eyes and hugged her mother.

The next morning, the women walked to the big house for breakfast. The guest house was fully stocked with food items, but they preferred company to solitude. Jayne, who was not a morning person, was feeling moody. These friends of hers, who insisted on greeting the sun each morning, continually puzzled her. She complained the sun came up in essentially the same fashion every morning and didn't require an audience to do its work. "I prefer to ease into my day," she explained. Nevertheless, she tromped across the compound with the others and settled in for breakfast, which was already on the table as the arrived.

Caton poured a fresh cup of coffee for Susan and held the pot as if asking if anyone else wanted a refill. "Last night," he said, while returning the pot to the coffee maker, "I intended to invite all of you to attend the Sunday church service in Cloudcroft, but I was distracted and never mentioned it. But, if it's not too late, the classes begin at ten o'clock, and we'll be there until noon or close to it. It would mean a lot if you would join us."

Susan cast questioning looks at Lily and Jayne. "Personally, I'd like to go. Girls, do you care to accompany me?" She blinked at them expectantly.

Lily glanced at Jayne, who rolled her eyes and emphatically stated, "I have no interest in ever stepping foot in a church again. I'd sooner burn in hell, which is the choice I've made. Thank you, but no." Her smile was betrayed by her tone of finality.

Lily, somewhat surprised by Jayne's outburst, seemed uncertain. After glancing from her mom to Jayne, Lily declined. "I'll keep Jayne company."

Soon, Caton pulled Blue Boy out of the driveway with Susan seated in the front seat. The truck rattled its way through the forest.

Mrs. Davis was a worrier. "I hope the girls will be fine at the house by themselves."

"They'll be fine," Susan replied, trying to settle her concerns. "They're used to being on their own."

"It'll be a little after one o'clock before we return," she replied, unconvinced. "They'll be hungry if they wait on us."

Caton grinned and chimed in, "I left some liver on the counter so they could cook their own meal. I'm sure they'll be happy when we return."

"Liver?" Mrs. Davis scowled. "Well, that's fine for us, but I doubt that those refined women will want liver. Really, Mr. Harvey, what were you thinking?"

Lily and Jayne had the run of the house for four hours. Lily was content to read a book while Jayne searched in vain for a television. "What's wrong with this man? Has he no television? I'll bet Dr. Death has a TV," Jayne said flippantly.

"Don't call him that," Lily replied softly. "What happened is no laughing matter."

Jayne shrugged. "Well, he's a complicated man. But at least he's a man." She glanced at Lily. "How'd you miss seeing him for who he was?"

Lily inhaled sharply as she considered her response. "You know? There's good and bad in all of us. Jack has so much potential, but his demons are stronger than he is. I think once he gets his life back on track, he'll make a fine husband for the right woman. There's more good in him than bad. Really."

"Fine," Jayne said patiently, "but you didn't answer my question."

Lily thought about it. "In my heart, I knew who he was, but I refused to see the warning signs. They were there—I just ignored them. Maybe I was worried I'd never find someone to love me, and I was willing to settle."

Jayne nodded. "Yeah, I get it."

"Well," she said, trying to make herself feel better, "my mother liked him first."

"Susan said he reminded her of Rodney. I wonder why."

Lily exhaled slowly. "Because my ex-husband was very similar. They're both dominant personalities. Why do I keep making the same mistakes?"

"I don't know. You went without a man in your life for like—forever," she said with feigned disgust. "Once you light the fire of passion, it's a hard flame to put out."

"Passion?" She looked up. "I vaguely remember passion. In the early years, I adored everything about Rodney. My friend, Clarisse, didn't like Rodney from our first date. She tried several times to persuade me away from him." Lily smiled at the memory. "It seems the more she tried to talk me away from him, the more I held firm. If I had only listened to her …"

"Oh, sure, if only! Listen to you." Jayne stared at her with a mostly friendly look of bemusement. "If you hadn't married Rodney, you wouldn't have divorced and left London. You wouldn't have joined the Boston Symphony and met me." She batted her eyes at Lily who smiled in response. "And you wouldn't be sitting here in this magnificent house."

"When you put it that way …"

"What? You wish you'd never made mistakes? Well, you're Mary Poppins compared to me. I've continually made mistakes from my teenage years. I used to steal from my parents and chase boys all over town. I was arrested once for shoplifting. After college, from which I graduated with a four-year hangover, I went from man to man." She frowned. "I've contracted two STDs." She waved a hand at Lily, who leaned forward in concern. "They're nothing I can die from, but they sure made my life miserable. Anyway, I'll never be able to have a man like Caton, and I don't deserve a man like him. So, stop whining about the one mistake you made and move on with your life. Honestly, I get so tired of hearing about someone's minor incident and them thinking they're a victim."

Lily was amazed. "Gee, Jayne, I've never heard you preach before. You might be good at it." Her tone softened. "And I had no idea there was so much pain in your life."

Jayne smirked and turned the conversation. "Why didn't you go to church with Caton?"

Lily was uncertain. She started to answer, then wavered. "Honestly? I don't know. In my mind, so you wouldn't be here by yourself." She pressed her lips tight with regret. "Do you think Caton was offended?"

"Wouldn't you be?"

She slowly nodded. "Probably. I should've gone with him." She frowned, regretting her decision.

"Well, there's always next time. I'll be going home in a few days, and you won't have me as an excuse."

"I don't need an excuse."

Jayne's eyebrows rose sharply. "Then why didn't you go to church?"

Lily was silent.

"See, this is what I'm talking about." Her voice was bursting with ire. "All you perfect people, who have no true issues, should come see me for a reality check. I went to church when I was a little girl. In fact, my father was the associate pastor at our church." As she spoke, bitterness filled her voice and her eyes narrowed. "One day, when I was a brand-new teenager, I went to the pastor to ask his advice about a boy I was interested in, you know, as a boyfriend. The pastor closed the door to his office and molested me, and my father was in the room next door."

Lily was astonished. "Oh, Jayne, I'm sorry."

Jayne's glare hardened. "It gets worse. After that, I told my father about what happened, and he punished me for …" she faltered and swallowed, then her voice cracked, "for lying!" Her breathing was shallow for a few seconds. "I was so upset, and I didn't know what to do. So, I went and slept with the boy I liked." Tears rolled down her cheeks. "He was an older boy, apparently experienced. Thirty seconds later, we were done, and he told me to take a hike." She stopped and wiped her face with a tissue. "I felt so dirty, and I hated myself. I saw my parents as frauds and the church too. They made me go to services until I embarrassed them to the point they wouldn't let me return. A few years later, a lawsuit was filed against the pastor for molesting little girls. My father was named in the suit, because he had covered up for him."

Lily had no response, so she sat next to Jayne and placed a hand on her shoulder.

"But don't use me as an excuse, because I don't need that kind of attention in my life."

"If I'd known …"

"What?" Jayne interrupted. "You'd have gone with them? I doubt it. You didn't want to go, and you know it."

Lily drew her shoulders higher. "Maybe," she replied softly.

"Listen, I know God sees no value in me, but you have no excuse."

"No, Jayne," Lily pleaded. "You're wrong about God seeing no value in you."

"And what do you know about it?" she demanded, her eyebrows lifted in defiance.

Lily nodded. "Okay." She lifted her hands in defeat. "I admit I know nothing, but for some reason, I believe God loves us."

"If God loves me, then why did my pastor rape me in church?"

TO BE CONTINUED

ABOUT THE AUTHOR

TRAVIS W. INMAN grew up in the ranch country of West Texas and worked as a cowboy for his first twenty years. He graduated from seminary in Dallas, Texas, and later served a year in the mission field in Mexico and South America. He returned home and married Sarah, his wife and sweetheart for more than twenty-five years.

Over the years, Travis has applied his skills to a variety of fields, ranging from marketing and real estate to criminal justice and law enforcement. He served in the United States Army where he overcame a devastating injury and was able to walk again despite the odds.

Writing is a life-long passion for Travis. His short stories and poems have been selected for publication in a variety of newspapers and on Internet sites. Travis's writing includes children's literature, action adventure, short stories, one-act plays, love stories, westerns, sci-fi, thrillers, and drama.

Travis and Sarah Inman reside in the mountains of New Mexico, where they homeschool their kids, and enjoy a quiet, rural lifestyle.

You can learn more about this story and the art portrayed in this journey on his blog, The Blundering Discoverer, www.traviswinman@blogspot.com and more about him at www.traviswinman.com

www.ingramcontent.com/pod-product-compliance
Lightning Source LLC
Chambersburg PA
CBHW030301200626
46816CB00002BA/722